Edmond de Goncourt, Jules de Goncourt

Renée Mauperin

Edmond de Goncourt, Jules de Goncourt

Renée Mauperin

ISBN/EAN: 9783743454637

Printed in Europe, USA, Canada, Australia, Japan

Cover: Foto ©Andreas Hilbeck / pixelio.de

More available books at **www.hansebooks.com**

RENÉE MAUPERIN.

A REALISTIC NOVEL.

BY

EDMOND AND JULES DE GONCOURT.

ILLUSTRATED WITH DESIGNS BY JAMES TISSOT.

NOTICE.

"RENÉE MAUPERIN" is more of a novel than any other of
the Brothers de Goncourt's works of fiction.   It is a somewhat complicated story, the characters in which are studied
with great knowledge of the surroundings and the period
selected by the authors.   For many people, those who
prefer analysis to art, this is Messieurs de Goncourt's
masterpiece.   The authors' object has been to depict a
phase of contemporary middle-class life.   Their heroine,
Renée, the most prominent personage of the story, is a
strange girl, half a boy, who has been brought up in the
chaste ignorance of virgins, but who has divined life.
Spoilt by her father, she has grown upon the dunghill of
advanced civilization with an artistic soul and a nervous,
refined temperament.   She is the most adorable little thing
imaginable, she talks slang, she paints and acts, her mind
is awake to every form of curiosity, and she is possessed of
masculine pride, straightforwardness, and honesty.   By her
side there is her brother, who is also marvellously true to
life: a serious young man, the type of properly regulated
ambition, the outcome of the manners and customs which
have resulted from Parliamentary rule.   He is one of those
very sharp fellows who make love to mothers in view of
marrying their daughters.   Then comes the whole gallery
of middle-class folks of either sex, all delineated with one

stroke of the pen, with a delightfully fine touch and without any approach to caricature. These people are enriched and satisfied revolutionists who have become conservatives, and who, of all their hatreds, only retain their animosity for Jesuits and priests. Some chapters of the book are of a comic character attaining to perfection, satirical without violence, extremely true to life. The tragedy begins in the second part of the work. Renée's brother has assumed a noble name in view of furthering his matrimonial plans. But a nobleman of that name is still living, and, having learnt through Renée of her brother's action, he challenges the young man and kills him. Then Renée, horrified by what she has done, slowly dies of heart disease, her distressing agony lasting through nearly one-third of the volume. Never has the approach of death been studied with more painful patience; and one finds here all the authors' literary art, all their power of happy expression employed to depict even the most fleeting tremors of the disease. I know of nothing that is more touching or more terrible.

ÉMILE ZOLA.

RENÉE MAUPERIN.

I.

" You do not like society, mademoiselle ? "

" You will not repeat what I say ? It chokes me. That is the effect the world has upon me. Perhaps it is that I have been unlucky. I have fallen among serious young men, friends of my brother; young 'text books' I call them. To the girls I meet I can only talk of the last sermon they have heard, of the last piece of music they have been studying, or of the last dress they have worn; my conversation with my contemporaries is limited."

" You spend all the year in the country, do you not ? "

" Yes. But we are so close to Paris. Have you seen the new piece at the Opéra-Comique ? Is it pretty ? "

" Yes, mademoiselle, it is charming; the music is admirably written. All Paris was there the first night. I ought to explain to you that I never go to a play except on a first night."

" Could you believe that the Opéra-Comique is the only theatre to which I am ever taken, besides the Français—and only there when they play a masterpiece. They bore me to extinction those masterpieces! To think that they will not allow me to go to the Palais-Royal! But I read all the pieces that are played there, nevertheless. It took

me ever so long to learn ' Les Saltimbanques ' by heart.
You are very fortunate; you can go everywhere. A few
evenings ago a great discussion was raised between my
sister and my brother-in-law on the subject of the masked
ball at the opera. Is it true that it is impossible to go
there ?"

" Quite impossible. Good gracious !"

" Come now, if you were married, would you take your
wife there ?—just once—only to see what it is like ?"

" If I were married I would not even take there——"

" Your mother-in-law ? Is it really as bad as that ?"

" Well, mademoiselle, you see that, firstly, the company
is decidedly——"

" Miscellaneous ? Yes, I know that. But one finds
that everywhere. But all the same one goes to La Marche,
and one finds there a variegated company. Those ladies
you know—they are odd—who drink champagne in their
carriages—and the Bois de Boulogne again ! Oh how dull
it is to be a girl; don't you think so ?"

" Upon my word, mademoiselle ! I don't see why. On
the contrary, I think——"

" I should like to see you turned into one ! You would
soon find out then what a bore it is always having to
behave 'properly.' I will give you an example. When
we are dancing, do you suppose that we may talk to our
partners ? ' Yes, no,' ' no, yes '—that is all we may say.
We have to keep to those monosyllables the whole time.
That is being well behaved ! There is one of the charms
of our existence ! And it's all like that in everything.
'Proper' is another word for simpleton. And then to be
condemned to chatter with one's own sex. When one has
the misfortune to run away from them to the society of
men—I have been well scolded by mamma for that ! One

more thing which is not 'proper,' and that is reading. It is only two years since I have been allowed to read the stories published in the newspapers. Then I am made to skip all the crimes which are reported; they are not 'proper' reading for me! It is the same with the accomplishments that we are allowed to have; they must not go beyond a certain point. Beyond a duet and a lead pencil, everything is regarded as affected and exaggerated. For instance, I paint in oils, and by so doing I make my family miserable. If they had their way, I should be only painting roses in water colours. But what a stream there is here. It is difficult to hold on."

This conversation took place in an arm of the Seine, between La Briche and the island of St. Denis.

The girl and the young man who were thus talking were in the water. Tired of swimming, carried away by the stream, they had taken hold of a rope which fastened one of the barges anchored off the island. The strength of the water swung them about quite gently at the end of the tightened and quivering rope. They floated down a short distance, and then came up again against the stream. The water flowed round the chest of the girl, filled her woollen bathing-gown up to the neck, then threw behind her a little wavelet which became, a moment later, nothing but a drop of dew ready to fall from the tip of her ear. As she was holding on to the rope, a little above the young man, her arms were out of the water, her wrists turned back that she might the better grip the rope, her back against the black side of the barge. Some instinct of modesty made her body shrink at every moment from that of her companion which was pushed against her by the stream. In her hanging and shrinking attitude she somewhat resembled one of those sea-goddesses who are sometimes twisted by carvers round the prows of ships. A slight tremor, caused by the movement of the river and the coldness of her bath, imparted to her something of the living undulation of the water.

"By the way," she began again, "it must be very improper for me to be bathing with you. If we were at the sea-side it would be very different. We should nevertheless be dressed exactly as we are now; we should have come out of a hut exactly as we have come down from the house; we should have walked over the shingle exactly as we walked across the bank; we should be in the water up to our chins exactly as we are here; the waves would toss us about exactly as the current does here;—but it would not be the same thing at all: the water of the Seine is not 'proper!' I am beginning to be very hungry. Are you?"

"Well, mademoiselle, I think I shall do honour to my dinner."

"I must warn you, I do eat."

"What do you mean, mademoiselle?"

"Yes, at meal-times, I am absolutely without poetry. I should be only deceiving you if I hid from you the fact that I have a good healthy appetite. You belong to the same club as my brother-in-law, do you not?"

"Yes, I belong to the same club as Monsieur Davarande."

"Have you many married men amongst the members?"

"Very many, mademoiselle."

"It is extraordinary—I never can understand why a man should marry. Had I been a man I should have never dreamed of marrying."

"Happily you are a woman, mademoiselle."

"Ah, yes! There is another of our misfortunes! We cannot remain bachelors, we poor women; but will you tell me why a man joins a club when he is married?"

"Well, a man must belong to some club in Paris—at least every man who is in society must—if it is only that he may have somewhere to smoke."

"What! are there still in existence women who refuse to make any allowances for smokers? I would allow anything—even a halfpenny pipe!"

"Have you any neighbours near you?"

"We are very unsociable, and make few friends. There are the Bourjots at Sannois, and we go there sometimes."

"Ah, the Bourjots!—but here there is nobody to make friends with?"

"Yes, there is the priest. Ha, ha! the first time he dined with us he drank the water out of his finger-glass! But it is very naughty of me to say that. He is such a good man, and he always brings me flowers."

"Riding would be a great distraction for you, I think. Are you fond of it?"

"Oh, yes, I adore it! It is my chief pleasure. I fancy I could not get on at all without it. What I like above everything is coursing. I was brought up to that in papa's country. I am mad about it. Do you know that one day I remained seven hours in my saddle without once getting down."

"Oh, I know what it is, mademoiselle. I course a great deal every year in Le Perche, with Monsieur de Beaulieu's pack. Perhaps you have heard of it? It is a pack that he got over from England. Last year we had some splendid sport there. The Chantilly hunt must be within reach of you here?"

"Papa and I never miss a day. We had a glorious day the last time we were out. At one moment we all met—there were at least forty horses, and you know how excited they become when they are together; we went away at full gallop—I need say no more than that! It was on that day that we saw the fine sunset over the pond. The air, the wind in one's hair, the hounds, the horns, the trees which seem to fly past one's eyes—it is just as if one were tipsy. At those moments I am brave enough for anything."

"Only at those moments?"

"Yes, in truth, only on horseback. For I must acknowledge that I am not brave on foot, that I am very much afraid of the dark, that I don't at all like thunder, and that I am very glad that three people have failed us for dinner to-night."

"And why, mademoiselle?"

"Because we should have been thirteen. You would have seen me commit any meanness to secure a fourteenth. Ah, here comes my brother with Denoisel in the boat. Look how beautiful all this is just at this moment!"

And, with a look, she made him notice the Seine, with its two banks and the sky.

Little clouds, violet, grey, and silver, were tumbling and playing about on the horizon, some of them with flashes of light just touching their crests, and seeming to produce an effect of sea-foam in the far-off sky. Out of these clouds rose the sky itself, infinite and blue, splendid, and already beginning to pale, as at the hour when the stars are lighting themselves up behind the day. Right above their heads hung two or three clouds, hovering over them, solid and motionless. A bright light was poured down upon the water, sleeping here, twinkling there, lighting up the ripples of the river in the shadow of the boats, just touching here a mast, and there a rudder, catching as it passed the orange petticoat or the pink cap of a washer-woman.

The country and the outskirts and suburbs of the town all met on the two banks of the river. Long lines of poplars showed here and there between the detached houses, which marked the end of a town. One saw low cottages, hoardings, gardens, green shutters, wine-shops painted red, with acacias in front of their doors, old barrels lying on their side, and here and there blinding peeps of white walls; then there came the hard lines of factories built of brick, with their roofs of tiles or zinc, and their large call bells. Smoke rose straight out of the mouths of their chimneys, and its shadow fell upon the river like the shadow of a column. On one chimney was written "Tobacco." On a plaster wall one saw the words, "Doremus, called Labiche, boat-builder." Over a canal, blocked up with barges, a revolving bridge raised its two black arms into the air. Fishermen were casting and drawing in their lines, wheels were creaking, carts were coming and going. Towing-ropes were being dragged along over the earth, which was rusty, hardened, blackened, dyed every colour by the coal-dust, the residuum from mineral works, and by deposits from chemical factories. A vague, indeterminate smell of grease and sugar, mixed with the emanations from the water and the smell of tar, rose from the candle factories, the glue factories, the tanneries, the sugar refineries, which were scattered about on the quay amongst thin, dried-up grass. The noise of foundries and the screams of steam-whistles broke, at every moment, the silence of the river. It was at once a picture of Asnières, Saardam, and Puteaux, one of the Parisian landscapes of the banks of the Seine, such as Hervier loves to paint, which are dirty and bright, miserable and gay, populous and full of life, where Nature passes every now and then between the buildings and the factories, as a blade of grass passes between the fingers of a man.

" Is not that view beautiful ? "

" Well, frankly, mademoiselle, I cannot excite myself up to any pitch of enthusiasm over it—it is fine up to a certain point."

" Yes, it is beautiful. I assure you it is beautiful. Two years ago in the Exhibition there was a picture in exactly that style. I don't know how it is, but there are some things that I feel."

" You have an artist's nature, mademoiselle."

" Pooh ! " was the only answer of the young lady, as she plunged into the water. When she reappeared on the surface, she began to swim towards the boat which was coming to meet her. Her hair, which had come undone, was soaked as it half floated behind her ; she shook it so as to scatter round her the drops of water.

Evening was coming down. The sky was slowly tinging itself with pink. A breeze had sprung up over the river. On the tops of the trees the leaves were shivering. A little windmill, which served as a sign to an inn, began to turn its sails.

As the swimmer reached the steps put out for her at the stern of the boat, one of the rowers said to her: " Well, Renée, and how did you find the water ? "

" Very pleasant, thank you. Denoisel."

" You are a nice young woman, upon my word." said the other ; "you are going to the devil. I was getting quite uneasy about you. And what have you done with Reverchon ? Ah ! here he comes."

II.

CHARLES LOUIS MAUPERIN was born in 1787. Son of a barrister, who was renowned and honoured in Lorraine and the Barrois, he entered upon a military career at the age of sixteen, as a cadet at the Military School of Fontainebleau. Appointed sub-lieutenant in the 35th regiment of line-infantry, afterwards lieutenant in the same corps, he distinguished himself in Italy by his extraordinary bravery At the battle of Pordenona, when already wounded, he was surrounded by a body of the enemy's cavalry, who called upon him to lay down his arms. He replied to their demand by an order to charge, killed with his own hand one of the horsemen who threatened him, and opened a passage with his men; finally, he succumbed to numbers, and, receiving on his head two new sword cuts, he fell back in his blood, and was left for dead. From captain in the 2nd Mediterranean regiment he became chief aide-de-camp to General Roussel d'Hurbal, and with him went through the campaign in Russia, where he had his right shoulder broken by a shot the day after the battle of Moskova. At twenty-six years of age, in 1813, he was an officer of the Legion of Honour, and in command of a squadron. In the army he was considered to have the finest future before him of any of the young superior officers, when the battle of Waterloo came to break his sword and his hopes. Put on half-pay, he entered, with Colonels Sauset and Maziau, into the Bonapartist conspiracy, known as the "*Bazar Français*." As a member of the directing committee, he was condemned

to death by default, but was concealed by some friends,
who helped him to escape to America. During the voyage
he did not know how to pass his time, and began to study
for a travelling companion of his who was going to take
his doctor's degree in America, and, on his arrival, he
passed his examination in the other's place. He remained
for two years in the United States, and at the end of that
time, by the brotherly friendship and the high influence of
some of his old comrades who had returned to active service, he obtained his pardon, and permission to return to
France. He came home, and took up his abode in the little
town of Bourmont, in company of his mother, who in-
habited a house there belonging to his family. This mother
was an excellent old woman, such as the 18th century
produced in the provinces, who was always ready with a
joke, and was not afraid of a little taste of wine. Her son
adored her. He found her suffering from an illness, on
account of which her doctors had forbidden her any stimulants; he gave up wine, liqueurs, and coffee, so as not to
tempt her, and to alleviate her privation by sharing it. It
was out of tenderness for her, out of respect for her desires as an invalid, that he took a wife. He married, without any strong inclination, a cousin of his own, who was
pointed out to his choice by his mother as possessing a
little bit of property, some land which marched with his
own; in fact, by all the ties which, in the country, bind
and unite families.

After his mother's death, as nothing kept him in the
little town where he felt his sphere was limited, and as he
was forbidden to live in Paris, Monsieur Mauperin sold his
house at Bourmont, and the property that he had in the
neighbourhood, with the exception of a farm at Villacourt,
and went to live with his young wife on a large property

that he bought in the depths of the Bassigny, at Morimond. There were there some remains of the great abbey,
a piece of ground worthy of the name which the monks had
given it—Mort-au-monde (Dead to the world)—a corner
of rural and magnificent nature, terminating in a lake of
a hundred acres, and in a forest of oaks whose age was
forgotten, fields enclosed in canals banked with freestone,
where the fresh water ran embowered by trees, where there
was a vegetation which had been abandoned since the Revolution, and which was as luxuriant as that of the back-
woods, where there were springs in the shade, wild flowers,
paths made by animals, and ruins of gardens upon ruins of
buildings. Here and there some stones survived. The
door remained, and the bench at which the soup used to be
given away to beggars; here the apse of a chapel without
a roof, there the seven stages of the walls, like those of
Montreuil. The pavilion at the entrance, built at the beginning of last century, was alone still standing entire,
almost intact : it was there that Monsieur Mauperin established himself.

He lived there until 1830, solitary and lost in study,
plunged in his books, and drawing therefrom an immense
education, a vast store of learning of all kinds: filling his
mind with the works of historians, philosophers, and politi-
cians, and ransacking all the mechanical sciences. He
never left his books but to take the air to freshen his head,
or to fatigue his body by long walks of eighteen miles
across the fields and woods. In the neighbourhood the
people were accustomed to see him walk like this; from
afar off the peasants recognised his step, his long buttoned-
up overcoat, his great cavalry officer's legs, his head, which
was always slightly bent, and the branch broken off a vine
which served him for a walking-stick.

B

At election times only did Monsieur Mauperin leave his laborious and secluded life: then he appeared in every corner of the department. He drove about in a light cart, inflamed with the fire of his soldier's voice all meetings of electors, and ordered an onslaught upon all the Government candidates; it was war over again to him. Then, the election over, he would leave Chaumont and come back to his daily avocations, and to the obscure tranquility of his studies. Two children were born to him, a boy in 1826, a girl in 1827. The Revolution of 1830 broke out; he was returned to Parliament. He came into his new life full of American theories, which gave him a point of resemblance with Armand Carrel. His speeches, which were excited, to the point, soldierly, and full of matter, created a sensation. He became one of the inspirers of the *National* newspaper, of which he had been one of the founders, and primed it with articles attacking the budget and the management of the finances. The Tuileries made advances to him; some of his old comrades, who had become aides-de-camp of the new king, approached him with offers of a high military position, of an important command, of a future for which he was still young enough. He refused absolutely. In 1832 he signed the protest of the Opposition to the words, "subjects of the king," used by Monsieur de Montalivet, and he fought against the system until 1835.

That year his wife gave him a child, a little girl, whose arrival disturbed his whole being. His two first children had only caused him a cold joy, a happiness without diversion. Something was wanting in them which makes the delight of a father and the merriment of a fireside. They had both made themselves loved by Monsieur Mauperin, without being adored by him. The hope of the father that he would be gladdened by them had been disappointed.

Instead of the son of his dreams, a real baby, a little scamp,
a little rascal, one of those pretty little devils in whom old
soldiers find once more their own youth, and seem to hear
again, as it were, the noise of gunpowder, Monsieur Mauperin had had to do with an orderly, well-behaved, little
boy—" a young lady," as he said; and it had been to him
a great cause of sadness, mixed with some shame, that his
heir was this little man who never broke his playthings.
He had the same trouble with his daughter: she was one
of those little girls who are born women. She seemed to
play with him in order to amuse him. She had scarcely
had any childhood. At five years old, when a gentleman
came to see her father, she ran away to wash her hands.
One had to kiss her only in certain places, and one would
have said that she had come into the world with the fear of
being rumpled by the caresses and love of her father.

All the tenderness of Monsieur Mauperin, which had
been thus repressed, and which had been for a long time
saving itself up and concentrating itself, went out to the
cradle of the new-comer, whom he had christened Renée,
after her mother, who bore that old Lorraine name. He
passed his days in delicious nonsense with his little Renée.
At every moment he took off her little cap to see her
silky hair. He taught her to make little faces, which
charmed him. He taught her to show how fat she was,
by pinching with her little fingers the flesh of her little
thighs. He would lie down with her on the carpet when
she was rolling, half naked, with the pretty indifference of
childhood. At night he would get up to look at her asleep,
and passed hours in listening to the first breath of life,
which is like the breathing of a flower. When she awoke,
he came to catch her first smile—that smile of tiny girls
which comes out of the night as out of Paradise. His

happiness momentarily increased to delight: he seemed to love a little angel.

What fun he had with her at Morimond! He used to drag her round the house in a little carriage, and would turn round, at every step, to see her laughing until she cried, the sun shining on her cheeks, nursing in her hand her little pink, supple, and crumpled-up foot. Or else he would carry her away with him on his long walks. He would go into a village, and make the child kiss her hand to the people who touched their hats to him, or he would go into a farm-house to exhibit the beautiful teeth of his little daughter. Often the child would fall asleep in his arms as in the arms of a nurse.

At other times he would carry her off into the forest, and there, under the trees full of nightingales, at the hours of the end of the day, when the voices of the woods are louder than those of the roads, he experienced ineffable happiness in hearing his baby, penetrated with all the sounds through which he was walking, by her little voice, murmuring and cooing, as if to answer the birds and the heavens which were singing to her.

Madame Mauperin, on the other hand, had not received this last daughter so warmly. She was a good woman and a good mother, but she was eaten up by the pride of provincial people—the pride of money. She had arranged to have two children; the third was one too many, and put out her calculations for the two others, and especially did her coming nibble away a little of the fortune of the son. This little girl represented to her mother the division of the united lands, the necessity of sharing their wealth, and consequently a falling from their present position and a lessening of the importance of the family in the future.

Soon Monsieur Mauperin was allowed no rest: the mother of his children was perpetually assaulting the politician, reminding the father that it was his duty to look after the fortune of his children. She tried to detach him from his friends, his party, his fidelity to his ideas. She laughed at him for a simpleton whose scruples prevented him from making the most of his position. Every day the same scenes were enacted—attacks, entreaties, reproaches—the terrible battle of the fireside against the conscience of a member of the Opposition. At last Monsieur Mauperin begged his wife to allow him two months' respite for reflection: he also wished his Renée to be rich. At the end of the two months he resigned his seat in Parliament, and came to La Briche to establish a sugar refinery.

Twenty years had passed since then. The children had grown up and the business had prospered. Monsieur Mauperin was making money fast out of his refinery. His son had been called to the bar. His elder daughter was married. Renée's portion was ready.

III

THE party had returned to the ground-floor of the house In a corner of the drawing-room, hung with chintz and decorated with bouquets of wild flowers in little baskets fastened to the wall, Henry Mauperin, Denoisel, and Reverchon were talking. Near the chimney-piece, Madame Mauperin was receiving, with great demonstrations of affection, her son-in-law and her daughter, Monsieur and Madame Davarande, who had just arrived. She fancied herself obliged, under existing circumstances, to put forth all her family tenderness, and to make an exhibition of her mother's heart.

The rustling caused by the embraces of Madame Mauperin and Madame Davarande was scarcely over, when a little, old gentleman, who had quietly entered the drawing-room, said, "How d'ye do?" with his eyes to Madame Mauperin, as he passed before her, and went straight to the group to which Denoisel belonged.

This little, old man wore a black coat. He had white whiskers, and carried a portfolio under his arm.

"Do you recognise that?" said he to Denoisel, as he carried him off into a bow window, and half opened his portfolio under his eyes.

"That?—I know nothing but that—it is the 'Mysterious Swing,' engraved after Lavreince."

The little man smiled: "Yes, but look at it."

And he again opened his portfolio, but only so that Denoisel could just get his nose into it.

"An artist's proof, too—an artist's proof! Do you understand?"

" Perfectly."

"And with a margin, too! It is a brilliant specimen— eh? But you may be sure the scoundrels did not make me a present of it! They ran up the price!—and it was a woman, too, who did it—"

" Nonsense!"

"Yes, a *cocotte*, too, who asked each time how much I had bid. That rascally auctioneer kept saying, ' It is madame's.' At last, at a hundred and thirty-five francs— oh, I would not have paid a penny more for it."

" I believe you—I wish I had known that, for I know a proof exactly like that at Spindler's the painter's, and with bigger margins, too. Spindler does not care about Louis XVI. I could have had it for the asking."

" Upon my word! and an artist's proof like mine? Are you quite sure of that?"

" An artist's proof before even—yes, it is in a less advanced state than your's. It is before——"

And the phrase which Denoisel finished in the ear of the old man caused his face to brighten up with pleasure, and made his mouth water.

At this moment Monsieur Mauperin came into the drawing-room with his daughter. He had given her his arm. She, with her head thrown a little back, languid and coaxing, was leaning on his arm, and was gently rubbing her hair on his sleeve, like a child wanting to be carried.

" How are you?" she said, kissing her sister. Then she put her forehead up to her mother, shook hands with her brother-in-law, and running to the man with the portfolio: " May I see, godfather?"

" No, goddaughter, you are not old enough yet." And

he gave her a little friendly tap on the cheek.

"Ah! the things that you buy are always like that," said Renée, turning her back on the old man, who began to tie up the strings of his portfolio with those knowing knots, familiar to the fingers of collectors of engravings.

"Well, what news has anyone got for me?" suddenly exclaimed Madame Mauperin, as she turned towards her daughter. She had made Reverchon take a chair quite close to her, so close that her gestures and her dress touched him, seemed to caress him. "You were carried away by the stream? I am sure you were in danger! Oh, that river! I cannot understand how Monsieur Mauperin allows——"

"Madame Mauperin," replied her husband, who with his daughter was turning over the leaves of an album on the table, "I allow nothing, I tolerate."

"Coward!" said Mademoiselle Mauperin in a low voice to her father.

"But, mamma, I assure you," intervened Henry Mauperin. "I assure you there was no danger. They were carried a little way by the stream, and they preferred to hook themselves on to a boat to being carried down a mile or two. That is all. You see——"

"You reassure me," said Madame Mauperin, upon whose countenance serenity had settled at each word of her son. "I know you are so careful. But do you see, Monsieur Reverchon, our dear Renée is so careless! I am always in terror about her! Oh, see, her hair is still wet. Come here, and let me dry it."

"Monsieur Dardouillet!" announced a servant.

"One of our neighbours," said Madame Mauperin to Reverchon in an undertone.

"Well, and how are you getting on?" asked Monsieur

Mauperin of the new comer, as they shook hands.

"Pretty well, pretty well; three hundred new stakes to-day."

"Three hundred?"

"Three hundred. I think it will not be amiss. Do you see, from the greenhouse, I cut straight down to the piece of water, on account of the view. A slope of a foot and a half, not more. If we were on the ground I should not need to explain it to you. On the other side, you know, I go back one yard up the alley. When that is done, Monsieur Mauperin, do you know that there will not be an inch of my land that has not been turned up?"

"But when do you mean to plant, Monsieur Dardouillet?" asked Mademoiselle Mauperin. "For three years now you have had workmen in your garden: are you never going to put in any trees?"

"Oh, the trees, mademoiselle, are nothing. There is always time for them. The most important thing is, first, the plan of the ground, the slopes, and then, afterwards, the trees, if you like."

Some one had come in by a door opening from an inner apartment into the drawing-room. He had made his bow without being noticed. He was present without attracting any attention. His head was honest, and his hair tumbled like a pen-wiper. This was Monsieur Mauperin's cashier, Monsieur Bernard.

"Are we all here? Has Monsieur Bernard come down? Ah, there he is!" said Monsieur Mauperin when he noticed him. "Suppose you were to ring and order dinner, Madame Mauperin. These young people must be hungry."

The respect due to fresh appetites had passed away. Chatter followed the silence of a dinner, which begins with the noise of spoons in the soup plates.

" Monsieur Reverchon," began Madame Mauperin. She had seated the young man next to herself, on her right, and one would have said that her amiabilities were rubbing themselves against him. She heaped attentions and flatteries upon him. She had a smile spread over her whole face, and even her voice was not that of every-day ; it was a high treble voice, which she put on on occasions of great ceremony. Her eyes travelled perpetually from the young man to his plate, and from his plate to a servant. The mother had her eye upon a son-in-law.

" Monsieur Reverchon, we recently met an acquaintance of yours, Madame de Bonnières. She spoke most highly of you, most highly."

" I had the honour of meeting Madame de Bonnières in Italy. I was even fortunate enough to be able to render her a slight service."

" Did you rescue her from brigands ? " cried Renée.

" No, mademoiselle, it was much less romantic. Madame de Bonnières was in a difficulty about a hotel bill. She happened to be alone. I saved her from being too much robbed."

" I call that a story of robbers," said Renée.

" One might make a play out of it," said Denoisel, " and a new play—how the discount of a bill brought about a marriage. And I have a pretty title for it : ' A Quarter-of-an-hour's Romance—of Rabelais.' "

" Madame de Bonnières is a very pleasant person," continued Madame Mauperin. " I think her face—Do you know her, Monsieur Barousse ? " added she, turning towards Renée's godfather.

" Oh, certainly, madame ; she is very agreeable."

" Godpapa, how can you ?—she looks like a satyr," said Renée. And as soon as the word had left her lips, and seeing people smile, she felt herself become scarlet. "Oh, only as to her head, I mean!" she added hastily.

"That is what I call recovering oneself," said Denoisel."

"Did you stay long in Italy, Monsieur Reverchon?" asked Monsieur Mauperin, to create a diversion.

"Six months."

"And your impression?"

"It is a very interesting country, but a very uncomfortable one. I never could get accustomed to drink my coffee out of a glass."

"Travelling in Italy," said Henry Mauperin, "is to my mind the most melancholy thing—the least practical thing one can do. What agriculture! What commerce! On the occasion of a masked ball, in Florence, I asked a waiter in a restaurant if they were to remain open all night. 'Oh, no, sir; we should have too many people,' was his answer. That was not told to me; I heard it myself. That condemns a country. When one thinks of England, of that collective and individual power of initiative; when one has seen, in London, the real genius for business of the English citizen; in Yorkshire, the returns of a large farm—there's a people indeed."

"I agree with Henry," said Madame Davarande; "England is so distinguished! the people are so polite! I like their plan of introducing people to each other. And then the way they have of giving you your change wrapped in paper. And besides their stuffs have so much character! My husband brought me home a poplin gown from the Exhibition. Ah, mamma, you know that I have settled upon my new cloak. I have been to Albéric. It was very funny. Imagine, he has a cloak put on to your shoulders, and then he begins to walk round you, and with an ebony ruler he points out the places where it does not fit by just tapping you—there! like that! little, tiny taps that he gives—and at every touch of his ruler his assistant makes a little chalk mark. Oh, Albéric is a man with a great deal of character! Besides that, he stands alone. There is no one but him; his cloaks are so smart. I recognised two by him at the races yesterday. But he does know how to charge."

"Oh, these men can make what they like," said Reverchon. "Edouard, my tailor, has just retired with a fortune of three millions."

"That is capital," said Monsieur Barousse; "I am always delighted when I see things like that. It is the hard-workers who have the fortunes nowadays! It is the greatest revolution since the beginning of the world"

"Yes," said Denoisel, "a revolution which reminds one of the speech of the famous robber, Chapon: ' Robbery, your worship, is the finest commerce in the world.'"

"Were the races brilliant?" asked Renée.

"There were a great many people at them," answered Madame Davarande.

"Very brilliant, mademoiselle," said Reverchon. "The Diana Stakes was a first-rate race. Cock's-tail, who started at 35, was beaten by Basilicate by two lengths. It was most exciting. The race for the Hack's Cup was very fine too, although the ground was rather hard."

"Who is that Russian lady who always drives four horses, Monsieur Reverchon?" asked Madame Davarande.

"Madame de Rissleff. Her horses are splendid—of the pure Orloff breed."

"You really ought to become a member of the Jockey Club, Jules, for the sake of the races," said Madame Davarande, turning to her husband. " I think it is so common to have to herd with all the rest of the world.

Really, for a woman who respects herself there is nothing like the Jockey Club Stand."

" How admirably your cook has done these mushrooms," said Monsieur Barousse ; " she has surpassed herself. She is a real Francatelli. I must congratulate her as I go out."

" I thought you never ate mushrooms," answered Madame Mauperin.

" I never did in 1848. I did not until the 2nd of December. Do you think that during all that time the police had nothing else to do but to inspect mushrooms? But since order has been restored——"

" Henrietta," said Madame Mauperin to Madame Davarande, " I want to scold your husband; he is neglecting us. It is almost three weeks since we saw you last, Monsieur Davarande."

" I am very sorry, dear mother, but if you knew all I have had to do. You know that I am very intimate with George. His father is very busy in Parliament. As President of the Cabinet, the work falls upon George. He has a thousand things to do which he can only pass on to friends and to persons whom he can trust. There was that first appearance at the opera; it was a very important matter, and required negotiations, interviews— such goings and comings. It was necessary to avoid a conflict between the two ministries. Oh. I assure you that we have been very busy latterly. He is so pleasant that I cannot——"

" So pleasant ? " said Denoisel; " he ought at least to pay your cab hire. It is quite two years since he promised you a sub-prefectship."

" My dear Denoisel, it is much more difficult than you fancy ; and besides as I do not wish to go too far from Paris. Besides, I may tell you, between ourselves, that it is almost settled I have good reason to hope that within a month——"

"Of whose first appearance are you talking?" asked Barousse.

"Of Bradizzi's," said Davarande.

"Bradizzi! wonderful! said Reverchon. She dances with a lightness! A few days ago I was in the director's box, on the stage: one could not hear her feet fall as she danced."

"We expected to see you last night, Henry," said Madame Davarande to her brother.

"I was at my debating society," said Henry.

"Henry has been appointed secretary," said Madame Mauperin, with pride.

"Ah." said Denoisel. "your Aguesseau debating society. Does that still go on, your little talkey-talkey? How many members have you?"

"Two hundred."

"And all statesmen? It is alarming! And upon what had you to report?"

"On the National Guard Bill."

"You refuse yourself nothing," said Denoisel.

"I am sure that you do not belong to the National Guard. Denoisel," said Monsieur Barousse,

"Certainly not."

"But yet it is an institution."

"So the drummer-boys say, Monsieur Barousse."

"And I would bet that you never vote."

"On no account."

"Denoisel. I am sorry to say it. you are a bad citizen. I am not angry with you, it is in your blood. but the fact remains."

"How a bad citizen?"

"Well you are always in opposition to the laws."

" I ? "

" Yes, you. Without going back very far, I will give you an instance, your uncle Frederick's money: the inheritance that you left to his natural children."

" Well ? "

" That is what I call an illegal, a culpable, a deplorable action. What says the law? It is clear; it says that children born out of wedlock cannot inherit. You were not unaware of that; I had told you, your solicitor had told you, the code told you What do you do? you make over the property to the children! You send the code. the spirit of the law, everything, in fact, to the right about! But, Denoisel, to abandon your uncle's fortune in that manner is pandering to bad habits; it is an encouragement to——"

" Monsieur Barousse, I know your feelings upon that subject. But what would you have? When I saw those three wretched little boys, I said to myself that the cigars I bought with their money would never taste good. No one is perfect."

" All very fine, but that is not the law. When the law says something it says it with some object, I suppose. The law is opposed to immorality. What will happen if people take to imitating you ? "

" You need not be afraid of that, Barousse," said Monsieur Mauperin, smiling.

" No one should set a bad example," answered Barousse, sententiously. Then turning again towards Denoisel, he continued ; " Understand me clearly, Denoisel, I do not think less well of you for doing it. On the contrary, I respect your disinterestedness; but as for telling you— you did well—no! It is so with your whole life: your life is not regular. Why, hang it, everyone works !

Everyone does something—goes into some public office, or in some way pays his debt to his country. If you had done that early in life you might by now have had a place worth three or four thousand francs a-year."

" I had something better than that offered me, Monsieur Barousse."

" Better than that?" said Barousse.

" Better than that," quietly answered Denoisel.

Barousse looked at him with stupefaction.

"Seriously, continued Denoisel, I had a splendid prospect once—for five minutes. You shall hear. On the 24th of February 1848, I did not know what to do with myself. Storming the Tuileries in the morning upsets all the rest of one's day. It occurred to me that I would go and see a friend of mine who was in a government office on the other side of the river. I arrive; nobody there. I go upstairs into my friend's room; no friend there. I light a cigarette and wait for him. A gentleman enters while I am smoking. He finds me seated and fancies I am employed in the office. He wears no hat; I presume that he also belongs to the house. He asks me very politely if I can tell him the way to some room that he wants. I show him; we return. He asks me to write something whereof he points out to me the gist. I take my friend's pen and I write. He reads, and is delighted. We talk; he finds that I know how to spell. He shakes hands with me and observes that I wear gloves. In short, at the end of a quarter of an hour he begs me earnestly to be his private secretary. It was the new minister."

" And you did not accept?"

" My friend came in—I accepted for him. He afterwards obtained an excellent appointment in the Privy 'Council Office. Nevertheless it was pleasant to have had even half-a-day of supernumeraryship."

They had by this time come to the dessert. Monsieur Mauperin had drawn towards him a dish of cakes, into which he thoughtlessly plunged his hand.

" Monsieur Mauperin?" said his wife, signalling to him with her eyes.

" I beg pardon, my dear—symmetry—you are quite right—I was not thinking;" and he replaced the dish.

" You have such a mania for disarranging things."

" I was wrong, my dear; I was wrong. Do you see, gentlemen, my wife is an excellent woman; but on the question of symmetry — symmetry is one of my wife's religions."

" You are ridiculous, Monsieur Mauperin," said Madame Mauperin, blushing at being caught committing a gross provincialism, and then she said sharply to her daughter: " Bless my soul, Renée, how badly you hold yourself. Sit up, my dear child."

" That's it," muttered the girl to herself. " Mamma avenging herself upon me now."

" Gentlemen," said Monsieur Mauperin, when they were all in the drawing-room, " you know that smoking is allowed here. We owe that to my son. He was so lucky as to obtain that concession from my wife."

" Coffee, godpapa?" asked Renée of Monsieur Barousse.

" No," replied he. " I should not sleep——"

" Here," said Renée, finishing his phrase. " Monsieur Reverchon?"

" No, thank you, mademoiselle."

She came and went about the room, and the steam from the cups, as she carried them, mounted into her face like the hot breath of the coffee.

" Is everyone helped?"

c

She did not wait. "Tra-tra, tra," the piano threw into the drawing-room the first bars of a polka. Then stopping: "Are we going to dance? Suppose we were to dance? Oh, let us dance!"

"Let us smoke quietly," said Monsieur Mauperin.

"Yes, daddy;" and quickly recommencing her polka, she danced it herself, turning about on the music-stool, and only holding on to the ground by the tips of her toes. She played without looking, her head turned towards the room, animated, smiling, the excitement of dancing in her eyes and on her cheeks, like a little girl who, while she plays that others may dance, follows them and dances with them. She worked her shoulders. Her body undulated as though in the arms of her partner, her waist marked the rhythm. In her feet there was a slight suggestion of a step. Then she turned herself again to the piano; she began to beat time gently with her head; her eyes followed her hands over the black and white keys. Leaning over the music that she was playing, she seemed alternately to beat the notes or to caress them, to speak to them, to scold them, to smile at them, to rock them, to send them to sleep. She leant upon the noise, she played with the melody; her little movements were sometimes tender, sometimes passionate. She stooped and raised herself again, and the top of her mother-of-pearl comb at one moment flashed in the light, at the next was buried in the dark masses of her hair. The two candlesticks on the piano, rattling with the noise, threw their light on her cheek, or crossed their flames on her forehead or her chin. The shadow of her earrings, two coral balls, trembled unceasingly on the skin of her neck, and her fingers ran so rapidly over the piano that one could only see something pink and undefined, which seemed to fly.

"And that is her own," said Monsieur Mauperin to Reverchon.

"She has had lessons from Quidant," added Madame Mauperin.

"Ha! I have done now!" And, leaving the piano, Renée went and stood in front of Denoisel. "Tell me a story, Denoisel, to amuse me; anything you like."

And she remained standing before him, her arms crossed, her head slightly thrown back, the weight of her body on one leg, with an impertinent little look and a sort of impudent courage which added to the somewhat cavalier grace of her dress; she wore a collar of white piqué, a neck-tie of black riband; the lappets of a white waistcoat fell back over her cloth gown, cut in the shape of a coat; on the front of her skirt she wore pockets like those of a greatcoat.

"When will you cut your wisdom-teeth, Renée?" asked Denoisel.

"Never!" and she began to laugh. "And how about my story?"

Denoisel looked round to see that no one was listening, and then, lowering his voice, began: "Once upon a time there were a papa and mamma, who had a little girl. The papa and the mamma, who wanted to see her married, brought to their house several very nice gentlemen, but the little girl, who was very nice also——"

"Oh, how stupid you are! I am going to do some work now."

And, taking her work-basket, she went and settled herself near her mother.

"Are we not to have any whist this evening?" asked Monsieur Mauperin.

"Certainly, my dear," replied his wife, "the table is

ready.   You see there are the candles waiting to be
lighted."

" Gone !" cried Denoisel into the ear of Barousse, who
was beginning to slumber by the fire-place, nodding his
head like a traveller in a stage-coach.   Monsieur Barousse
jumped up.   Denoisel offered him a card.   " The King of
Spades ; proof before letters !   They want you to play a
rubber."

" You are not too tired this evening, I hope, mademoiselle ? " said Reverchon, coming nearer.

" I, sir ?   I could dance all night !   I am made like
that."

" You are making something very pretty there."

" This ?   Oh, yes, very pretty.   It is a stocking I am
knitting for one of my poor children.   It is warm, and
that is all you can say for it   I must admit that I am not
good at needlework.   To do embroidery or wool-work,
one must give one's attention, while this—you see only
my fingers work—once you have got it started it seems
to go alone ; one's mind is free to think of the Grand
Turk, if one chooses."

" Look here, Renée," said her father ; " this is curious.
I lose in vain ; I cannot recover myself."

" Ha, ha, that is very good ; I shall keep that for my
collection." answered Renée.   Then, all of a sudden :
" Denoisel ! come here !   Will you come here ?—nearer
—there—nearer.   Will you come at once ?   And now,
on your knees——"

" Are you mad ? " cried Madame Mauperin.

" Renée," said Denoisel, " I believe you have sworn an
oath to make me miss any chance of marrying."

" Renée, come, come ! " said Monsieur Mauperin, from
the card-table, in a fatherly voice.

" Well, what is the matter ? " said Renée ; and, so saying, she playfully threatened Denoisel with a pair of
scissors. " Now, if you stir ! Besides, Denoisel's hair is
always so untidy ; it is so badly cut. There is always a
great ugly curl falling over his forehead. It makes every
one squint to look at him. I am going to cut off his curl.
Ha, now he's afraid ! But I am a first-rate hair-dresser ;
ask papa ! " And thereupon she cut vigorously twice or
thrice into Denoisel's hair, went up to the fire-place, shook
off the hair on to the hearth, and turning round : " Did
you think I wanted to steal a lock ? " she said.

She had paid no attention to the touch that her brother
had given her with his elbow as he passed. Her mother, an
instant before crimson, was now quite pale. She had not
noticed it. Her father, as the whist was over, came towards
her with an embarrassed and cross look. She took the
cigarette that he had just begun, put it to her lips, drew
one puff, and, throwing it away, quickly turned her head,
coughed, blinked, and exclaimed—

" Pah ! how nasty it is ! "

" Really, Renée," said Madame Mauperin, in a severe
and melancholy voice, " really, I do not understand you !
I have never seen you behave in such a manner before."

" Bring some tea," said Monsieur Mauperin to a servant
who came in answer to the bell.

IV.

"ALREADY a quarter-past ten!" said Madame Davarande. "We have only just time to get to the station. Renée, will you send for my hat?"

Everyone got up. Barousse, at the noise, awoke, and the little group of guests from Paris started for Saint-Denis.

"I will come with you," said Denoisel; "the walk will do me good."

Barousse led the way; Davarande following with his wife. Henry Mauperin and Denoisel closed the procession.

"Why don't you sleep here?" said Denoisel to Henry; "you could return to Paris to-morrow."

"No," answered Henry, "I do not wish to. I have some work to do to-morrow morning. I should only reach Paris late, and my day would be lost."

They were silent. Some words of Barousse, singing the praises of Renée, reached them now and again in the silence.

"Tell me, Denoisel; I fear it is all over; what do you think?"

"I think so."

"Well, my dear fellow, will you have the kindness to tell me why you lent yourself to all the follies that entered my sister's brain this evening? Your influence over her is great, and——"

"First of all, my boy," said Denoisel, pulling at his cigar, "allow me to open a historical, philosophical, and social parenthesis. We have done, have we not?—when I say 'we,' I mean the majority of the French people—with the pretty little misses who used to talk like dolls with springs inside them, who used to say 'papa!' 'mamma!' and who, when they danced, never lost sight of the authors of their being. The little, shy, childish, timid, stammering miss, who was taught not to know anything, who did not know how to stand upright nor how to sit down, is done with; it's old, worn-out; a thing of the past. She was the kind of bread-and-butter miss of the Gymnase Theatre. Nowadays it is quite a different matter. The plan of cultivation has been changed: young women used to be like espalier apple-trees: now they grow alone in the teeth of the wind. People expect a girl to form her own impressions, and to be able to express herself in her own language. She can talk, and she must talk about everything. That has become part of her manners. She is no longer required to display innocence, but intellectual originality. As long as she shines in society her parents are charmed. Her mother takes her to lectures. Has she a talent? How it is fostered and cherished! Instead of poor daily governesses, she has lessons from real masters, professors of the Conservatoire, painters who have exhibited. Her mind takes an artistic turn, and her parents are delighted thereat. Tell me, is that or is it not a faithful picture of our young middle class women of to-day?"

"Whence you conclude?"

"Now, then," continued Denoisel, without answering, "add to that fine education which I have described, but which I do not judge, please observe—add to that, I say, an excellent, good fellow of a father, who is kindness and tenderness personified, who encourages all this emancipation by his weakness and his adoration; suppose that this father has smiled at all the impertinences, all the pretty little naughtinesses of this boy in petticoats; that he has, little by little, allowed his daughter to assume these manly qualities wherein he discovers, with pride, a reflection of his own heart——"

"And so you—you, my dear fellow, who know so well what my sister is, how she has been brought up, the style she has adopted—thanks to the spoiling of my father—all the difficulties in the way of her marriage, it is you, I say, who this evening allowed her to play a number of unseemly tricks, when you could, with those few words which you, and you alone, can say to her, have stopped her completely."

Denoisel, the friend to whom Henry Mauperin thus spoke, was the son of a man who came from the same part of the country as Monsieur Mauperin, and who had been his schoolfellow and companion-in-arms. Monsieur Mauperin and his father had been side by side in the same battles; their blood had mingled on the same fields; in the retreat from Russia they had both bitten into the same piece of horse-flesh.

A year after his return to France, Monsieur Mauperin lost this friend who, on his death-bed, made him guardian of his son. The child found his father over again in his guardian. While at school, he had passed all his holidays at Morimond, and the Mauperins' house had become to him a home. When Monsieur Mauperin's children were born it seemed to Denoisel that he had until then missed a brother and a sister; he felt like their elder brother, and became a child again to play with them.

His preference was naturally for Renée who, when quite a small child, began to worship him. She was already quick-tempered and obstinate; he alone could make her listen and obey. By the time she was grown up he had become the moulder of her character, the confessor of her mind, the director of her tastes. And his influence over the young girl had increased day by day with his familiarity with her in that house where his room was always ready, his place at table always laid, and where he could come to pass a week at any time.

" There are days," began Henry again, " on which my sister's nonsense does not signify; but this evening, before that man—I am sure it will put an end to the marriage. An excellent match—he had very large expectations. He is a capital fellow from all accounts, pleasant, well educated."

" Do you think so? He frightened me on your sister's account. And that is why I behaved with her as I did to-night. That man only possesses the commonest refinement—refinement made out of the vulgarisation of all that is eloquent. He is, both physically and morally, a fashionplate, a tailor's model. There is absolutely nothing in a little mannikin like him. He, a husband for your sister? But how the deuce do you expect him to understand her? By what power do you expect him to discover what a depth of generous, noble, and fine feeling there is in her under her eccentricity? Do you fancy that they would have one idea in common? God bless my soul! Your sister might marry no matter whom, and I would not say a word against it so long as he were intelligent, and were possessed of a strong character and a personality of his own, something capable of governing or moving the nature of a woman like her. A man may often have great defects

which keep alive the heart of a woman. There would be
the chance, with a bad husband, that she might devote
herself to him out of jealousy; an ambitious and busy
man like yourself would give her occupation, excitement,
dreams of her own future. But a little mannikin like
that! for ever! She would be perfectly wretched; she
would die of it. The truth is that your sister is not made
like other women, and it is no use blinking the fact. Her
nature is refined, open, full of chaff and very tender. At
bottom she is of a melancholy disposition, mixed with
noisy spirits."

"What in the world do you mean by that?"

"I will tell you—I mean——"

"Henry, make haste!" cried Davarande from the plat-
form, "we are just off. I have got your ticket."

V.

Monsieur and Madame Mauperin were in their room. The clock had just struck midnight, gravely, slowly, as if to mark its sense of the solemnity of this intimate and conjugal hour, which, while it is the *tête-à-tête* of married life is at the same time the cabinet council of the household; an hour of transformation and of magic, at once commonplace and diabolical, which recalls the story of the woman who was metamorphosed into a cat. The shadow of the bed falls mysteriously upon the wife, and invests her with a sort of charm. Some remains of the sorceries of a mistress come to her at that moment. Her will awakes by the side of that marital will which sleeps. She draws herself up, she scratches, she scolds, she sulks, she teases, she struggles. Alternately she caresses and claws her husband. She derives her power from her pillow: at night she puts on her strength.

Madame Mauperin was arranging her curl-papers before the looking-glass by the light of a single candle. She was dressed only in her chemise and her petticoat. Her fat figure, above which her little arms moved about with a gesture as though she were crowning herself, threw on to the wall the fantastic outline of an undressed person of fifty, and caused to tremble on the paper at the end of the room one of those corpulent shadows such as Hoffmann and Daumier seem to paint together in the bedrooms of old couples—Monsieur Mauperin was already in bed.

"Louis," said Madame Mauperin.

"What?" was his answer, given in that tone of weariness, of indifference, of regret, of the man who, with his eyes still open, has begun to taste the sweetness of the horizontal position.

"Oh, if you are asleep!"

"I am not asleep at all. What is it?"

"Oh, dear me, nothing! I thought that Renée's behaviour this evening was most shocking—that is all. Did you happen to notice it?"

"No, I did not remark anything."

"It is a craze. There is really no sense in it. Come, did she not say anything to you? Do you know anything? For I am always left out of all your little confidences—your secrets: I am always the last person in the house to hear anything. But you, oh yes—you are told everything. It is very lucky that I was not born jealous, do you know?"

Monsieur Mauperin, without answering, pulled the sheet up over his shoulder.

"You are certainly asleep," said Madame Mauperin, in the sharp and vexed tone of a woman who expects a reply to her attack.

"I have already told you that I am not asleep."

"But don't you see, Monsieur Mauperin? Oh these clever men—how odd it is. And it comes home to you, too; it is your business as much as mine. Do you understand that another marriage has come to nothing? A marriage which offered everything—fortune, family—everything. I know the precise moment at which these things come to nothing—we may go into mourning for this one. Henry was talking to me about it this evening. Naturally the young man had said nothing to him; he is too well-bred for that. But Henry is convinced he is drawing back. One can feel that sort of thing—one sees it in their manner."

" Well, and what do you expect me to say to you, supposing he does draw back?" And Monsieur Mauperin sitting up in bed, stretched his hands along his legs. " He will draw back. We can find other young men like Reverchon. He is not unique—while girls, like my daughter——"

" Bless my heart! Your daughter—your daughter."

" You do not do her justice, Theresa."

" I! I do her every justice. Only I see her as she really is, and not with your eyes. She has faults, grave faults, and you have encouraged them; caprices, whims, like a child of ten years old. Do you suppose that ever since I have been trying to get her married I have not suffered from her indecision, her wants, a heap of ridiculous fads. And then her way of looking over people who are introduced to her. She is terrible in interviews of that kind. We have already seen her pluck at least ten candidates."

At these last words of Madame Mauperin, a flash of vanity played over Monsieur Mauperin's fatherly face. " Yes, yes." said he, smiling at the recollection, " the truth is that she is infernally sharp. Do you remember that unlucky prefect : ' That old cock,' as she said. I can hear her say it now as soon as she had looked at him."

" Very funny in truth, and quite proper into the bargain. And that is the sort of wit to catch husbands with, believe me. It encourages other people to come forward, does it not ? I am certain that Renée has, in the world, a reputation for spitefulness A few more pretty speeches like that—and you will see how many offers your daughter will have. I married Henrietta off so easily   This one is my cross."

Monsieur Mauperin had taken his snuff-box off the table beside his bed, and seemed occupied in turning it round between his finger and thumb.

" Well," recommenced Madame Mauperin, " it's her own look-out. When she is thirty and has refused every-body, when she finds no one who cares to marry her, notwithstanding all her wit, her good qualities. and all the rest of it, then she will begin to reflect—and so will you."

A pause ensued. Madame Mauperin allowed her hus-band time to fancy that she had done. Then changing her tone : " I have now to talk to you about your son."

At this Monsieur Mauperin, who had hitherto remained bent down under the weight of his wife's words, raised his head ; he half smiled with malicious good humour.

There is, among the middle-classes, the highest as well as the lowest, a kind of motherly love which rises to passion and lowers itself to idolatry. One may often meet mothers in that class, whose affections prostrate themselves, whose hearts, as it were, kneel down before a son. It is no longer motherly love, hiding its weak-nesses, armed with its rights, jealous of its duties. careful for the hierarchy and discipline of the family, surrounded by respect and authority. The son, connected with his mother by every familiar link, receives from her attentions which resemble homage, and caresses which are almost servile. Of him the mother dreams ; for he is not only the heir. but he is the future of the family, to whom he holds out the prospects of all the good fortunes of the middle-class. its advance. its progressive ascent from generation to generation. The mother glories in what

he is and in what he will be. In him she centres all her
ambitions, to him she gives her worship. This son seems
to her to be of a superior creation; she is amazed at
herself for having borne him; one might almost say
that, in her heart of hearts, are intermixed the pride and
the humility of the mother of a god.

Madame Mauperin was a typical mother of the modern
middle-classes. The merits, the face, the mind of her
son were to her as those of a divinity. His person,
his attractions, all that he said or did was sacred to her.
Before him she knelt in meditation; as compared to him,
other people did not exist for her. The world seemed to
begin and end with her son. In her eyes he was the
perfection of everything, the most intelligent, the most
beautiful, and above all, the most distinguished-looking of
mankind. He was short-sighted, and wore glasses. She
would never acknowledge that his eyes were in the least
degree affected.

When he was there, she watched him speak, walk, sit
down; she smiled at him when his back was turned. She
loved the very wrinkles of his coat. When he was not present, she would often remain for minutes together in an
arm-chair; an idea of infinite sweetness would, little by
little, lighten and soften her face; her looks would be happy,
her eyes full of memory, her heart full of introspection. If
anyone addressed her at such a moment, she would seem
to wake from sleep.

This mania of maternal love was hereditary. Madame
Mauperin came of a stock which had always borne its sons
this hot, violent, almost frenzied affection. The mothers
of her family had been furiously mothers. Her grand-
mother had left behind her a legend in the district of the
Haute-Marne: it was related that she had disfigured with

a live coal a child who was said to be more beautiful than
her own.   At the first little illnesses of her son, Madame
Mauperin almost went mad; she cursed all strong children;
she wished God to kill them if her son were to die.   Once
he was seriously ill; she passed forty-eight nights without
going to bed; her legs swelled from fatigue.   When he
began to run about he was allowed to do as he pleased.
If anyone complained that he had beaten the village boys,
she said, in a melancholy voice: " Poor darling!"

As the child grew older, the mother's heart seemed to
go before him, and already to fill with hopes the road that,
as a man, he would have to travel.   She thought of all the
heiresses in the department whose ages were about the
same as his.   She saw him living in castles, on horseback,
hunting in a red coat.   She dazzled herself with illusions
and anticipations.

School-time came, and with it separation.   Madame
Mauperin struggled for three months to be allowed to
keep her child, and to have him taught by a tutor under
her eye.   But her husband was firm.   All that Madame
Mauperin could obtain was the choice of the school.   She
chose the softest she could find—one of those schools for
rich people at which the children are allowed cakes when
they go out for a walk, and where the masters set more
lessons than punishments.

He remained there seven years, and during that time
Madame Mauperin did not let one day pass without going
to see him during his play-hour.   Rain, cold, fatigue,
illness—nothing stopped her.   In the parlour, in the play-
ground, other mothers pointed her out to each other.   The
child would kiss her, take the cakes that she had brought
him, and, saying that he had a lesson to finish, would hasten
to return to his play.   But that was enough for his mother.

She had seen him. He was well. She thought unceasingly of his health. She loaded him with flannel. During his holidays she stuffed him with meat—beef-steaks, of which she gave him all the fresh gravy to make him big and strong. She bought him a little mat for fear the benches at school should be too hard for him. Each pupil was provided with a separate room; she furnished his as though it were a man's. At twelve years old he had a dressing-table of rose-wood.

The child became a young man, the young man left school, and Madame Mauperin's passion only increased with all the pride that a mother feels in a son, whose figure is changing and whose beard is sprouting. Forgetting that she paid the tradesmen's bills, she marvelled at the manner in which her son dressed, did his hair, and at the boots he wore. In his tastes, in the luxury of his habits, in his appearance, in his life, there was an elegance before which she fell down and worshipped, as though she herself were not the source and the treasurer thereof. Her son's servant was not quite a servant. His horse was not merely a horse; it was her son's horse. She was always warned beforehand if her son was going for a drive, so that she might have the satisfaction of seeing him get into the carriage and start.

Every day she became more and more taken up with this son. With no distractions, with nothing to occupy her thoughts, never reading, growing old beside the husband who had brought her no love, and whom she had always felt to live a life apart from her—immersed in study, in politics, and in business; having beside her only one daughter, to whom she had never given all her heart, she had ended by staking her whole life upon Henry's chances, all her vanity on his future.

D

And her only thought—her thought of every waking hour, whether by day or by night—her one idea, was how to get this adored son married—married well, in such a rich and brilliant manner as to avenge her, and recoup her for all the sadness and obscurity of her existence, for her life of saving and solitude, for all her privations as wife and woman.

" Do you know exactly how old your son is, Monsieur Mauperin? " asked Madame Mauperin.

" Henry? Let me see ; Henry must be——He was born in 1826, was he not ? "

" Oh, how like a father to ask ! Yes, 1826—the 12th of July, 1826."

" Ah, then, he is twenty-nine years of age. So he is ! Twenty-nine."

" And you quietly stay where you are and do nothing ! You don't give a thought to his future career ! You say, Yes. he is twenty-nine.' quite quietly ! Anyone else would take some steps—would look about. Henry is not like his sister ; he wants to be married. Have you ever thought of trying to find him a suitable wife ? No more than you have for the King of Prussia ! It was just the same with your eldest daughter. I ask you, what did you do to help on her marriage ? It really seemed as though it were all one to you whether she found a husband or whether she did not ! Didn't I have to urge you to make you stir in the matter ! Ah ! you may wash your hands of that marriage ; your daughter's happiness need not weigh upon your conscience. No doubt, without me, you would have found such a husband as Monsieur Davarande, who worships Henrietta. Such a man of the world, too ! —a model husband."

And Madame Mauperin, blowing out the candle, slid into

bed beside Monsieur Mauperin, who was turned towards his corner with his nose close to the wall.

"Yes," she continued, as she stretched herself under the sheets, "a model! Do you suppose that all sons-in-law would pay us as much attention as he does? He does all in his power to be pleasant to us. You make him eat meat if he dines here on a Friday; he does not complain. And so good-natured! A short time ago I wanted to match some wools for my work, and——"

"Pardon me, my dear, but what were we talking about? I warn you that I am rather sleepy to-night. It began with your daughter. Now you have started the chapter of Monsieur Dwarande's perfections. I know that chapter well. It will last till to-morrow morning. Come now; you want your son to marry, do you not? That's it. Very well; find him a wife. I ask nothing better."

"And a great deal of help I shall have from you in the matter! You will take a lot of trouble about it! You so much like disturbing yourself!"

"Upon my word, my dear, you are unjust to me! If I remember rightly, I gave a proof of my good disposition about a fortnight ago. Do you call it nothing to go and hear an opera which bored me to death; to eat ices at night, which I particularly dislike doing; talk about nothing to a provincial who publish d on the Boulevards, at the top of his voice, what his daughter's fortune would be? You will tell me that it all came to nothing! But was it my fault that this good gentleman wanted for his daughter what he called a 'fine male'? Is it my fault, and mine alone, that our son is not a Hercules?"

"Monsieur Mauperin!"

"Upon my soul it is quite true. According to you I

am guilty of everything. You would make me pass for a selfish——"

" Yes indeed, like all men!"

" Thank you for them."

" No, it is a part of your nature; one must not be angry with you for it. It is only mothers who worry themselves. Ah, if you were like me! If you had before your eyes, day and night, a picture of all that may happen to a young man. I know very well that Henry is steady; but an entanglement is so soon made—a bad woman—any wretched creature, no matter who; one sees it every day. I should go mad! Look here, Mauperin, suppose we were to try to get at Madame Rosières—eh?"

There was no answer. Madame Mauperin resigned herself to silence, turned this way and that, sought for sleep and only found it at daybreak.

VI.

"Hulloa, where in the world are you going to?" said Monsieur Mauperin to Madame Mauperin next morning, as she was putting on a black lace mantle before her looking-glass.

"Where am I going?" repeated Madame Mauperin, as she fixed the cloak on one of her shoulders with one of the two pins that she had in her mouth. "Does my cloak fall too low? Do look."

"No."

"Pull it a little."

"But how smart you are!" said Monsieur Mauperin, stepping backwards a little and looking at his wife's toilet, which was all black and of the most elegant severity, in good taste, and almost austere.

"I am going to Paris."

"So you are going to Paris? And pray what are you going to do in Paris?"

"Dear me, how tiresome you are, always asking, 'Where are you going? What are you going to do?' I suppose you want to know, don't you?"

"Clearly, so that is why I asked the question."

"Well, my dear, I am going to confession," answered Madame Mauperin, dropping her eyes.

At this answer Monsieur Mauperin became silent. During the first part of their married life, his wife had been pious to the extent of going to church once every Sunday; later on, she had accompanied her daughters to the cate-

chism classes; and there ended all the religious duties that
he had ever seen her perform. For the last ten years he
had felt that she was, like himself, indifferent, naturally and
ingenuously. After the first moment of stupefaction had
passed, he opened his mouth to speak to her, looked at her,
and said nothing; then, suddenly turning sharp round on
his heels, he walked straight out of the room, humming a
sort of tune to which nothing was wanting save the air
and the words.

Madame Mauperin reached a fine, cheerful house in the
Rue de la Madeleine, and mounted to the fourth floor; there
she rang at an unpretending door; her bell was answered.

"The Abbé Blampoix?"

"Will you walk in, madame?" said a servant, who had
a Belgian accent, a black livery, a respectable appearance,
and who bowed low. He conducted Madame Mauperin
through an ante-room faintly perfumed, then through a
dining-room full of sunlight where one place was laid at
table. Then Madame Mauperin found herself in a drawing-room gay with scented flowers. Above a harmonium
which was handsomely ornamented with brass-work, hung
a copy of Correggio's picture of "Night." On another
wall there hung in a mourning frame, the "Communion
of Marie-Antoinette and her guards at the Conciergerie,"
lithographed from a legend. Little tokens of all sorts, a
number of things which resembled New Year's presents
covered the brackets. A miniature copy in bronze of Can-
ova's "Magdalen" stood on the table in the middle of the
room. The furniture, covered with embroidery of different
patterns and colours told its own tale and showed what it
was: presents from various pious women to the priest.

Men and women were waiting there, opening the door of
the study, remaining inside a few minutes, coming out

again, bowing and disappearing. The last of these people, a woman, remained a long time. When she came out again, Madame Mauperin could not see her face for the thick veil which covered it.

The priest was standing by the fire-place when Madame Mauperin entered. He held the skirts of his cassock stretched out before the fire, like the tails of a coat.

The Abbé Blampoix had neither cure of souls nor parish. He had a following and a specialty; he was the priest of the world, of the great world and the fashionable world.

He heard all the drawing-room confessions, he directed all the well-born consciences, he consoled such souls as were worth the trouble. He brought Paradise and salvation within the reach of learned and rich people. " Every one has his part in the vineyard of the Lord," he would often say, when he seemed to groan and to bend under the burden of saving the Faubourg St. Germain, the Faubourg St. Honoré, and the Chaussée d'Antin.

He was a man of sense and wit, an easy-going priest, who adapted everything to the precept : " The letter killeth, but the spirit giveth life." He was tolerant and intelligent. He knew how to understand and how to smile. He measured out faith according to people's temperament, and only insisted upon little doses at a time. He sweetened penance, planed away the knots from the cross, sanded the way of salvation. From the hard, ugly, rigorous religion of the poor, he detached, as it were, the pleasant religion of the rich—light, easy, elastic, suiting itself to things and to persons, to all the demands of society—to its customs, to its habits, and even to its prejudices. Out of the image of God he managed to make something comfortable and elegant.

The Abbé Blampoix had all the charm of a priest who is

cultivated, talented, and refined. He knew how to mingle conversation and confession; how to put salt into his exhortations, and pleasantness into his unction. He knew how to move and how to interest. He was acquainted with all the words which touch, the words which caress, and the words which tickle. His voice was musical, his style flowery. He called the devil the " prince of evil," and the eucharist the " divine nourishment." He abounded in periphrases as highly coloured as pious engravings. He could talk of Rossini, and quote Racine; he said, " The Bois," for the Bois de Boulogne. If he spoke of divine love it was in language that excited his listeners; if of the vices of to-day, it was in a piquant style of his own; if of the world, he used the language of the world. Now and then the most modern fashionable expressions and the most intimate words in the language appeared in his spiritual discourses, like fragments from a newspaper in an ascetic book. He was impregnated with the odour of the century. His cassock smelt, so to speak, of all the pretty faults which had approached it. He was profound and sharp on all subtle temptations; and his tact, his discernment, and his delicacy in all matters of sensual casuistry were admirable. Women raved about him.

His first step—his appearance almost in the ecclesiastical career, had been marked by a seduction, a transporting of souls, a success which reached the proportions of a triumph and almost of a scandal. At the end of a year, during which he had conducted the catechism class in the parish of ——, the archbishop called him to other duties, and replaced him by another priest; thereupon the class rebelled. All the young girls refused to see or to listen to the new-comer. These little hearts and these little heads were all in a ferment. There were tears among the whole flock; a real outbreak of regrets, which in a short time developed into open resistance. The eldest girls of the class carried on the struggle during several months. They agreed amongst themselves not to attend the classes any more; they even went so far as to refuse to give to the priest the missionary-box of which they had charge. They were appeased with great difficulty. The fortune that all this announced to the Abbé Blampoix had never failed him. His reputation spread rapidly. The power which, in Paris, touches everything, even a priest's cassock—I mean fashion —took him up and started him. People came to him from all sides. The small fry of sins went to others; to him people only brought their choice sins. Around him one heard the rustling of fine names, great fortunes, pretty contritions, and smart gowns. Mothers consulted him before taking out their daughters; girls went to him for advice before going out. He could give or refuse leave to wear a low dress; he decided the height of ball-dresses, and what books might be read; to him people applied for a list of novels or of plays that they might see. He prepared for the first communion, and he performed the marriage ceremonies. He baptised the children, and listened to confessions of adulteries committed in the heart. Women who were misunderstood at home came to groan to him over the material nature of their husbands, and he gave them a little ideal something which they could take back with them. Despairs and great sorrows had recourse to him, and he ordered them a journey to Italy, the distractions of pictures and music, and a good confession in Rome. Women who were separated addressed themselves to him to arrange matters quietly for them, to enable them to return home. He was called upon to act as peace-maker between loving wives and jealous mothers-in-law. He pro-

vided mothers with governesses; to young women he gave
ladies'-maids of forty. Young married women learned
from him how to retain their happiness and their husbands
by the discretion and the delicacy of their toilet, by their
cleanliness, by their neatness, and by the fineness of their
linen. " My dear child," he would occasionally say, " an
honest woman must have a little odour of an actress about
her." His experience entered into the hygiene of marriage.
Maternity recommended itself to his knowledge, pregnancy
listened to his foresight ; he could decide whether a woman
ought to be a mother, and whether a mother ought to
nourish her child.

This fashion, this part that he played, this intimate
handling of women's souls; this possession of all secrets,
these confidences and acquaintances ; these constant
communications with the promoters and treasurers of
good works, authorised by the requirements and interests
of charity; all the influences which a clever, discreet,
and helpful priest can amass—and in Paris they are
many—had given to Abbé Blampoix one of those great
powers which spread underground. Interests, like everything else, came and confessed to him. Social ambitions
had recourse to his good nature. And almost all
people with daughters to marry addressed themselves
to this priest who had no political convictions, who was
widely known in all grades of society, and so situated
that he had wonderful means of bringing old names
together or crossing old families, of adapting conveniences,
of balancing positions, of uniting money to money, or old
titles to new fortunes. One would have said that marriages
in Paris possessed an occult providence in this rare man,
who was in himself a priest and a lawyer, an apostle and
a diplomat, Fénélon and Monsieur de Foy.

The Abbé Blampoix had a private fortune of forty thousand francs a-year, of which he gave half to the poor. He had refused a bishopric to remain what he was: a priest.

"Whom have I the honour of addressing?" said the abbé, who seemed to be searching for a name in his memory.

"Madame Mauperin—mother of Madame Davarande."

"I beg your pardon, madame; you are not one of those whom one quickly forgets. But pray sit down in this arm-chair."

And seating himself opposite to her, with his back to the light, he continued: "The marriage which gave me the opportunity of making your acquaintance, is a very pleasant recollection to me, I mean the marriage of your daughter and Monsieur Davarande. Between us, madame, you and I, you with your mother's affection, I with the poor lights of a humble priest, brought about a truly Christian marriage, which responded at once to all the need of religion in that dear girl, to all the need of her heart, and to all the requirements of her position in the world. Madame Davarande is one of my model penitents; I am thoroughly well pleased with her. Monsieur Davarande is an excellent fellow who shares, what is so rare now-a-days, the religious sentiments of his wife. One's soul rests with pleasure upon homes so happy, so distinguished as theirs is, and I feel certain beforehand that you have not come to me on their account."

"Quite true, sir; I am very happy as regards them —their happiness is a great joy in my life. It is such a responsibility to marry one's children. No, I do not come on their account; it is on my own."

"On your own, dear madame?"

And the abbé threw a sly glance at her which he withdrew immediately.

"Ah! sir, years bring many changes. Until my age one is distracted by many things; one has the world, society—and it all amuses one. One forgets one's troubles, one likes it all, one believes in it, one leans upon it—one imagines that one will never want anything else. Well, sir, I have reached the age at which one does want something else. You understand me—I feel the emptiness of the world. Nothing interests me. I wish to return to what I have abandoned. I know how indulgent you are, and how charitable. I am in want of your advice, your hand to bring me back to the performance of all those duties which I have too long neglected, without ceasing nevertheless to know and to respect them. You understand those troubles, sir?"

While she was thus speaking, with that flow of words which belongs to a woman, and especially to a Parisian, which is vulgarly called "gab," Madame Mauperin's eyes, which avoided those of the priest as if they felt them in the shadow, had fallen mechanically upon some light apparently moved by his hands, glittering in a sunbeam, shining in the middle of this room, which was the room of a man of business, severe, solemn, and cold. This light came from a jewel case, with the diamonds in which the priest's fingers were playing.

"Ah, that!" said the priest, catching Madame Mauperin's glance and answering her thought without answering her phrase, "that surprises you, does it not? Yes, it is a jewel case—diamonds, and fairly good ones too." He handed her the necklace. "It is curious, is it not, that this should be here? But how can it be helped? That is our modern society. We have to mix with a little of all sorts—A sad scene! I have not yet recovered from it—tears, sobs—perhaps you heard them? An unhappy young woman rolling at my feet, mother of a family, madame. Alas! so runs the world—see to what the love of dress and of all that helps to please may lead one. People go on spending, spending till at last they can only pay the shops the interest on their bills. Yes, madame, that happens; I could give you the names of the shops. They always hope to be able to pay the capital some day—they count upon a son-in-law to whom they can tell all, and who will be only too happy to pay his mother-in-law's debts. But meanwhile the shops get impatient—and one fine day they threaten to disclose everything to the husband—then, oh! then! imagine the misery. Do you know that just now a person was threatening to throw herself into the river? I have had to promise to find thirty thousand francs. But I beg your pardon, madame. I am talking of my own affairs. Let us return to you, and your's——You had a second daughter—a charming girl. I prepared her for her first communion. Let me see what was her Christain name?"

" Renée!"

" Exactly; that's it. A very intelligent child—very quick; an exceptional nature. She is not married?"

" No, sir, and it is a great trouble to me; you don't know what a curious character she has. She is not the least like her sister. She has one of those natures that are most trying to a mother. I had much rather she were less clever. We have tried to make the most suitable matches for her; she refuses them giddily, madly. It was only yesterday—— Besides which her father spoils her so terribly."

" Ah, that is a pity! You would never believe what a

motherly interest one takes in children whom one has brought to Jesus and to Mary. But you tell me nothing about your son—a charming fellow, who is doing very well, and who is old enough now to think of marrying if I remember rightly?"

"Do you know him, sir?"

"I had the pleasure of meeting him once at the house of his sister, Madame Davarande, when I went to see her during her illness; for you must know that the only visits we ever pay are those to the sick. And besides, I hear on all sides good accounts of him. You are a happy mother, madame; your son practises his religion. At Easter he communicated at the Jesuit Church. I daresay he did not tell you that that he was one of a number of truly Christian young men of the world, who waited nearly all night to make their confessions, so great was the crowd! Yes, one would not believe it, but, thank God, it is a fact. Young men, in the best society, waited until five in the morning to confess. I need not tell you how much the Church is touched by such zeal; how grateful she is to those who, in these sad times of demoralisation and unbelief, give her this consolation and pay her this homage; in short, how we, her servants, are favourably disposed towards these young men who show such goodwill and so good an example, and how ready we are to give them all the little help in our power, and to support with the little influence that we may have in families——"

"Ah, sir, you are too good—and our gratitude, mine and that of my son—if you would only occupy yourself with him. It was a happy thought of mine to come and see you. Dear me! I came to you as a woman, but I also came as a mother. My son is an angel, sir. And then you can do so much!"

The priest shook his head with a smile of denial in which modesty was mingled with melancholy : " No, madame ; you exaggerate. We are far from being what you say. Sometimes we succeed in doing some small good, but even that is very difficult ! If you knew how little influence a priest has nowadays ! People are afraid of him ; they keep out of his way ; they will not meet him except in church, nor speak to him outside the confessional. Why, you yourself, madame, would be surprised if your director mixed himself up in your everyday affairs. So prejudiced is the world against us that it is always on the defensive, trying to keep us at arm's length."

" Goodness ! here it is one o'clock already. I saw your table laid as I came in. I am ashamed of myself. You will let me come back in a few days."

" My luncheon is made to wait," said the Abbé Blampoix. Then turning towards a writing-table covered with papers near him, he signed to Madame Mauperin to sit down again. An instant of silence, during which nothing was to be heard but the rustling of the papers as the abbé turned them over, followed. It ended by the abbé drawing a visiting card, with the corner turned down, out of a heap of papers. He turned it towards the light and read: " Three hundred thousand francs, stocks, government bonds. Fifteen thousand francs a-year the day of marriage. Father and mother dead. Six hundred thousand francs on the deaths of uncles and aunts who are unmarried and will not marry. Young— nineteen ; charming—prettier than she thinks." " Think that over," said the priest, replacing the card among his papers. " You see—well I have—yes, I have at this minute an orphan with five-and-twenty thousand francs a-year the day she marries. But that would not do,

Her guardian wants influence. He is one of the second-class referendaries in the audit-office, and will only give his ward to a son-in-law who can obtain his nomination as first-class referendary. Ah, wait a minute; this might do." And, as he turned over his notes, he continued: " Twenty-two years of age; not pretty; accomplished, intelligent, dresses well; father, fifteen hundred thousand francs; three children; fortune secure. The house in the Rue de Provence, where the offices of the ' Security' insurance company are, belongs to him; property in the department of the Orne; two hundred thousand francs in government stocks;—a solid man, of Portuguese origin. The mother counts for nothing in the house. No relations, and the father would be angry if you tried to see the few there are. You see I hide nothing from you. They meet together once a-year, at dinner, and that is all. The father will give his daughter three hundred thousand francs, and wishes her to live with him."

And, turning over his notes again: " Yes," he went on, " that is all that I have at this moment likely to suit you. Now talk it over with your son, dear madame. Consult your husband. I am entirely at your service. If you can, the next time I have the honour to receive a visit from you, will you bring me a few figures, a little memorandum, which might give me an idea of your intentions as regards your son? And do bring your daughter to see me; I should be delighted to see that dear child again."

" Would you be so kind, sir, as to name an hour at which I should inconvenience you somewhat less than I have done to-day ? "

" I belong, madame, to all who have need of me, and I am too much honoured. I would only ask you not to come in about a fortnight's time. I shall then be quite in the country, and shall only come into Paris once a week. Yes, I have been obliged to make up my mind to it; by the end of the winter I find myself so worn out. I have so much to do—and besides these four floors kill me. But it cannot be helped—one must pay something for the privilege of having one's own chapel, the precious permission to say mass in one's own house. You know that no one may sleep over a chapel. But while I think of it, why not come and see me in the country, at Colombes? It would be a little outing. I have fruit trees—my only vanity as a land-owner. I would offer a simple luncheon, dear madame, to you and to your charming daughter. Will not your delightful son do me the pleasure of coming with you?"

VII

A QUARTER of an hour later, a servant in a red waistcoat opened, in answer to Madame Mauperin's bell, the door of some first floor rooms in the Rue Taitbout.

"Good day, George; is my son in?"

"Yes, madame, monsieur is in his room."

Madame Mauperin had smiled at her son's servant. As she passed them, she smiled at his rooms, his ornaments, his furniture.

She went into his study, where Henry was writing and smoking. He said, "Hulloa!" took the cigar out of his mouth, threw his head on to the back of his arm-chair to be kissed by his mother, then beginning to smoke again: "Is it you, mamma; in Paris to-day? You had not told me you were coming. What has brought you?"

"Oh, some business, some visits—you know I am always behindhand. How comfortable you are here."

"Ah, true! you have not seen my new arrangements."

"But, dear me, how comfortable you know how to make yourself. Only you understand it. Are you sure it is not damp here?" And Madame Mauperin laid her hand upon the wall. "Tell George to open the windows whenever you go out, won't you?"

"Yes, yes, mother," said Henry in the bored tone in which one answers a child.

"Oh, why have you those things? I do not like your having them"—Madame Mauperin had just noticed two

duelling swords over a book-case—" Only to look at them.
When one thinks—"

Madame Mauperin shut her eyes for an instant and sat
down. " You do not know how your odious bachelor life
makes us tremble. If you were married I think that I
should no longer be so tormented. I wish I could see you
married, Henry."

" I too, I assure you."

" Really ? Come now, you can have no secrets from your
mother, you know. I am afraid, when I see you as you are,
handsome, witty, possessed of all that can please, you who
so deserve to be loved! Well, I am afraid—"

" Of what ? "

" That—that you may have some reason for not—"

" For not marrying, do you mean ? Some chain I suppose."

Madame Mauperin nodded her head.

Henry burst into a fit of laughter.

" Oh, my dear mamma, if I did have one I would soon
file it through! A man who respects himself wears no
other."

" Well, then, will you explain to me about Mademoiselle
Herbault ? It was you who broke it off."

" Mademoiselle Herbault ? The introduction with my
father at the opera ? Ah, not that one! Yes, yes, Mademoiselle Herbault—the dinner at Madame Marquisat's, do
you mean ?—the last one, in short ? An ambush into
which you let me walk without any warning! I must say
that you are simple. I am announced, Monsieur Henry
Mauperin! in a sonorous voice, which seemed to say :
'Here is the future husband!' I find all the candles
lighted in the drawing-room. The mistress of the house,
whom I had only seen twice in my life, overwhelms me

with smiles; her son. whom I don't know, squeezes my hand. In the drawing-room are also a mother and daughter, who seem not to see me. Very good! Naturally, I take the young lady into dinner; provincial family, fortune all in farms, tastes simple. I see all that with the soup. The mother, on the other side of the table, keeps her eyes fixed on us; such a mother, in such a gown. I ask the daughter if she had seen the ' Prophète ' at the opera ? "

" Yes, it is splendid—especially that effect in the third act. Ah, yes! that effect—that effect."

She had not seen it any more than I had. Untruthful to begin with. I amuse myself by teasing her a little about it. That makes her cross. We go into the drawing-room.

" What a pretty gown; have you noticed it?" says the mistress of the house to me. " Would you believe it. I have known that gown for five years? Emmeline takes such care of her things! So much method!"

Miserly curmudgeons, who wanted to catch me.

" Do you think so? Nevertheless, our information—"

" A woman who makes her gowns last for five years! That is enough for me! One can fancy her fortune in a woollen stocking! One can fancy her property, two-and-a-half per cent., repairs, taxes, lawsuits, tenants who pay no rent, a father-in-law who regards you as unsaleable property! No, no, I am not young enough for that. I want to marry, but to marry well. Leave me alone, and you will see. Let me be. I am not one of those who are caught by a—' *She has such beautiful hair, and she is so fond of her mother !*' Do you see. mamma, without appearing to do so, I have thought a great deal about marriage. What is the most difficult thing to obtain in the world? what does one pay the highest price for? what does one fight for and only obtain by conquest?

what can one only get by a stroke of genius, of luck? by meannesses, by privations, by untiring efforts, by persever- ance, by resolution, by energy, by boldness, by work? It's money, is it not? To be rich is to be happy and honoured; it is the best means of securing the respect of the public. Well, I have seen that there is a method by which one may arrive at all that, at money, directly and immediately, with- out fatigue, without struggles, without genius, simply, natu- rally, honourably; that means is marriage. I have also observed this, that one need not be either suprisingly hand- some, nor astonishingly witty, to make a rich marriage; all that one wants is the will, to will it coldly and with all one's strength, to stake everything upon that card; in a word, to make one's marriage one's career. I have observed that in playing that game it is no more difficult to make a remark- able marriage than an ordinary one; to marry a fortune of two hundred thousand francs than one of twelve hundred thousand; that depends simply upon one's calmness and one's luck; one's stake is the same. In these days, when tenor singers can marry eight hundred thousand francs a year, arithmetic is at fault. That is what I wanted to say to you, and I am sure you have understood me."

Henry Mauperin added, taking the hand of his mother, who was open-mouthed with astonishment, admiration, almost respect: "Do not worry yourself; I will marry well, and perhaps even better than you expect."

And when his mother was gone, he took up his pen again, and continuing the article he was engaged upon for the *Financial Review*, wrote: "The trajectory of humanity is a spiral, not a circle."

VIII

HENRY MAUPERIN, like many young men of the present day, was not the age of his life, but the age of his time. The coldness of youth, the distinguishing feature of the second half of the nineteenth century, was imprinted upon his whole person; he appeared serious, and one felt that he was frozen. He possessed in himself all the elements generally omitted in the French temperament, which constitute in our history those sects without enthusiasm, and those parties without youth, yesterday jansenism, to-day doctrinarism. Henry Mauperin was a young doctrinaire.

He belonged to the generation of children who are astonished at nothing, amused at nothing, who go without excitement to a theatre, and come home without being dazzled. When still quite a boy, he was well behaved and serious. At school it never occurred to him to dream in class, his head in his hands, his elbows on a dictionary, his eyes looking forward into the future. He had none of the temptations of the unknown, and of those first visions of life which fill with commotion and delight sixteen-year old imaginations, between the four walls of a courtyard with barred windows, from which the balls rebound, but over which the thoughts fly. In his class there were some sons of political personages, and to these he attached himself. When he got higher up in school, he began to think of what club he would belong to.

When he left school, Henry continued well behaved, and

hid himself. His bachelor life made no stir. He was never
to be met where people play, nor where they drink, nor
where they compromise themselves in any way, but in grave
drawing-rooms he was to be found, attentive to and anxious
for the comfort of middle-aged women. What would
elsewhere have been disadvantageous to him, was of use
to him there. His coldness was treated as an attraction,
his seriousness was one of his charms. Men's charms
have their fashions. The reign of Louis Philippe, with its
great fortunes made in the universities, had just accustomed
the large political and literary circles of Paris to value in
their men of society, that I know not what of the peda-
gogue's gown which every professor, even when he has
become a minister, wears about him in the world. Amongst
the women of the highest middle classes the taste for
language which suggests the schools, for science fresh from
a desk, for a sort of learned amiability, had succeeded to the
taste for more lively, witty, gay qualities of mind. A pedant
frightened nobody, even when old; when young, he charmed,
and report said that Henry Mauperin charmed greatly.

He had a practical mind. He professed the worship of
the useful, of mathematical truths, of positive religions,
and of exact sciences. He took pity upon art, and main-
tained that Boule furniture was never better made than
now. Political economy, that science that leads to everything, appeared to him, when he made his entry into
society, as a vocation and a career, and he became a
resolute economist. On this dry study he brought to bear
an intelligence narrow indeed, but patient and laborious,
and every fortnight he launched in a leading Review, some
solid article, stuffed with figures, which the women skipped,
and the men pretended to have read.

Political economy, by the interest it takes in the poor

classes, by its preoccupation for their comfort, by the
algebraical accounts that it keeps of their sufferings, had
naturally tinged Henry Mauperin's mind with liberalism.
His opposition was not very decided; his opinions were
only ahead of governmental principles, in that mass of
convictions which go to meet the future, prepare the way
for them, and make advances to all that may happen. He
limited his war against power to a word, a veiled allusion,
of which he sent the interpretation into society by means
of his friends. At heart he was rather coquetting with the
actual state of things than in opposition to it. Drawing-
room friendships and society acquaintanceships kept him
within reach of government influences, and on the border-
land of administrative patronage. He prepared the work,
and corrected the proofs for a high functionary who had
scarcely time to do more than put his name to his books.
He was on very good terms with the prefect of his department, hoping, through him, to push himself into the Municipal Council, and thence into the Chamber. He excelled
in all double games, all compromises, all arrangements
which gave him a hold upon everything, without making
him quarrel with anything. A Liberal and an economist,
he had found means to disarm the mistrust and the hostility
which the Catholics felt for his person and his doctrines.
Amongst them he had gained for himself some indulgence
and some sympathies; he had succeeded in making himself
agreeable to the clergy, and in flattering the Church by
reconciling spiritual with material progress, political with
religious faith, Quesnay with St. Augustine, Bastiat with
the Gospel, statistics with God. Then, in addition to this
programme, this alliance between religion and political
economy, he had a substratum of religion, certain habits of
piety, hidden indeed but regular, which gained for him the

affectionate esteem of the Abbé Blampoix, and made him side secretly with the believing and practising section of society.

Henry Mauperin had taken his rooms in the Rue Taitbout, in order to give evening parties to young men — serious evening parties round a table resembling a writing-desk, at which his guests discussed natural rights, public assistance, productive forces, and the multiplicability of the human species. Henry tried to turn these parties into a sort of debating society He sorted his men, and picked out the elements from which to compose the great salon which he meant to have in Paris as soon as he was married. He attracted thither the authorities and notabilities of political economy; he called to the honour of a sort of presidency, different members of the Institute, whom he pursued with his civilities and requests, and who should, according to his plans, some day call him to sit next to them in the section of political and moral sciences.

But it was in all that he got out of the association that Henry had displayed all his talents, all his skill. He had attached himself, at first starting, to the great means of achieving success practised by all cyphers, which makes a man to be no longer one, but a unit bound up with a number. He had joined himself to associations of every kind. He had affiliated himself to the Aguesseau debating club, and had slipped in amongst all the young men who were learning to speak, getting up the tricks of the rostrum, going through their oratorical apprenticeship, learning the way to become statesmen, preparing for the parliamentary struggles of the future. Clubs, re-unions, and banquets of old fellow-students, lawyers' meetings, societies of historians, geographers, men of science, charitable and good works, he had neglected none of them. Everywhere, in all

the centres which make the individual shine, and which also
make him benefit by the collective influence of a number,
he had shown and multiplied himself, increasing his acquaintance, tightening connecting links, cultivating friendships and sympathies which might carry him far, throwing
out far and wide the roots of his ambitions, marching on
from charitable works to philosophical meetings, gradually
increasing his importance, his subterranean notoriety, with
the intention of ending one fine day in a name with which
the political world should ring.

Nothing was wanting in him for the perfect performance
of this part. Talkative and restless, he made all the noise
which leads to success in our present age; he was a
splendid mediocrity.

In society, he rarely quoted his articles. But he
generally and naturally put one hand into his waistcoat,
after the manner of Monsieur Guizot in the portrait of
him by Delaroche.

IX

"Hulloa!" exclaimed Renée, panting like a child who has been running, as she entered the dining-room at eleven o'clock—"I thought everyone was down. What has become of mamma?"

"She is in Paris—on business," answered Monsieur Mauperin.

"Ah! and Denoisel?"

"He has gone to see that garden-planning maniac, and will have stayed to breakfast. Let us begin."

"Good morning, papa!" And instead of sitting down, Renée going up to her father, threw her arms round his neck and began kissing him.

"Come, come, you mad child," said Monsieur Mauperin. And he smiled as he struggled.

"Let me give you a baby kiss, see, like this,"—and she pinched his cheeks together in her fingers.

"What a child you are, upon my word!"

"Look at me, so that I may see whether you love me a little."

And Renée, moved a step backwards from her father, whose head she still held at arm's length. They looked into each other's eyes, lovingly, deeply.

The long window of the dining-room was wide open and gave entrance to the brightness from outside, the scents and the noises of the garden. A ray of sunshine danced upon the table, touching the china and glinting in the glasses.

A light breeze made itself felt in the outside air; shadows of leaves fell softly upon the floor. One could hear indistinctly the noise of wings in the trees, birds playing among the flowers far off.

"Only our two selves. How delightful!" said Renée, unfolding her napkin. "Oh, the table is too big; I am too far away."

And taking up her glasses she came and sat beside her father.

"Since I have my papa all to myself to-day, I intend to thoroughly enjoy him," she said, as she brought her chair close to his.

"You remind me of the days when you always hunted in my pockets for your dinner. But you were eight years old then."

Renée began to laugh.

"I got a scolding yesterday," continued Monsieur Mauperin, after a moment's silence, laying down his knife and fork upon his plate.

"Ah!" merely said Renée, raising an innocent glance to the ceiling, then dropping upon her father her caressing eyes: "Really, poor papa. And why? What had you done?"

"You had better not ask me that again. You know better than I do. What do you mean, you bad child?"

"Oh, if you are going to scold me, papa, I shall get up and kiss you." And, as she spoke, Renée half rose.

"Sit down, Renée, if you please," said Monsieur Mauperin, in a voice which he tried to make severe. "You will admit that yesterday, my dear child—"

"Oh, papa, are you going to say 'you' to me instead of 'thou' on such a fine day?"

" But really," said Monsieur Mauperin trying to remain dignified in face of the little impertinent look of his daughter, in which caress was mingled with defiance,—" Will you explain to me? for evidently you did it on purpose."

Renée, winking her eyes maliciously, nodded her head affirmatively two or three times.

" I intended to speak seriously to you, Renée."

" But I am quite serious, I assure you—and when I have told you that I acted as I did quite on purpose."

" And pray why? Will you tell me?

" Why? yes I will, but on the condition of its not making you too conceited. It was because—because—"

" Because what? "

" Because I am much fonder of you than I am of the gentleman who was here yesterday, there!—but much fonder, you know! "

" In that case we must not let people come here. If that young man was displeasing to you. We did not force you. It was you who allowed matters to go so far. We thought, on the other hand, your mother and I, that this marriage—"

" Pardon me, papa. If I had refused Monsieur Reverchon at first sight, straight away, you would have considered me giddy, foolish, idiotic. I can hear now all that mamma would have said. But as matters now stand, what have you to scold me for? I saw Monsieur Reverchon, more than once, I gave myself plenty of time to appreciate him, and I finally convinced myself that I felt towards him an antipathy, which may perhaps be very stupid, but which nevertheless—"

" But why not have told us so? We would have found a thousand ways of breaking off."

" Papa, you are ungrateful. I saved you that trouble

The young man disappears without your having anything to
do with it. It is all my doing. And that is all the thanks
I get for my devotion! Another time—"

"Listen to me, dear child. If I speak to you in this tone,
it is because your marriage is at stake. Your marriage. I
have been a long time making up my mind to the idea of
separating from you. Fathers are selfish, you see. They
would like their daughters never to fly away. It is so
difficult to them to picture their happiness without your
smile, their house without the sound of your dress! But
one must make up one's mind to it. It seems to me now
that I shall love my son-in-law. You see I am getting old,
my dear Renée,—" and Monsieur Mauperin took the two
hands of his daughter into his own—"Your father is sixty-
eight my child. I have only just time to see you happy.
Your future, believe me, is my constant thought; it worries
me. Your mother also loves you dearly, I know, but
between your character and hers there is—and then if
anything were to happen to me! One must look things
straight in the face, and at my age—do you see, the idea of
leaving you without seeing you with a husband and
children—affections which might replace in your heart the
affection of your poor, old father who would be with you
no longer."

Monsieur Mauperin could not continue; his daughter
was embracing him, choking with sobs, crying on his
shoulder.

"Oh, it's wicked, wicked—" said she in a stifled voice.
"Why speak of it? Never! never!" And with a
gesture she chased the vision from her thoughts.

Monsieur Mauperin had taken her on to his knees. He
put his arms round her, kissed her forehead, and said:
"Don't cry any more."

She went on repeating, "Never! wicked!" as though fighting with the end of a bad dream. Then drying her eyes on the back of her hand, she said to her father:

"Let me go and cry a little, all alone" and ran away.

"Dardouillet is certainly mad," said Denoisel, coming in "I thought I should never get away from him again—ah, you are alone?"

"Yes, my wife has gone to Paris. Renée has just gone upstairs."

"You look worried, Monsieur Mauperin."

"I? It's nothing. A little scene with Renée. I have just had one on account of this marriage, this Reverchon. I was stupid enough to tell her that I was in a hurry to see my grand-children—that fathers are not immortal. Thereupon, the poor child is so easily upset, you know. She is now crying in her room. Don't go there. Leave her time to get over it. Meanwhile I am going to look after my workmen."

Denoisel, left alone, lighted a cigar, took a book, and went to read on a bench in the garden. He had been there quite two hours when he saw Renée coming. She had on her hat, and on her animated face a sort of joy seemed to be sparkling, a sort of tender and loving excitement.

"You have been out? And where do you come from?"

"Where I come from?" repeated Renée, untying the ribbons of her hat. Well, I will tell you, because you are my friend." And taking off her hat, and raising her head with the pretty movement of a woman shaking back her hair:

"I have been to church, and if you wish to know what I have been doing there. I have been praying God to let me die before papa. I knelt before a large statue of the

Virgin—don't laugh at me—it would hurt me to be laughed at by you. It was perhaps the sun, or perhaps from looking at her for so long. I do not know—but at one moment I fancied she went like this." And Renée nodded her head in sign of yes. "I am very happy all the same—and my knees are hurting me nicely too, by the way—for I prayed kneeling all the time, without a chair, without anything, on the pavement. Ah, I prayed in earnest that time. They cannot refuse me that!"

X.

A FEW days later Monsieur and Madame Mauperin, Henry. Renée, and Denoisel, were sitting, after dinner, in the garden which stretched behind the house, squeezing itself in between the walls of the buildings belonging to the refinery. The principal tree in the garden was a fir-tree. Roses had grown up amongst its lower branches, and its green arms swayed them to and fro. Near the tree was a swing. behind it a shrubbery composed of lilacs and horn-beam; in front of it, a circle of turf, a bench, and a little basin with a margin of white stone, and a fountain which played no longer; it was full of water plants, and at the bottom, in the little water that remained, some black salamanders were swimming.

"Are you still thinking of your private theatricals. Renée," asked Henry of his sister, "or has that plan been given up?"

"Given up? no; but how can I help it? it is not my fault. I would willingly act on my head. But I can get nobody—and unless I play a monologue—Denoisel has refused. It is no use asking a grave man like you," she said to her brother.

"I will gladly act." said Henry.

"You, Henry?" said Madame Mauperin, surprised.

"But men are never difficult to get." continued Renée: "one can always find men to act. But the women—there's the rub—I see none to act with me."

F

" Oh." said Henry, " if we think over all our acquaintances we shall easily find some one, I bet."

" Let us see — Monsieur Durand's daughter — eh ?
Monsieur Durand's daughter.   They are at Saint Denis
—it would be convenient for the rehearsals.   She is rather
a stick, but it seems to me that for the part of Madame
de Chavigny—"

" So you are still bent upon playing ' The Caprice'?" said
Denoisel.

" And what of that, old morality? since I shall act with
my brother."

" And the proceeds of the performance will go to the
poor, I hope ? " said Denoisel.

" Why so ? "

" Because you will thereby predispose your audience to
be charitable."

" We shall see, monsieur, we shall see.   Mamma, what
do you say to Emma Durand ? "

" Those people are not in our set, my dear child,"
hastily rejoined Madame Mauperin ; " it is all very well
to see them from time to time, but we know where they
come from—from the Rue St. Honoré.   Madame Durand
used to go and take orders at the doors of her customers' carriages, and meanwhile, Monsieur Durand used
to slip out by a back door and take the servants to drink
at the nearest wine-shop.   That is how the Durands made
their fortune ! "

Although at heart an excellent woman, Madame Mauperin
rarely lost an opportunity of running down, with the most
superb expressions of contempt and disgust, everyone of
her acquaintance.   It was not from a love of evil-speaking,
nor for the pleasure of backbiting or calumniating, nor was
it from envy ; but she refused all consideration to people,

She even denied them the wealth they were supposed to have, simply from a supreme middle-class pride, from a conviction that, except her blood, there was no such thing as good blood in the world; except her family, no respectable family; except her own people, nothing but scoundrels; except her own possessions, nothing solid; except what she had got, nothing merited.

"And to think that my wife can tell a story of that kind of every creature we know!" said Madame Mauperin.

"Well, papa, suppose we try that pretty little Remoli girl?"

"Ask your mother. What have you to say, Madame Mauperin?"

"The little Remoli girl! Why, my dear, you know—"

"I know nothing."

"What? The story of her father, don't you know? A wretched Italian stucco-maker. He came to Paris without a shilling; bought, no one knows how, a hovel and a bit of land at Montparnasse, and found there, on his land, a real Montfaucon! He sold upwards of eight hundred thousand francs' worth of stucco! And then he cheated on the Stock Exchange. Bah!"

"It seems to me," said Henry, "that you are hunting very far afield. Why not ask Mademoiselle Bourjot? They are at this moment at Sannois."

"Mademoiselle Bourjot?" asked Madame Mauperin.

"Naomi?" chimed in Renée; "of course I should be delighted. But I fancied her cold to me this winter. There is something wrong. I do not know."

"What is the matter with her is that she will some day have three hundred thousand francs a-year," interrupted Denoisel; "and mothers watch over such daughters as that. They are not ready to allow them to become too intimate with girls who have brothers. She has learned her lesson, that is all."

" And then they are always so haughty, those people ! One would think they were descended from—"

And Madame Mauperin suddenly broke off to ask Henry—

" But all the same, they have always been very kind to you, have they not, Henry ? Madame Bourjot is always very pleasant to you."

" She has even complained to me, more than once, that she did not see you oftener at her parties, and that you did not let Renée see so much of her daughter."

" Really ? " said Renée, quite happy.

" Mauperin," said his wife, " what do you say to Henry's proposal, Mademoiselle Bourjot ? "

" What objection do you expect me to make ? "

" Then," said Madame Mauperin, " Henry's idea is carried unanimously. We will go there on Saturday. Will you come too, Mauperin ? Henry, you will go with us ! "

A few hours later every one was in bed. Henry Mauperin alone awake, was walking up and down his room, puffing at a cigar that was out. One would have said that from time to time he smiled at his thoughts.

XI

FREQUENTLY, during the day-time, Renée would go and
paint in a little studio, built out of the remains of a greenhouse, hidden in a corner of the garden, of rustic appearance,
and looking as though it were part of the shrubbery, overgrown with ivy, partaking of the nature of a ruin and a nest.

On a table, covered with an Algerian cloth, there were
on the day in question a Japanese vase, covered with blue
designs, a lemon, an old red almanac, with the arms of
France upon its cover, and two or three other bright-
coloured objects grouped as naturally as possible to make
a picture, in the full glare of the sunlight that pierced the
glass roof. Renée, at the table, was painting all this on
a canvass, of which the other side had already done duty,
with brushes as fine as pins. The skirt of her gown, of
white piqué, stood out in large folds on either side of the
stool on which she was seated. As she came through the
garden, she had gathered a white rose, and had fastened
it into a tuft of hair, just above her ear. Her foot, peeping
out from under her petticoat, and shod with an open slipper,
displayed a glimpse of her white stocking, as she rested it
upon the cross-bar of her easel.

Near her, Denoisel, watching her at work, was trying his
hand on a sketch of her profile on a page of an album which
he had picked up in a corner.

" Well, you are a good model!" exclaimed he, sharpen-
ing his pencil. " I would as soon try to catch an omnibus

as your likeness. You are never still. If you fidget like that—"

" Look here, Denoisel, no nonsense with your portrait. I hope you are going to flatter me a little."

" No more than the sun. My conscience is that of a camera."

" Shew me," said she, leaning over towards Denoisel, and holding her maul-stick and palette crossed on her breast. " Well, I must be beautiful." And she turned to her painting again. " Am I really, really like that ? "

" A little. Now, Renée, tell me honestly. What do you think you are—beautiful ? "

" No."

" Pretty ? "

" No—no."

" Ah ! this time you thought before you answered ? "

" Yes, but I repeated it twice over."

" Good. Well, if you think yourself neither beautiful nor pretty, I am sure that you neither consider yourself—"

" Ugly ? No; that is true. It is very difficult to explain to you. There are days on which, when I look at myself, I think myself—how shall I put it ? Well, I am pleased with myself. It is not my face, I know very well ; it is a look which I have on those days, something that is in me, and which I feel passes into my features. I do not know what it is—happiness, pleasure, excitement, emotion —call it what you will ! There are moments, I fancy, when I deceive my neighbours pretty thoroughly. But, all the same, I should like to have been beautiful."

" Dear me, dear me."

" It must be so pleasant, I think. I should like to have been tall, with very black hair. It is stupid to be so fair. It is like having a white skin. I should like to have a skin

like Madame Stavelot—I declare I should—rather orange.
I like that; it is to my taste. And then it would have
given me pleasure to look at myself in my glass. I should
have made a beautiful outline in bed. When I walk about
barefoot on the carpet, when I get up, I feel that I should
like to have feet like those of statues that I have seen—it
is my idea!"

" And so you would not care to be beautiful for others?"

" Yes and no; not for everybody—only for those I love.
One ought to be ugly for people who are indifferent to one,
or for those one does not like: do you not think so? They
would only have their deserts."

Denoisel had begun to sketch again. " What a curious
wish it is of yours to be dark!" said he, after a minute's
silence.

" What would be your dream?"

" If I were a woman, I should wish to be a little woman,
neither fair nor dark."

" Chestnut, then?"

" And plump—oh, plump as a quail."

" Plump? Ah, I breathe again! For a moment I feared
you were going to propose to me. It was lucky that the
sun shining on your head reminded me that you were
forty."

" You do not make me older than I am, Renée; that is
my age. But do you know how old you are in my eyes?"

" No?"

" Twelve; and you will always remain so."

" Thank you, my friend; I am glad to hear it," said
Renée; " for now I can say to you all the nonsense that
comes into my head. Denoisel," continued she, after a
pause, " were you ever in love?" And stepping back from
her canvas, she looked at it sideways, her head inclined

towards her shoulders, to see the effect of the colour she had just used.

"Come, you are beginning well!" answered Denoisel. "What a question to ask!"

"What is the matter with my question? I ask it you as I should ask you anything else. I can see nothing wrong in it. May one not ask that in society? Come, Denoisel; you allow that I am twelve years old. Very good; but I am also twenty. I am a girl, true; but if you fancy that girls of my age have never read any novels or sung any songs, that's all nonsense, that is—an affectation of inno-cence. After all, it's just as you like. If you do not think me old enough, I will withdraw my question. But I thought we were men talking to each other just now."

"Well, since you wish to know—yes, mademoiselle, I was once in love."

"Indeed! And what effect did being in love have upon you?"

"My dear child, you have only got to read again the words you have already read: you will find that effect described on every page—"

"Yes, and it is exactly that which makes me curious. Every book I read is full of love—nothing but that—and in real life one never sees it; at least I never do. I see, on the contrary, the world doing very well indeed without it. There are days upon which I ask myself whether it was not invented simply for the sake of books—if it is not the creation of authors' brains."

Denoisel began to laugh: "Tell me, Renée, since we are talking like men, as you say, perfectly frankly and openly, like old friends, will you allow me, in my turn, to ask you whether you have ever felt, not love, but a kindness for anyone?"

"No, never," answered Renée, after an instant's reflection. "But I—I am not a good example. I believe that those things come chiefly to people with empty, unoccupied hearts and minds—people who are not filled, possessed, guarded by an affection which seizes and keeps you entirely; such, for instance, as the love one feels for a father."

Denoisel did not answer.

"You do not believe in that as a preservative?" continued Renée. "I assure you, I search my memory vainly. I have made a most thorough and complete examination of conscience: I swear it. Well, in my childhood, I can find nothing—no, nothing at all. But I had little friends who were no older than I. When no one was looking they used to kiss the tops of the caps of the little boys who played with us. They used to collect the stones of the peaches that these little boys had eaten and keep them in a box, and I remember very well that they used to sleep with these boxes under their pillows. By the way, Naomi, Mademoiselle Bourjot used to do that a great deal. But I played quite innocently."

"And later on, when you were no longer a child?"

"Later on? I was always a child in those matters. No, I can remember nothing, not the faintest impression; that is to say—I am going to be very honest with you—I felt once a beginning, a quite little beginning of what you say, a little of that emotion which I afterwards recognised in novels. And do you know for whom?"

"No."

"For you—oh! it only lasted an instant. I soon learned to love you very differently—and much better too—with esteem and gratitude. I loved you for correcting me of my faults of a spoiled child, for having opened my mind, for having raised me to appreciate fine things, noble things, generous things, you did all that by chaff, but by chaff that laughed at everything that was ugly, everything that was mean, everything that was disgraceful, everything that was underhand and cowardly. You taught me to play at ball and to be bored by fools. I owe to you much of what I think, much of what I am, some of the little that I am worth; I wanted to return it to you in a good and solid friendship; giving you cordially, as to a comrade, some of the same kind of love that I feel for my father." And at these last words Renée's voice assumed a solemn, grave tone.

"What in the world is that?" asked Monsieur Mauperin, who came in at this moment, and casting his eyes over Denoisel's sketch; "that my daughter. It is an abominable libel." And taking up the sketch-book he began to tear the page across.

"Oh, papa!" cried Renée; "I wanted to keep it—as a souvenir."

XII.

A LIGHT carriage, drawn by one horse, carried the Mauperin family to Sannois. Renée had taken the reins and the whip out of the hands of her brother who was smoking beside her.

Cheered by the drive, the fresh air, the movement Monsieur Mauperin joked about all they saw on the road, and gaily nodded to everyone whom they passed. Madame Mauperin was silent and self-absorbed. Buried in herself, she was preparing and working up her amiability to the proper pitch before arriving at the country house for which they were bound.

" Well, mamma," said Renée, "you are quite silent. Are you not enjoying yourself?"

" Yes, very much, very much," answered Madame Mauperin; "but the fact is that this visit bores me a little—and without Henry—Madame Bourjot is sometimes so cold. There is a frigidity in their house. All the same, they cannot impose upon me—Their millions! I know very well where they got them from; they came from a business which they bought from a wretched working man for nothing, for a few pence."

" Come now, Madame Mauperin," said her husband, " they must have bought more than one at that price."

" Well, nevertheless. I am never comfortable in those people's house."

" You are really very good to occupy yourself about them."

" But we say ' rot ' to their fine airs," interrupted Mademoiselle Mauperin, whipping up the horse as she spoke, which drowned the word she had used with the noise of his hoofs.

Madame Mauperin's uneasiness was quite to be accounted for. Her discomfort was justifiable. Everything, in the house whither she was going, was combined to frighten people, to make them feel small, to crush, to penetrate and overpower them with a sense of their own inferiority. Their exhibition of wealth was studied, and their riches received the most careful stage-mounting. Opulence aimed at the humiliation of others by every means of intimidation at its command: by the showy or refined forms of luxury, by the height of its ceilings, by the impertinent looks of its footmen, by its hall porter with his silver chain, by the plate off which it ate, by a number of princely habits which made the mother and daughter, even when they were quite alone, dine together in low gowns, as in a little German court.

The Bourjots enjoyed the tone of their household, and supported it. The spirit of their home, of their everyday life, was, so to speak, incarnate in them. The man, with all that he had borrowed from English gentle people, his manners, his clothes, his curled whiskers, his veneer of good breeding, the woman with her mannerisms, her supreme elegance, all the hardness of the upper middle class, each of these represented admirably the Pride of Wealth. They seemed to wish to bring themselves down to the level of other people by their disdainful politeness, their condescending amiability. Even their tastes exhibited a sort of insolence. Monsieur Bourjot possessed neither pictures nor works of art ; he had made a collection of precious stones, which included a ruby worth five-and-twenty thousand francs, and was one of the finest in Europe.

Society had got over all this exhibition of wealth, and the Bourjots' house, brought into fashion and into light by a powerful opposition, was one of the three or four great houses of Paris. It had filled after two or three winters spent at Nice by Madame Bourjot, under pretext of delicate health, and during which she had turned her house into a hotel for travellers to Italy, opening it to all comers who were great, or rich, or celebrated, or well-known. On the days on which she gave her great concerts, at which Madame Bourjot would show off her fine voice and her really remarkable musical talent, European celebrities met Parisian reputations; the scientific world, the philosophical world, the æsthetic world, rubbed shoulders with the political world which was represented by a compact body of Orleanists and a band of liberals out of work, amongst whose ranks Henry Mauperin had figured continually during the past year. Amongst these were to be found a few legitimists, brought by the husband into his wife's drawing-room: for Monsieur Bourjot was a legitimist.

Under the Restoration monarchy he had been a Carbonaro. Son of a draper, his origin, his very name of Bourjot had, at the outset of life, exasperated him against the nobility, the landed gentry, the Bourbons. He had conspired. He had first made the acquaintance of Monsieur Mauperin at various secret meetings. He took part in every rising. At that time he used to quote Berville, St. Just, and Dupin the elder. After 1830 he quieted down, and then contented himself with grumbling at the royalty which had robbed him of his Republic. He read the *National*, pitied the people, despised the Chambers, abused Monsieur Guizot, flew into a passion over the Pritchard affair.

Suddenly 1848 arrived; the landowner started up, terrified and ousted the Carbonaro of the Restoration, the liberal of Louis-Philippe's reign. The fall in the Funds, the depreciation of house property, socialism, increased taxation, the threats contained in the Public Debt Accounts, the days of June, all the terrors, in fact, that a revolution has for the owner of a five-franc piece, upset Monsieur Bourjot, while at the same time they gave him fresh ideas. His opinions changed all at once, and his political conscience veered round entirely on its own axis. He precipitated himself towards the doctrines of order, he threw himself into the arms of the Church as into those of the police, he hastened towards Divine Right as towards the safeguard of authority, and as the guardian appointed by Providence to watch over his cash-boxes.

Unfortunately for Monsieur Bourjot, in his sudden and sincere conversion, his education, his youth, his past, his whole previous life struggled, fought, and rebelled. When he came round to the Bourbons, he could not return to Christ. And the old mammon still broke out sometimes in attacks, in pranks, and in old songs. As one came near him one felt that he still was something of a Voltairian. In him Béranger, every now and then, superseded De Maistre.

"Give the reins to your brother, Renée," said Madame Mauperin, "I do not wish them to see you driving."

They had arrived at some magnificent gates near which stood two large gas lamps which were lighted every evening and left to burn all night. The carriage drove over the red sand of an avenue, passed some large bushes of rhododendrons and arrived at the steps of the front-door. Two servants opened the glass doors of the marble-paved hall, whose high windows were screened by a large curtain of exotic shrubs. Thence, the Mauperins were shewn into a drawing-room hung with crimson silk, with nothing on the walls save one picture, the portrait of Madame Bourjot in

a ball-gown, signed " Ingres."   Through the open windows
a stork was visible near a piece of water, the only animal
that Monsieur Bourjot would tolerate in his park, and that
merely on account of its heraldic outline.

When the Mauperins entered the drawing-room, Madame
Bourjot, seated alone on a sofa, was listening to her
daughter's governess, who was reading aloud to her;
Monsieur Bourjot, leaning against the chimney-piece, was
playing with his watch-chain; Mademoiselle Bourjot,
seated near the reader, was working at an embroidery
frame.

Madame Bourjot, with her large eyes of rather steely
blue, her arched eyebrows, the droop of her eyelids, her
aristocratic and rather prominent nose, the haughty pro-
jection of the lower part of her face, and her imperious
manner, reminded one of the young Georges in the part of
Agrippina.   Mademoiselle Bourjot had strongly pencilled
brown eyebrows.   Through her long, curved eyelashes one
could see two blue eyes, bright, deep, and dreamy.   A
slight down, which was almost white, showed itself when
she was in a strong light, just above her lip, near the
corners.   The governess, poor thing, had one of those
battered-looking faces; she was an old woman who had
been knocked about, worn out by life, outwardly as well as
inwardly, and had no more effigy than an old halfpenny.

" But this is really delightful," exclaimed Madame
Bourjot, rising and going as far as a particular join in the
parquet floor just in the middle of the drawing-room.
" Our dear neighbours.   A charming surprise!   It seems to
me an age since I have had the pleasure of seeing you, dear
madam, and were it not that your son has had the goodness
not to neglect us, and to come to my Monday evenings,"
—here she shook hands with Henry, who bowed—" we

should not have known what had become of you, what had
happened to this charming child—and her mamma."

"Oh, madame," said Madame Mauperin, seating herself
at some distance from Madame Bourjot, "you are much too
kind."

"Do come and sit here," said Madame Bourjot, making
room for her on the sofa beside herself.

"We have put off coming from day to day; we all
wanted to come together."

"It was very wrong of you," answered Madame
Bourjot; "we are not a hundred miles away, and it is
a sin not to let those two children"—pointing to Renée
and Naomi—"who grew up together, ever see each other.
What! haven't you kissed each other yet?"

Naomi, who was still standing, offered her cheek coldly
to Renée, who kissed her much as a child bites at a fruit.

"Dear madame," said Madame Bourjot to Madame
Mauperin, "what a long time it seems since we used
to take them to those classes in the Rue de la Chaussée
d'Antin, which bored us nearly as much as they did the
children. I can see them now, playing together. Your
little girl, like quicksilver—a regular imp! And mine—
oh! they were like day and night. But your's always
carried the day. Bless me! do you remember the mania
they had at one time for acting charades? how they used
to get all the napkins in the house to dress up in?"

"Ah, yes, madame!" said Renée, laughing and turning
to Naomi, "the best we ever acted was *Marabout*, with
Marat in a bath too hot for him, who kept repeating, '*Je
bous! je bous!*' (I am being boiled! I am being boiled!)
Do you remember?"

"Oh, I remember it well," said Naomi, suppressing a
smile with difficulty; "but you made up that one."

" Well, madame, I am enchanted at finding you so favourably inclined beforehand to what I am going to ask you; for my visit is an interested one. I come precisely with the object of bringing our two children together. Renée is dying to get up some private theatricals—and naturally she thought of her old friend to help her. And if you would allow your daughter to act with mine. It will be an intimate little family party."

At the first words of Madame Mauperin's request, Naomi hastily withdrew her hands from those of Renée, into which, as they were talking, she had let them fall.

" I thank you very much for this idea, dear madame," answered Madame Bourjot. " I thank also your charming Renée. You could not have asked me anything which would give me greater pleasure, or be more agreeable to me. Besides, I think it will be very good for Naomi. She, poor child, is so timid—it is most unlucky. It will accustom her to talk, and take her out of herself. It will also be an excellent spur to her mental powers."

" But, mother, you know my memory is so bad. And the mere idea of acting. I should be terrified. No, I will not act."

Madame Bourjot raised her cold eyes, and looked at her daughter.

" But, mother, if I could. But I shall spoil the whole play, I am sure."

" You will act. I desire it, mademoiselle."

Naomi hung her head.

Madame Mauperin, embarrassed, had, in order to give herself a countenance, let her eyes fall upon a Review which was lying open on a table near her.

" Ah," said Madame Bourjot, recovering herself, " you will find a friend there; it is your son's last article. And when do you think of having the play?"

G

"But, madame, I am so sorry to be the cause—to be disagreeable to your daughter."

"Please don't talk of that any more. My daughter is always afraid of making up her mind."

"All the same," chimed in Monsieur Bourjot, from the other end of the drawing-room, where he was talking to Monsieur Mauperin and Henry, "if Naomi has such a strong feeling against it."

"On the contrary, she will be very grateful to you," said Madame Bourjot to Madame Mauperin, without noticing Monsieur Bourjot's interruption. "We are always obliged to force her to amuse herself. And now, tell me, when is the play to be acted?"

"Renée," asked Madame Mauperin, "When do you think?"

"It seems to me we shall want a month for our rehearsals at two a week. We would make our days and hours suit Naomi." And Renée turned to Naomi who remained silent.

"Very well," said Madame Bourjot, "Then let us say Mondays and Fridays, if that suits you, at two o'clock, shall we? Mademoiselle Gogois"—and Madame Bourjot turned to the governess, "You will accompany my daughter. Monsieur Bourjot, you hear me, you will give the orders about the carriage, the horses, and the servant, to go to La Briche. You need only keep 'Terror' and John for me. There. Now you are going to stay to dinner?"

"We are extremely sorry. It is impossible. We have some people coming to us to-day."

"Allow me to say that I wish those people were at Jericho. But I do not think you have yet seen Monsieur Bourjot's new conservatories. I am going to make you a bouquet, Renée. We have one flower. There are only two like it. The other is at Ferrières. It is a—but I must tell you it is very ugly. This way."

"Shall we come in here?" said Monsieur Bourjot, pointing to the billiard-room, which they could see through the unground glass. "Monsieur Henry, we will leave you to look after the ladies. Here we may smoke," continued he, offering a cigar to Monsieur Mauperin. "Shall we have a game?"

"Yes, by all means," said Monsieur Mauperin.

Monsieur Bourjot pulled up the blinds of the billiard-room.

"Twenty-four up?"

"Twenty-four up."

"You have no billiard-room at home, have you, Monsieur Mauperin?"

"Dear me, no. My son never plays."

"Are you looking for the plain ball?"

"Thank you; and as my wife does not think it a proper game for a girl—"

"Will you begin?"

"Oh, I am very much out of practice. Besides I was always a muff."

"You leave nothing for me—good! Now I have broken my cue—the only one I could ever play with," and Monsieur Bourjot gave vent to a round oath. "Those scoundrelly workmen! they haven't a scrap of conscience! one can get nothing properly done now. Hulloa, you're getting on; three I have to mark you. The truth is that we are at their orders now. A few days ago I wanted to have some lamps hung up. Well, Monsieur Mauperin, I could not get a man to do it. It was some feast day—I don't know what feast—and they would not come. They are great lords nowadays. You fancy perhaps that they bring us all they kill or catch? When they get a good thing they eat it. In Paris, I know what it is—four, by jove! All they earn goes to the café. They will spend twenty francs on a Sunday. The locksmith here has bought a gun by Lefaucheux; and has taken some shooting. Ha, two for me, at last—and what wages they ask now; they charge me five francs for reaping. I have some vines in Burgundy; they offered to work them for me on the hire-system, by which means they would have obtained possession of them at the end of three years. That is where we are drifting to. Some day, happily I am too old to live to see it, but in a hundred years it will be impossible to get a servant—there will be none left. I often tell my wife and daughter that they will some day be obliged to make their own beds—five—six—you are playing very well. We have been killed by the Revolution, do you see." And Monsieur Bourjot began to hum—

> ' Zonzon, zonzon, zonzon,
> Zonzon, zonzon.'

"You did not entertain those ideas thirty years ago, when we met for the first time, do you remember?" said Monsieur Mauperin, with a slight smile.

"That is true. I had some better ones—too good they were at that time"—said Monsieur Bourjot, leaning with his left hand on his cue. "Ah, I was young then! I should rather think I did remember. Gad, it was at Lallemand's funeral! The best blow I ever gave with my fist in my life, a nasty one to parry! I can still see the nails in the boots of that bescarved commissioner of police when I bowled him over to get across the boulevard! At the corner of the Rue Poissonnière I fell into the arms of a patrol; they gave me a tolerable thrashing to begin with. I was with Caminade—you knew Caminade well? He was a good fellow; it was he who used to go and smoke his meerschaum pipe, worth fifteen hundred francs, at the mission lectures in the Church of the Petits-Pères, and who used to take a girl out of the Palais Royal with him for company. He had the good luck to escape. I was driven to the police station by blows from the stocks of their guns. Happily, Dulaurens noticed me—"

"Dulaurens, did you say?" said Monsieur Mauperin. "He belonged to the same 'venta' as I did. If I remember rightly he sold shawls, did he not?"

"Yes, and you know how he finished?"

"No, I have lost sight of him."

"Well, one fine day—it was after all the other doings—his partner runs away to Belgium, carrying with him two hundred thousand francs. They send detectives after him: no results. My good Dulaurens goes into a church and makes a vow that he will reform if he gets his money back. He gets it, and his piety is now disgusting. I see nothing of him now. But at that time he was pretty keen, you know. Well, as I pass him, I tip him a wink. I had at home twenty-five guns and five hundred cartridges. By the time the police arrived he had cleared out everything. That did not save me, however, from three months in the prison of La Force, in the *new buildings*, and from being called up two or three times, at dead of night, to be examined with a possibility always of being shot. You have been through it all, too: you know what it was. And all that to reach socialism at last! All the same, one speech which was made to me ought to have enlightened me. After I came out of gaol, one of my fellow-prisoners came to see me at Sedan. He said to me: 'What is this that I hear about you? It appears that your father has property and money, and yet you have joined us. I thought you had nothing.' When I think, Monsieur Mauperin, that even that did not open my eyes! The fact is that, at that time, I was convinced that all those with whom I was acting wanted simply what I wanted: equality in the eyes of the law, no more privileges, the end of the Revolution of '89 against the nobility. I thought we should stop there. Eleven—did I mark you your last? I think not. Let us call it twelve. But when I saw my republic, upon my soul I was disgusted. When I heard, in February, two men coming away from the barricades and saying to one another: ' We ought not to have come out of that until we had got five thousand francs a-year!' And then the right to work, and progressive taxation, an iniquity, the hypocrisy of communism! But with their progressive taxation," exclaimed Monsieur Bourjot eloquently, as he interrupted his phrase. " I defy them to find anyone who will take the trouble to make a fortune. Thirteen, fourteen, fifteen—capital! Oh, you are too good for me. All that upset me, you see."

" Perfectly," said Monsieur Mauperin.

" Where is my ball? There? It completely upset me; it actually made a legitimist of me. I have slipped my cue again! Only—"

" Only? "

" Only there is one thing. Ah! upon that point, by George! I have never changed my opinions. I don't mind saying this to you; but anything that has to do with a priest, in my eyes—eighteen, come; I am beaten. We asked this one here to dinner because he is a good fellow; but the priests. When one has known one of them, as I have, who broke his leg one night in trying to clamber over the wall of the seminary. A lot of Jesuits, to my mind, Monsieur Mauperin.

' Black men, whence do you come?
We come from beneath the earth.'

Ah. that's the man for my money! *The god of good people!*
And all the rest of them; and Judas:

> ' My friends, don't let us talk so loud :
> I see Judas, I see Judas.'

Twenty-one; you only want three more. Now, in the
country round my iron-works, there is a bishop who is a
capital fellow. Well, all the humbugs hate him. Ah !
if he were a bigot, or a hypocrite, if he were to go to
mass—"

" I have never seen Madame Bourjot so pleasant," said
Madame Mauperin when they had all got into the carriage.

" An odd chap, that Bourjot !" said Monsieur Mauperin.
" What is the use of a billiard-table to him? Why, I
could have given him twelve points."

" I," said Renée, " found Naomi quite odd. Did you
notice. Henry, how she refused to act ? "

Henry did not answer.

XIII

Naomi had just come into the Mauperins' drawing-room, followed by her governess, with a little troubled, restless, almost shamefaced manner. From the door she allowed her eye to travel all around the room; then, as if reassured, and more at her ease, she had put up her forehead to be kissed by Madame Mauperin, and allowed herself to be warmly embraced by Renée. Renée, joking and laughing, with caressing and playful gestures, had taken the mantle off her shoulders, untied her ribands and removed her hat.

"Upon my word!" said she, twisting round on the end of her little thumb the pretty hat of white net, trimmed with pink primulas. "Monsieur Denoisel, whom you must have seen I think in old days—that does not make us any younger—and whom I now introduce to you as our stage manager, professor of elocution, prompter and scene-shifter —all that at once!"

"I have not forgotten how kind Monsieur Denoisel was to me when I was a little girl."

And Naomi, blushing with emotion at this recollection of childhood, offered to Denoisel, with a gesture of pretty awkwardness, a timid hand whose fingers squeezed themselves close one to the other.

"Oh, what a lovely frock!" began Renée walking round her, "You are quite lovely!" And as she spoke she lightly tapped her gown of shot silk so as to smooth out the little wrinkles, and then, giving a final pull to her skirt, she made her a low curtsey and said: "You will make a beautiful Mathilde. Do you know I shall be quite jealous of you? And raising herself again: "See, mamma, I told you so. She quite overtops me." She stood upright beside Naomi and put her arms round her waist: "Do you know that you are ever so much taller than I am?" And still holding her she drew her in front of a glass, stood close beside her, and tried to reach her shoulder with her own: "Do you see?" asked she.

The governess had effaced herself in a corner of the drawing-room. She was looking at the pictures in a book, which she, modestly, only half opened.

"Come, my dear children, had you not better begin to read the piece?" asked Madame Mauperin. "It is no use waiting for Henry. He will only come to the last rehearsals, when the actresses know their parts well."

"Oh, presently, mamma; let us talk a little. Come here, Naomi—here! We have a heap of secrets, so many things, to say to each other. It is such ages since we met."

And Renée and Naomi began one of those chattering little conversations, which sound like the noise of running water; one of those fresh, limpid, endless prattlings, which suddenly break off in a burst of laughter, and die away in a whisper. Naomi, who at first had been on the defensive, soon gave herself up to the pleasure of this effusion, to the thoughts of all in the past, of which Renée's voice reminded her. Each one, as after a separation, asked the other all that had happened to her, and where she had been. To listen to them, one would have said at the end of half-an-hour that they were two young women who were gradually renewing their spirit of childhood.

"I paint," said Renée; "and you—you had a fine voice?"

"Oh, don't talk of it," said Naomi; "I am made to sing.

Mamma will make me sing at her large parties; and you have no idea, when I see everyone looking at me, a shiver comes over me—I am terrified. The first few times I began to cry."

" Do you know that I have deprived myself of a green apple for you? you must eat it—you still like green apples, I hope?"

" No, thank you, thank you, dear Renée, I really am not hungry."

" Now then, Denoisel, what do you find so interesting to study out of window?"

Denoisel was watching the Bourjot's servant in the garden. He had seen him first dust the bench with a fine cambric pocket handkerchief, then spread the handkerchief over the green bars of the bench, sit down thereupon with the greatest precautions for the sake of his red plush breeches, cross his legs one over the other, produce a cigar from his pocket, and light it. At that moment he was watching him as he sat there smoking lazily and majestically, and casting round him, on the little property, the contemptuous glances of a man who serves in a chateau, and whose master owns a park.

" I? oh, nothing," said Denoisel, turning from the window; " I was afraid of being in your way."

" Oh, now we have told each other all our little adventures; you may come and talk to us."

" Do you know how late it is getting, Renée? If you mean to begin your rehearsals to-day—"

" Oh, mamma, it is so hot to-day. Besides, it is a Friday."

" And the year began on the thirteenth," said Denoisel seriously.

" Really?" said Naomi, turning towards him her eyes which expressed implicit faith in his statement.

"Don't listen to him, he is taking you in. He spends his whole time in jokes of that kind, does Denoisel We will rehearse next time you come, won't we? We have plenty of time."

"As you like." said Naomi.

"Very well, then, that is settled. Denoisel, be amusing at once ; and if you are very, very funny, I will give you a picture—one of my own doing."

"Another?"

"Well, you are polite. Thank you."

"Mademoiselle." said Denoisel to Naomi, "you shall judge of my position. I possess already a tomato and a parsnip from Mademoiselle's pencil—and as a pendant to that picture a slice of water-melon and a piece of cheese. I know it comes from the heart—but my room looks like a greengrocer's shop."

"See what men are." said Renée, laughing, to Naomi. "All ungrateful, my dear. And to think that some day or other we have to marry. Do you know that you and I are nearly old maids by now? Twenty years old. Dear me, how time flies! One used to think one would never be eighteen—and then all of a sudden one becomes eighteen, and one is that age no longer. Ah, well, it can't be helped. Mind you bring some music with you next time you come —we will play a duet. I don't know now if I can."

"And you will rehearse when?" (quand) asked Denoisel.

"In Normandy." replied Renée, making the kind of joke which of late years has risen from the studios and the stage to the mouth of society.

Naomi looked astonished like a person who hears what is said without understanding the meaning of the words.

"Yes." explained Renée to her. "Caen in Normandy. Ah,

you cannot make puns? I had a mania for it at one time. I was quite unbearable, was I not, Denoisel? And you go out a great deal? Tell me where you went this winter. Tell me about the balls you were at."

And Naomi answered, chattered, and, little by little, became quite animated. The smile had returned to her face, the ease to her manner. She seemed to open in this air of liberty, and under this warm breath of affection, near Renée, in the bright drawing-room happy and full of youth.

It was four o'clock. The governess jumped up as if moved by a spring. " Mademoiselle," said she : " it is time to go. You know there is a dinner party at Sannois to-night—and you must have time to dress."

XIV

"THIS time we have to work and not to play—we are to rehearse seriously," said Denoisel. "Mademoiselle Naomi, come and sit here. That's right; now we are ready—one —two—three."

He struck his hands together. "And away!"

"I do not think I am quite sure of the first scene," said Naomi, hesitatingly, "I don't think I quite know it. I know the other one better."

"The second? very good, let us try the second. I will do Henry's part: '*Good evening, my dear.*'"

Denoisel was interrupted by a shout of laughter from Renée.

"Oh, dear me!" said she to Naomi; "how funnily you are sitting. You look like a lump of sugar in the sugar-tongs."

"I?" said Naomi, embarrassed, and trying to improve her attitude.

"Will you kindly not worry the actors, Renée," said Denoisel, and, making a fresh start: "*Good evening, my dear, do I disturb you?*"

"Oh! and the purses?" cried Renée.

"Why, I thought that you were going to see to them."

"I? not at all—it was you on the contrary—you are a nice man to look after the properties, I must say. Tell me, Naomi, if you were married, do you think it would ever occur to you to give your husband a purse? Isn't it like a shopkeeper? Why not a smoking cap while you are about it?"

"Are we to rehearse or not?" said Denoisel.

"Look here, Denoisel, you say that exactly as if you wanted to go and smoke."

"I always want to smoke, Renée," said Denoisel "especially when I don't require it."

"But that is a vice, you know."

"I know. So I mean to keep it."

"But what pleasure can you find in smoking?"

"The pleasure of a bad habit; that explains many passions." And beginning anew with the appearance of Monsieur de Chavigny: "*Good evening, my dear, do I disturb you?*"

"*Me? Henry, what a question!*" said Naomi. And so the rehearsal began.

XV.

"THREE o'clock." said Renée, lifting her eyes from the sock she was knitting and looking at the clock. "I really begin to believe that Naomi will not come to-day. She is going to miss her rehearsal—we must fine her."

"Naomi?" replied Madame Mauperin. appearing to wake up. "She is not coming. Oh, did I not tell you? I don't know what has happened to my head, I forget everything now. Last time she was here she told me she would probably not be able to come to-day. They have people staying with them—I believe—I really am not sure."

"That is pleasant. I know nothing so tiresome as waiting for people who do not come. As soon as I woke this morning I said to myself: This is Naomi's day. I was looking forward to it. Oh, of course she won't come now. It is odd how much I miss her, since she has begun to love me again. I miss her as if she belonged to the house. I do not think she is lively—she wants vivacity. She is not up to much fun—and her intelligence is not brilliant—she is so easily taken in. Well, explain it as you will, all the same, I think she is charming—there is something so sweet about her—it seems to penetrate one—she rests one's nerves positively. She seems to warm the cockles of one's heart somehow, does she not? simply by being with one. I have known lots of girls who were really superior to her; but all the same, they had not what she has; one felt as dull as ditchwater in their company."

"Bless me, it's very easily understood," said Denoisel "Mademoiselle Bourjot has a very tender, loving nature. A sort of current of affection seems to pass from such natures to others."

"Yes, but when she was quite a little girl, I remember that she was just the same as she is now—so sensitive. Her facility for tears and kisses was extraordinary. She never seemed to do anything else. And she has not changed in looks a bit, has she? one might say that her beauty is composed of all the tenderness of her nature and all the childhood that still remains to her. She has one look in particular. One often feels malicious or spiteful in oneself; but when she looks at one all one's spitefulness seems to vanish, as if it were melted. I have never dared to play an unkind trick on her—and I was a terrible tease —once upon a time."

"But, all the same, such sensibility as that is very unusual," said Madame Mauperin.

"Oh no, it is easily explained," replied Denoisel. "Imagine a girl who, at her birth, loves as she breathes, instinctively, kept down by the coldness of a mother whom she humiliates and makes to blush; kept down by the egoism of a father, who has no other pride, no other affection, no other child but his money! Well, such a fool will resemble Mademoiselle Bourjot: in return for any little interest you take in her, she will give you this affection and these demonstrations of which you speak. Her heart will overflow of its own accord; and you will find in her the look that Renée has noticed—a look that seems to shine through a tear."

XVI.

The rehearsals had been going on for a fortnight when Madame Bourjot herself brought her daughter to Madame Mauperin's. After the first common-places, she expressed surprise at not seeing the principal actor.

"Oh, Henry has a prodigious memory!" said Madame Mauperin, "and in two rehearsals he will know his part perfectly."

"And how is it getting on?" asked Madame Bourjot. "I tremble, I must admit, for my poor Naomi. Are you at all pleased with her? I came chiefly to see you, but also because I was not sorry to judge for myself."

"Well, dear madame," said Madame Mauperin, "I think you will be made happy. You will find, I think, that your daughter's natural talent—her expression—I assure you she is charming."

The actors took their places, and began "The Caprice."

"You flattered her," said Madame Bourjot to Madame Mauperin, after the first few scenes; and, turning to her daughter, she went on: "You put no feeling into it, my dear child—you recite it. And yet I took you to see it at the Français. But, go on, please."

"Ah, madame," said Renée, "you will make the whole company nervous. We want a little encouragement."

"You need not speak for yourself, mademoiselle," returned Madame Bourjot. "If only my poor daughter could act like you."

" Well," said Denoisel to Mademoiselle Bourjot, " let us take the sixth scene, mademoiselle. We will take our stand upon that, because I think that you act it extremely well, and as my professional vanity is at stake—your mother will allow me ? "

" Oh, monsieur," said Madame Bourjot, " in all this I distinguish between the teacher and the pupil ; you are not responsible for—"

And, after the scene was acted :

" Yes, on the whole," said she, " that is fairly good—it will pass muster. It is a snivelling scene, which just suits her ; and, besides, she does as well as she can. In that particular there is no fault to be found with her."

" Oh, you are too severe," said Madame Mauperin.

" As severe as a mother should be," Madame Bourjot let fall, with a sort of sigh. " And you expect a very large audience ? "

" Oh, you know," said Madame Mauperin, " that on occasions of this kind one has always more people than one wants. There is always a certain amount of curiosity. We shall have fully one hundred and fifty people, I expect."

" Look here, mamma, why should not I make out a list ? " said Renée, wishing to spare Naomi, whose embarrassment was evident, the continuation of the rehearsal. " That would be a means of introducing our guests to Madame Bourjot. I am going to make you acquainted with our friends, madame."

" With pleasure," said Madame Bourjot.

" I must warn you that you will find the dish rather mixed. One's friends, I always think, look rather like people whom one has met in a stage-coach."

" That is charming, and very true," said Madame Bourjot.

Renée seated herself at the table, and, taking a pencil, began to write down the names of the people, chattering all the time as she did so.

"First, the family—we know them. Then, who? Let us see. Madame and Mademoiselle Chanut, whose teeth look like those bits of broken glass on the top of a wall, you know. Monsieur and Madame de Bélizard: they, you must know, have the reputation of feeding their horses on visiting cards."

"Renée, Renée! Come—what an opinion you will give of yourself," began Madame Mauperin.

"Oh, my reputation is already made. I have nothing to lose in that quarter. And besides, don't you suppose people give me as good as they get?"

"Let her go on, I beg," said Madame Bourjot to Madame Mauperin; "and then?" turning and smiling to Renée.

"Madame Jobleau. Ah what a wearisome woman that is with the story of her presentation to Louis Philippe at the Tuileries: '*Yes, sire, yes, sire, yes, sire,*' that is all she found to say. Monsieur Harambourg, who is upset by dust. In summer he leaves his servant in Paris to clean out the cracks in his parquet floor. Mademoiselle de la Boise, or the Policeman of Participles, an old governess, who in conversation will correct you upon the use of the subjunctive. Monsieur Loriot, President of the Society for the Destruction of Vipers. The Clouqemins, father, mother, and children, a family who go up like that—like panpipes. Ah! I had forgotten the Vineux in Paris; but it is useless to ask them; they only visit people who live on an omnibus route. And I was forgetting the Mechin trio—three sisters—the three graces of Batignolles. One is wanting, one is—"

And Renée stopped as she noticed the terrified looks that Naomi was casting in her direction, like a poor loving and helpless creature suddenly frightened and disquieted by all these malicious remarks.

Renée jumped up and ran to kiss her.

"Silly!" she said to her gently; "but all these are not people whom I love."

XVII.

HENRY only came to the last rehearsals. He knew the play; in a week he was ready. But the "Caprice" was too short to fill up a whole evening, and it was decided to finish up with a farce of some kind. Two or three little Palais-Royal pieces were tried, then abandoned, the company not being sufficiently numerous, and they fell back upon a sort of pantomine which was being played with great success at one of the theatres on the boulevards at the moment, and upon which Henry insisted despite the motiveless opposition of Mademoiselle Bourjot, and a resistance, which, from her timidity, was quite unexpected.

It seemed, too, that Mademoiselle Bourjot, since Henry had come, had completely changed her character. Renée occasionally thought she had no longer the same feelings. She felt a coldness in the friendship of her friend. She was surprised to find her contradictory, which she had never before known her to be. She was hurt besides at Naomi's manner to her brother; it was cold, and a slight touch of disdain rendered it almost contemptuous. Nevertheless, her brother was always polite and attentive to her, but nothing more. And even in all his scenes with Naomi he acted with so much reserve, so much restraint and stiffness, that Renée, fearing for the success of the performance, and afraid of the coldness of his acting, joked him about it: "Bah!" said he in reply, "I am like the great actors: I am reserving my strength for the first night's performance."

XVIII

A LITTLE stage had been erected at the end of the Mauperins' drawing-room. The footlights were hidden behind a screen of foliage and flowering shrubs. Renée, with the help of her drawing-master, had painted the curtain, which represented a view on the banks of the Seine. On either side of the stage hung a bill, on which were these words, written by hand :—

LA BRICHE THEATRE.

This Evening,

THE CAPRICE,

To conclude with

HARLEQUIN, A BIGAMIST.

And then followed the names of the actors.

On all the chairs in the house, which had been seized and arranged in rows before the stage, women in low gowns were squeezed together, mixing their skirts, their lace, the sparkle of their diamonds, and the whiteness of their shoulders. The folding-doors of the drawing-room had been taken down, and showed, in the little drawing-room which led to the dining-room, a crowd of men in white neckties, standing on tiptoe.

The curtain rose upon " The Caprice." Renée played with much spirit the part of Madame de Léry. Henry, as the husband, revealed one of those real theatrical talents which are often found in cold young men, and in grave men of the world. Naomi herself, carried away by Henry's

acting, carefully prompted by Denoisel from behind the
scenes, a little intoxicated by her audience, played her little
part of a neglected wife very tolerably.   This was a great
relief to Madame Bourjot.   Seated in the front row, she
had followed her daughter with anxiety.   Her pride
dreaded a failure.   The curtain fell, the applause burst
out, and all the company were called for.   Her daughter
had not been ridiculous; she was happy in this great
success, and she composedly gave herself up to the
speeches, opinions, congratulations, which, as in all repre-
sentations of private theatricals, followed the applause and
continued in murmurs.   Amidst all that she thus vaguely
heard, one sentence, pronounced close by her, reached her
ears, clear and distinct above the buzz of general conversation: " Yes, it is his sister, I know — but I think
that, for the part, he is not sufficiently in love with her
—and really too much in love with his wife; did you
notice it ?"   And the speaker, feeling that she was being
overheard by Madame Bourjot, leaned over and whispered
in her neighbour's ear.   Madame Bourjot became serious.

After a pause, the curtain went up again, and Henry
Mauperin appeared as Pierrot or harlequin, not in the tradi-
tional sack of white calico and black cap, but as an Italian
harlequin, with a white three-cornered hat, and dressed
entirely in white satin from head to foot.   A shiver of
interest ran through the women, proving that the
costume and the man were both charming; and the folly
began.

It was the mad story of Pierrot, married to one woman
and wishing to marry another, a farce intermingled with
passion, which had been unearthed by a playwright with
the help of a poet from a collection of old comic plays.
Renée, this time, acted the part of the neglected woman,

who in various disguises interfered between her husband and his gallant adventures, and Naomi that of the woman he loved. Henry, in his scenes of love with the latter, carried all before him. He played with youth, with brilliancy, with excitement. In the scene in which he avows his love, his voice was full of the passionate cry of a declaration which overflows and swamps everything. True, he had to act with the prettiest Columbine in the world: Naomi looked delicious that evening in her bridal costume of Louis XVI., copied exactly from the "Bride's Minuet," a print by Debucourt, which Barousse had lent for the purpose.

A sort of enchantment filled the whole room, and reached Madame Bourjot, a sort of sympathetic complicity with the actors seemed to encourage the pretty couple to love one another. The piece went on. Now and again Henry's eyes seemed to look for those of Madame Bourjot, over the footlights. Meanwhile, Renée appeared disguised as the village bailiff; it only remained to sign the contract; Pierrot, taking the hand of the woman he loved, began to tell her of all the happiness he was going to have with her

The woman who sat next to Madame Bourjot, felt her lean somewhat on her shoulder. Henry finished his speech, the piece disentangled itself and came to an end. All at once, Madame Bourjot's neighbour saw something glide down her arm: it was Madame Bourjot who had just fainted.

XIX

"Oh, do, pray go indoors," said Madame Bourjot to the people who were standing around her. She had been carried into the garden. "It is passed now, it is really nothing, it was only the heat." She was quite pale, but she smiled. "I only want a little air. Let Monsieur Henry only stay with me."

The audience retired. Scarcely had the sound of feet died away when: "You love her!" said Madame Bourjot, seizing Henry's arm as though she were taking him prisoner with her feverish hands: "You love her!"

"Madame." said Henry.

"Hold your tongue! you lie!" And she threw his arm from her. Henry bowed.—"I know all. I have seen all. But look at me!"—and with her eyes she closely scanned his face. Henry stood before her, his head bent.—"At least speak to me! You can speak at any rate! Ah, I see it, you can only act in her company!"

"I have nothing to say to you, Laura," said Henry in his softest and clearest voice. Madame Bourjot started at this name of Laura as though he had touched her. "I have struggled for a year, madame," began Henry, "I have no excuse to make. But my heart is fast. We knew each other as children. The charm has grown day by day. I am very unhappy, madame, at having to acknowledge the truth to you; I love your daughter, that is true."

"But have you ever spoken to her? I blush for her

when there are people there! Have you ever looked at her? Do you think her pretty? What possesses you men? Come! I am better looking than she is! You men are fools. And besides, my friend, I have spoiled you. Go to her and ask her to caress your pride, to tickle your vanity, to flatter and to serve your ambitions, —for you are ambitious, I know you! Ah, Monsieur Mauperin, one can only find that once in a lifetime! And it is only women of my age, old women, like me, do you hear me? who love the future of the people whom they love! You were not my lover, you were my grandchild." And at this word, her voice sounded as though it came from the bottom of her heart. Then immediately changing her tone :—" But don't be foolish! I tell you you don't really love my daughter, it is not true : she is rich!"

" Oh, madame!"

" Good gracious, there are lots of people. They have been pointed out to me. It pays sometimes to begin with the mother and finish with the dower. And a million, you know, will gild a good many pills."

" Speak lower, I implore you—for your own sake— someone has just opened a window."

" Calmness is very fine, Monsieur Mauperin, very fine, very fine," repeated Madame Bourjot. And her low, hissing voice seemed to stifle her.

Clouds were scudding across the sky, and passed over the moon looking like huge bats' wings. Madame Bourjot gazed fixedly into the darkness, straight in front of her. Her elbows resting on her knees, her weight thrown on to her heels, she was beating with the points of her satin shoes the gravel of the path. After a few minutes she sat upright, stretched out her arms two or three times wildly and as though but half awake; then hastily and with jerks, she pushed her hand down between her gown and her waistband, pressing her hand against the riband as though she would break it.   Then she rose and began to walk. Henry followed her.

"I intend, sir, that we shall never see each other again," she said to him, without turning round.

As they passed near the basin, she handed him her handkerchief:

" Wet that for me."

Henry put one knee on the margin and gave her back the lace which he had moistened.   She laid it on her forehead and on her eyes.   "Now let us go in," she said, " Give me your arm."

" Oh, dear madame, what courage!" said Madame Mauperin going to meet Madame Bourjot as she entered— "but it is unwise of you.   Let me order your carriage."

" On no account," answered Madame Bourjot hastily, " I thank you.   I promised that I would sing for you, I think. I am going to sing."

And Madame Bourjot advanced to the piano, graceful and valiant, with the heroic smile on her face wherewith the actors of society hide from the public the tears that they shed within themselves, and the wounds which are only known to their own hearts.

XX.

MARRIED for the sake of the social advantages of two great houses of business, united by a community of interests to a man whom she did not know, Madame Bourjot felt, at the end of a week, all the contempt that a woman can feel for her husband. It was not that she had formed any ideal requirements, or that she had brought into the married state any romantic notions of young girlhood. Singularly intelligent, of a serious turn of mind which had been formed and nourished by reading, by studies, and by a depth of knowledge which was almost that of a man, this woman asked nothing of the companion of her life save that he should be capable, that he should be a man upon whose head she could found all her ambitions and her pride as a married woman, a man, in short, with a future; knowing how to seize his opportunity in such a way as to crown his chances with a large fortune, able, through one of the holes of modern society, to jump into a ministry, into the Board of Works, or the Exchequer: all that fell to pieces in her hand with this husband whom day by day she discovered to be despairingly hollow, completely inefficient, empty of all which ought to have been in him and which was in her, whose mind she found to be narrow, whose character was mean and composed of all the violence and instability of a child's temper.

Pride had preserved Madame Bourjot from going wrong, pride which, besides, had been helped by circumstances.

During her first youth, Madame Bourjot, whose nature was cold, whose blood was southern, had had features too strongly defined to be beautiful. It was only when she was nearly thirty-four years old that she began to get stout, and then another woman suddenly seemed to appear in her; her features, while they remained pronounced became softer and more amiable; the hardness seemed to melt out of her countenance, and her face began to smile. Hers was an autumnal beauty such as age sometimes gives to certain women whose face of twenty years old one would like to see again, a beauty which makes one think of the youth that they have never had. Until that time, also, Madame Bourjot had never passed through any serious dangers or any very trying temptations. The society into which she entered by taste, her surroundings, the men who frequented her house and with whom she was on terms of friendly intimacy, were not such as to oblige her to defend herself seriously. They were, for the most part, members of the institute, clever men, literary men, political men; all of them seemed to be modest, rather worn out, and aged some of them by all that they had stirred up in the past, others by all that they were stirring up in the present. Any little attention pleased them, they wished for nothing, they were content to hear the rustle of a gown, a friendly word, or to see, by a look, that they were being listened to. Madame Bourjot had been surrounded by this academical adoration, and she had allowed it, without much danger, to rise up round her as though she had been the Egeria of the circle; it had been to her a flame with which she might play without fearing to burn her fingers.

But maturity came to Madame Bourjot. The great change in her appearance and figure was finished. Tormented by a superabundance of health, by an excess of life, it seemed as though her moral being lost the power that her physical being gained. While she admired her past, she felt less strength in her soul and less security in her pride. At this juncture Henry Mauperin was introduced to her. To her he seemed young, intelligent, serious, deep, armed for the victories of life, with all the cold and calculating qualities which she, before her marriage, had dreamed of finding a husband. At the outset, Henry seized the situation and foresaw his chances; his plans immediately threw themselves upon that woman as upon a prey.

He began to make love to her; and this woman, with a husband and a child, with her twenty years of virtue, with one of the best positions in Paris, scarcely allowed him time to attack her. She yielded at the first interview, she gave herself to him, like a common woman in a suburban restaurant, in a mad, stupid, almost grotesque manner, regardless of the ironical smiles of the waiters, who, at the sight of her forty years of age, had opened for her the door of a public dining-room.

Thenceforward her love became more furious as it was satisfied; it was one of those passions which take hold of women of that age, and seem to pass into their very blood. Henry, meanwhile, exerted all his genius in the endeavour to attach her to himself, and to chain her to her fault. Nothing betrayed him, nothing escaped him which could, for one moment, have shewn her that he was weary, or indifferent, or that there was in him that spice of contempt which every man feels after too easy a conquest, that sort of disgust which he feels for certain ridiculous situations in which a woman who loves places herself. He was always affectionate, and his emotion always seemed real. He had on Madame Bourjot's behalf the outbursts of tenderness and jealousy, the loving superstitions, the attentions, the kindnesses which a woman, after she has passed a certain age, no longer expects from love or from a lover. He treated her like a girl. He asked her to give him a ring which she wore in memory of her first Communion. He bore all the childishness, the vanity, all the mockery of passion in this mother of a family, without a symptom of impatience upon his face, or a trace of sarcasm in his voice. At the same time he took possession of the whole woman, and moulded her to his will by giving her pleasures for which she felt both gratitude and pride, as she might have done for a victory gained by her person over this young man, who appeared to be so cold. Having thus become the master of this woman, and having entire possession of her, Henry intoxicated her still more by showing her the apparent danger of their interviews, by the risks they ran in their meetings, by all the emotions of criminal romance wherewith he stupefied with fear and danger the imagination of this middle-class woman, who excited herself in her love by the thought of all she had to lose.

She came at last to living only through him and for him, by his presence, by the thought of him, by his future, by his picture, by all that she carried away from him after each of their meetings. When they parted, she would pass her hands two or three times through his hair, and then would put on her gloves quickly. And all that day, and the next, beside her husband, near her daughter, in her own home, she would smell the palms of her hands, which she had not washed; she breathed the perfume of her lover when she kissed the scent from his hair!

That evening, that treachery, that rupture at the end of one year broke down Madame Bourjot. She felt as if she had received her death-wound, and she found comfort in the thought. The next day she looked out for Henry. She was conquered—ready, if he had come, to beg his pardon, to acknowledge that she had been in the wrong, to implore him to forget, to be kind to her, to let her pick up the crumbs of his love. She waited a week: Henry did not come. She begged for an interview in order to recover her letters; Henry sent them to her. She wrote, begging him to see her for the last time, to bid him an everlasting farewell. Henry did not answer; but through his friends, through newspaper articles, and through gossip, he surrounded Madame Bourjot with rumours of a prosecution that had been commenced against him on account of one of his last articles on behalf of the poor classes. During a week he haunted her, waking and sleeping, with visions of police-courts, prisons, everything that the dramatic imagination of a woman foresees as the end of a trial; and when the Solicitor-General gave Madame Bourjot an assurance that the trial would not take place, ashamed of all her former terrors, quite overcome by her emotions, and at the end of her strength, she wrote to Henry:

"To-morrow at two o'clock. If you are not at home, I will wait on the staircase; I will sit upon a step."

XXI

HENRY was ready and waiting. He had dressed himself in a studiously careless costume, his apparent indifference was the result of anxious thought, his untidiness was intentional, in short his toilet was such that in it a young man would almost always look attractive.

At the hour mentioned in the letter he heard the bell. He went to the door; Madame Bourjot entered, and, passing before him with that familiar manner of women who know their way well, she went and seated herself upon a divan at the far end of his study.

At first neither spoke. There was a vacant place upon the divan; Henry pulled up a writing-chair, turned it round, and seated himself astride upon it with his arms crossed on the back.

Madame Bourjot had raised and thrown back her thick lace veil. Her head resting on the back of the divan, one hand lazily occupied in ungloving the other, she was looking at all that surrounded her, the pictures on the wall, the things on the chimney-piece. She heaved a little sigh as though she had been alone, then looking as though she had just remembered Henry, she said to him:

"Some of my life is here. All this is a little of myself."

And she stretched her ungloved hand towards him, of which Henry respectfully kissed the tips of the fingers.

"I beg your pardon," she continued. "I did not mean to speak of myself. I did not come here for that. Oh, do not fear, I am quite reasonable to-day, really. The first moment, oh, the first moment was hard, I acknowledge, my friend. It was a wrench," she said with a tearful smile;

I

"But that is all over now. I hardly suffer now, and I am quite strong, I assure you. Oh, of course I cannot wipe out everything in one day, and I do not mean to tell you that you are no longer anything to me—you would not believe me if I did. But what I can swear to you, and what you must believe, Henry, is that in my heart there is no longer any passion, there is no weakness now. The woman is dead, quite dead, and my feeling for you now is very pure."

The daylight troubled her as she spoke, as though it had been someone looking at her: "Will you pull down the blind for me?" she said, "the sun,—my eyes have been so troublesome the last few days."

And while Henry went to the window, she untied the strings of her bonnet, and let the large shawl in which she was wrapped slip from her shoulders. She continued, after the light in the room had been subdued: "Yes, Henry, after many struggles, many wrenches, which you will never know of; after nights such as I hope you may never have! by dint of praying and weeping, I have triumphed over myself; I thought of the happiness of my daughter without being jealous of her, of yours as the only one that is now allowed me on earth!"

"You are an angel, Laura!" said Henry; and leaving his chair he began to walk up and down the room as though much agitated. "But we must look at things as they are. You were quite right when you said that we ought to part for ever and never meet again. To live together! You cannot mean that! It takes so little to reopen wounds as slightly closed as ours are? And then, even if you are so sure of yourself, how do you know that I am sure of myself? How can I tell that this hourly intimacy, this temptation which will last all my life, near you in short," he said tenderly, "an opportunity, a surprise; how can I tell? and I am a honest man."

"No, Henry," said she, taking his hands, and making him sit near her. "I fear nothing from you, and I am not afraid of myself. All is finished. Upon what shall I swear it? And you will not refuse me. No, you would not refuse me the only happiness which remains to me, the only one, I repeat; I have only that now in the world! to see you, only to see you!" and throwing her arms round the young man's neck she embraced him so tightly that he could feel that she wore no stays.

After an embrace which lasted some seconds:

"Ah, this is impossible! Do not let us talk any more of it," said Henry hastily, as he rose.

"I will be strong," said Madame Bourjot gravely.

After this comedy of renunciation had been played out, both of them felt more at ease.

"Now," began Madame Bourjot, "listen to me, Monsieur Bourjot will give you his daughter."

"Really, Laura, you are mad."

"Do not interrupt me. Monsieur Bourjot will give you his daughter. I believe it is his intention to ask his son-in-law to live with him. But he would have perfect liberty: rooms, carriage, cook, all separate. You know how we live. Unless Monsieur Bourjot has changed his mind, *she* will have a million of francs down; and unless he is ruined, which is scarcely probable, she will have, when we are no longer here, from four to five millions."

"And how do you seriously expect Mademoiselle Bourjot, who has one million, and who will have five, to marry—"

"I am her mother," replied Madame Bourjot, in a decided tone; "and besides, do you not love her? Bless my heart, it is a convenience like any other." And Madame

Bourjot smiled. " You will **bring her happiness—you.**"

" But the world ? "

" The world ?   Child ! "

She slightly shrugged her shoulders. " We will close the world's mouth with truffles."

"Monsieur Bourjot ? "

" He is my business. Before two months are over he will be devoted to you. Only, you know him. He will require a title; he has always wanted a count for his daughter. All that I can do is to make him contented with the particle, with a simple "*de*." Nothing is easier now-a-days than to obtain permission to add to one's name the name of a wood, or of a property, or of a field, or of a bit of land somewhere or another. Have I not heard your mother speak of a farm called Villacourt that you have somewhere in the Haute-Marne? *Mauperin de Villacourt* —that would do very well. You know how indifferent I am to all that sort of thing."

" Oh, but it would be too absurd, with my principles, my liberalism, engaged as I am, and for myself."

" Nonsense; you will tell people it was a caprice of your wife. But everyone takes some title or another now ; it's like the Cross of the Legion of Honour !   Shall I speak to the Minister of Justice for you ? "

" By no means. No, I beg you. I did not know I had said anything which would make you think me disposed to accept. Indeed, I do not know, honestly. You will understand my wanting to reflect, to think it over, to see what is my duty, to belong more to myself and less to you, before giving you an answer."

" I will go and see your mother this week, my dear friend," said Madame Bourjot, rising and squeezing his hand. " Farewell," said she sadly, " life is a sacrifice ! "

XXII.

"RENEE," said Madame Mauperin one evening to her daughter; "would you like to come to-morrow to see the exhibition of Lord Mansbury's things? They say it will be very interesting. There is a picture there which ought to fetch more than a hundred thousand francs. Monsieur Barousse thought it would amuse you. He has sent me a catalogue and a ticket of admission. Does it suit you?"

"Indeed it does suit me," said Renée; "it suits me down to the ground."

Next day, Renée was surprised to see her mother superintend her toilet, busy herself about her, make her put on her best bonnet.

"You see that now these exhibitions are so fashionable," said Madame Mauperin, as she re-tied the strings of her bonnet; "you must be dressed like everyone else."

Although the exhibition was private, there was a crowd in the room in which was put out Lord Mansbury's collection, on the first floor of the large auction-rooms in Paris. The celebrity of the pictures, the very scandal of the sale itself, caused, people said, by the follies that Lord Mansbury had committed for one of the Palais-Royal actresses, had attracted all the usual visitors of the Hôtel Drouot, the world which fashion has brought there during the last few years, the would-be artistic boobies, the well-known collectors, and nearly every inquisitive person in Paris.

It had been found necessary to hang high on the walls, out of reach of the crowd, the three or four most precious pictures. In the hall itself, the sort of roar was audible which always accompanies the sales of rich men's goods—the buzzing of prices always rising, of desires being kindled, of follies breaking bounds, of bankers' rivalries, of vanities of rich men who are losing their tempers. A murmur of voices bidding on the sly ran from group to group. "The pot was getting hot," said the dealers.

At the door of the hall, Madame Mauperin and her daughter found Barousse leaning on the arm of a young man of about thirty years of age. This man had large, soft eyes, which would have been fine had they not been rather silly. His figure, which was already showing symptoms of future stoutness, made him look rather vulgar.

"Here you are at last, ladies," said Barousse; and, turning to Madame Mauperin, he continued: "Allow me to introduce to you my young friend, Monsieur Lemeunier. He knows the collection by heart, and if you require a guide, he will take you to all that is most worth seeing. I will, with your leave, go to run up the price of something in room No. 3."

They went round the hall. Monsieur Lemeunier conducted Madame Mauperin and her daughter to the pictures signed with the best known names, simply explained the subjects of them, and did not talk painting. Renée, in her heart, without knowing why, was grateful to him. When they had been all through the exhibition, Madame Mauperin let go of Monsieur Lemeunier's arm, thanked him, and bowed to him.

Renée wished to go into one of the side rooms. The first thing she saw on entering was the back of Monsieur Barousse, a back which displayed every emotion whereof a collector in the full swing of a sale could be capable. He was seated on the chair nearest to the auctioneer, close beside a female agent in a bonnet, and he was at every moment

jerking her elbow, pushing her knee, prompting her fever-
ishly as to the bids he would make and which he fancied
were a secret from the auctioneer, his clerk, and the public
generally.

"Come along, now; you have seen enough of him," said
Madame Mauperin after a short time. "And besides, this
is your sister's reception-day—it is not too late. We have
not been there this year; it will give her pleasure."

Renée's sister, Madame Mauperin's eldest daughter,
Madame Davarande, was essentially a worldly woman.
Society filled her life and her head. As a child she dreamed
of it. From the day of her first Communion she longed
for it. She married very young. She had taken the first
suitable man who had presented himself, without hesitation,
without any worry, at the first suggestion. It was not
Monsieur Davarande, it was a position that she was marrying. Marriage to her meant a carriage, diamonds, servants
in livery, invitations, acquaintances, drives in the Bois de
Boulogne. She had all that, did without any children,
loved her gowns, and was happy. To her the height of
happiness was to have to go to three balls a night, to have
forty cards to leave during an afternoon drive, to go from
one to another of her friends on their reception-days, and
to have a day herself.

As she gave all to the world, so Madame Davarande
borrowed all from it, her ideas, her judgments, her charities,
her formulas, her manners and affectations. Her opinions
were the same as those of all the women who had their
hair dressed by Laure. She thought what it was distinguished to think just as she wore what it was fashionable
to wear. Everything, from her gestures down to her
drawing-room furniture, from her favourite game of cards
down to her alms-giving, from the newspaper she read

down to the dishes she ordered her cook to prepare, aimed
at being in the fashion; fashion was her rule of life and
her creed. Wherever fashion led the way, thither she
followed even to the "Bouffes-Parisiens." She had
learned to know by sight and by name a few of the
celebrated women who drove in the Bois de Boulogne;
it sounded well to talk of them. She spelled her
name with a little *d*, an apostrophe, and a capital *A*,
d'Avarande. Madame Davarande was pious; to her, God
seemed fashionable. It would have appeared to her almost
as improper not to have a parish church as not to wear
gloves. She frequented one of those churches where the
smart marriages take place, where great names bow to each
other, where the chairs are painted with coats of arms,
where the verger is resplendent in gold embroidery, where
the incense smells of patchouli, where, on Sundays, after the
High Mass the porch resembles the corridor of the opera-
house when Mario has been singing. She went to hear the
sermons of preachers whom it would be unfashionable not
to have heard. She confessed, not in the public confessional, but in a convent. The name and appearance of a
priest were, to her, of the greatest importance in the
administration of the sacraments; she would not have
thought herself properly married had anyone but the Abbé
Blampoix performed the ceremony, and she doubted the
efficacy of any baptism which was not followed by the
gift of a two-hundred franc note to the priest in a box
of sweetmeats.

This woman, entirely given up to the world even in respect
of her church and her salvation, was absolutely, naturally and
fundamentally virtuous, without having, in her virtue,
either effort, or merit, or conscience. Living as she did in
a whirlpool, in a hot and unnatural atmosphere, open to all

the opportunities and solicitations of drawing-room life, she had neither enough heart to dream, nor enough mind to be bored. Desire and curiosity were not in her. She had one of those happy, narrow natures which have not in them the stuff whereof faults are made. She possessed that unassailable virtue that some women in Paris have; temptation passes them by and touches them not; she was virtuous just as marble is cold. Physically also, the world, as sometimes happens to lymphatic and delicate natures, wore out her strength, her nervous activity, and the movement of the little blood she had in her veins, by the excitement of visits and races, the work of amiability, the weariness of evening parties, the fatigue of night, the lassitude of the next day, and thereby left her without desire. There are certain women in society in Paris who, by their expenditure of life and of power, by their struggles between activity and gracefulnes, almost resemble those circus-riders and tight-rope dancers whose natural desires are killed by the fatigue of their performances.

Madame Mauperin and her daughter met Madame Davarande in her dining-room just as she was showing out, with much apparent friendliness, a pale man with blue spectacles.

"I beg your pardon," she said, coming back and kissing her mother and sister; "that is Monsieur Lordonnot, the architect of the Church of the Sacred Heart. I am coaxing him to collect for my poor. Last year he collected twelve hundred francs for me, do you know. That was very good; Madame Berthival has never yet got beyond eight hundred. So you are come at last; I am very glad to see you. Come in, I have nobody here to-day; Madame de Thésigny, Madame de Champromard, and Madame de Saint Sauveur, that is all; and two pleasant little men.

little de Lorsac, whom I think you know, mamma, and his friend, de Maisoncelles. Wait a minute," said she to Renée, giving a little pat to her hair so as to smooth it down. "your hair is all over the place." She opened the door of the drawing-room: "My mother and sister, mesdames."

Every one got up, bowed, sat down again, and looked at each other. Madame Davarande's three friends, sitting in deep arm-chairs in the soft attitudes that soft furniture gives, seemed quite tiny, almost hidden, as they were, by the fulness of their gowns and their huge petticoats which swelled out under their arms. Their clothes were delicious, their little bonnets were adorable, their gloves would have fitted a doll's hands, their bodices were cut by an artist among dressmakers, their whole toilet and the thousand little trifles of which it is composed, their pretty attitudes, the charm of their bearing, the little affectation of all their gestures, the little wilfulness of their movements, the rustling and noise of their silk gowns, they had all these things, and all that from which the Parisian woman draws her charm, and, without being beautiful, they managed to make themselves almost pretty by means of a smile, a look, details, appearance, glances, animation, a little suggestion of noisiness.

The two young men, Lorsac and Maisoncelles, glorying in their twenty years, pink and white, full of health, still somewhat doll-like, beardless and curled, rejoicing at being admitted to the reception of a young married woman, sat on the edge of their chairs, respectfully. They were two excellently brought up young men. They had just left a school kept by a priest who every evening asked them to a tea party in his billiard-room under the presidency of his sister.

The conversation began again.

" Henrietta," said Madame de Thésigny, speaking to
Madame Davarande, "shall we go to-morrow to see
Mademoiselle de Bussan's wedding? I hear that everyone will be there. People are talking a great deal about
this marriage."

" Then come and pick me up. What is the bridegroom
like? Do you know? Do you know him, Madame de
Saint-Sauveur ? "

" No, not at all."

" Is she making a good marriage ? "

" Shocking," said Madame de Champromard; he has
nothing. Fifteen thousand francs a year, all told."

" But," mildly said Madame Mauperin, "it appears to
me, madame, that fifteen thousand francs a year——"

" Oh! madame," answered Madame de Champromard,
" on such an income as that one could not afford to change
the setting of one's jewels in these bad times."

" Monsieur de Lorsac," said Madame Davarande, "are
you going to this wedding to-morrow?"

" I will go if you wish it."

" Very well, then, I do wish it. You will keep me two
chairs, otherwise one ruins one's gown. I suppose one
may go in pearl-grey, may one not ? "

" Certainly," replied Madame de Thésigny: " you may
go to this marriage in *moire antique* if you like. Monsieur
de Maisoncelles, two chairs also for me, please; don't forget."

De Maisoncelles bowed.

" And if you are very good, you shall lead my cotillon
on Wednesday."

De Lorsac blushed on behalf of de Maisoncelles.

" You do not go out much, mademoiselle ? " asked Madame de Saint Sauveur of Renée, who was sitting near her.

"No, madame, I do not like it," answered Mademoiselle Mauperin, somewhat drily.

"Julia," said Madame de Thésigny to Madame de Champromard, "tell us again about that beautiful young married couple's bedroom. Madame Davarande has not heard it. Do listen to this, my dear."

"Well, it was my linen draper who told me about it. Imagine, the walls are all panelled in white satin, bordered and trimmed round each panel with muslin and a ruching of satin riband. The sheets—I saw a pattern of them— are of cambric, fine as a cobweb! The mattresses are of white satin, edged with knots of sky-blue floss silk, which are visible through the sheets. And the most astonishing part of it all is that it is for an honest woman!"

"Ah, yes," said Madame de Saint Sauveur, "that is most astonishing. Now-a-days everything is done for those women. Have you heard of what has happened to me, in the country?—it is most disagreeable. I have a bad woman in my neighbourhood. We meet at church, where she has taken a sitting, if you please! Since she came into the place, all the prices have gone up. We cannot get a needlewoman now for less than sevenpence a day! Of course money is of no importance to these creatures: it costs them nothing. Besides, this intriguer is adored in the place. She visits the poor when they are sick, she finds situations for their children, she gives them sovereigns; before she came we could do our little charities cheaply, now it is no longer possible. It is unheard of, scandalous, and I told our priest so. And for this, Monsieur de Lorsac, we have to thank one of your cousins, Monsieur d'Orambeau. Remember me to him when you see him, and tell him what I have said."

Both the young men burst out laughing at this, and

simultaneously began to bite the tops of their sticks.

"And where have you come from?" asked Madame Davarande of her mother and sister.

"From the Sale Rooms," answered Madame Mauperin; "Monsieur Barousse dragged us off to an exhibition of pictures."

"Lord Mansbury's exhibition," said Renée.

"By-the-bye we must go to the Sale Rooms, Henrietta," said Madame de Thésigny; "we will go and have a peep at these old things, it is sure to be amusing."

"Have you seen the Petrucci's exhibition, my dear?" asked Madame de Saint Sauveur.

"Is she selling her things?" said Madame de Thésigny.

"I would have given anything to go there," said Madame Davarande. "If I had only known you were going."

"We were all there," interrupted Madame de Saint Sauveur, "It was extraordinary. There was a glass-case full of jewellery: a necklace of black pearls amongst other things. If only you had seen them! Three rows of them. No husband in the world could ever give one such things: they would need a national subscription."

"Shall we not see your 'husband?" asked Madame Mauperin of Madame Davarande.

"Oh no, he never comes to my afternoons, thank goodness!" and Madame Davarande, hearing someone enter behind her turned her head; it was Barousse, followed by the young man with whom Madame Mauperin had met him at the sale of the pictures.

"Here we are again," said he, placing upon a chair the portfolio without which he was never seen.

Renée smiled.

The chatter began again:

"Have you read the novel—*the* novel?"

" In the *Constitutionel?* "

" No."

" By; Ah, I can't remember the man's name.   It is called—wait a minute."

" Everyone is talking of it."

" You must read it."

" My husband will get it for me from the club."

" Is the new play amusing ? "

" I only like dramas."

" Shall we go and see it ? "

" Let us have a box."

" Friday ? "

" No, Saturday."

" Shall we have some supper afterwards ? "

" By all means."

" At the Provençeaux ? "

" Will your husband come ? "

" Oh, of course he will do as he is told."

Everyone talked, everyone answered, nobody listened. They all chattered together. Words, questions, answers mingled together in the noise; it was like the fluttering inside an aviary. The door opened.

" Please don't move, anybody," said a tall, thin young woman, dressed in black, as she entered. " I only just looked in as I passed. I have only one minute to stay."

She bowed to the ladies present, stood in front of the chimney-piece, her elbows on the marble, looked at herself in the glass, raised her petticoats slightly and stretched out towards the fire the thin sole of her little boot, and began : " Henrietta, I have come to ask you to do me a favour, a great favour.   You simply must undertake to send out the invitations for the ball that the Brodmers are going to give, you know these Americans who have just come, and who have taken an apartment in the Rue de la Paix at forty thousand francs a year."

"Ah, the Brodmers," said Madame de Thésigny, "yes, yes."

"But, my dear," said Madame Davarande, "it is very difficult. I do not know them. Do you even know who these people are?"

"Well, they are Americans who have made a huge fortune in cotton, or tallow, or indigo, or negroes, or something or another. But, I ask you, what in the world does that matter to us? And besides Americans are quite received, now. For my part, I only require of people who give balls two things, first that they should not belong to the police; and secondly, that they should provide a good supper. It appears that these people are going to do it well. The wife is prodigious. She talks the French of the primeval back-woods. They say that she can't wear a low gown because she was tattooed as a child. She is very funny, and will amuse you. They want to get smart people, you see. You will do it for me, won't you? I assure you that, had I not been in mourning, I would have sent out the cards 'with Baroness de Lermont's compliments.' Besides, I am sure they will do the thing handsomely. They will certainly give you something worth having."

"Good gracious! if I look after their invitations, I don't want their presents."

"How odd you are. But it is done every day; it is the commonest thing in the world. It would be like refusing to accept a box of bon-bons from one of those young men there on New Year's Day. Now, I am off. I will bring my savages to see you to-morrow. Good-bye, good-bye. By the way, I am dying."

And thereupon she disappeared.

" Is that true ? " Renée asked her sister.

" What ? "

" That people provide society for balls in that way."

" What; didn't you know that ? "

" I was in the same benighted state of ignorance," said the young man who had been brought by Barousse.

" It is very convenient for foreigners," said Madame Davarande.

" Yes, but tolerably humiliating to Parisians, it appears to me ; don't you think so, mademoiselle ?" And the young man turned towards Mademoiselle Mauperin.

" Oh, it's an understood thing," said Madame Davarande.

XXIII

MADAME BOURJOT had just arrived, with her daughter, at the house of the Mauperins. She had kissed Renée on the forehead, and seated herself on the sofa beside Madame Mauperin, near the fire.

" Young people," she said, turning towards the two girls, who were chattering in a corner, " suppose you were to let your mothers have a little talk. Renée, I confide Naomi to you ; take her out for a walk."

Renée seized Naomi round the waist, danced out of the room with her, picked up a Pyrenean hood off a chair in the hall and threw it over her head, put on a pair of tiny sabots, and began to run round the garden gaily, like a little girl, without letting go of her friend. Then, out of breath at last, she stopped short: " There is a secret ! there is a secret ! do you know the secret ?"

Naomi looked at her with two great, sad eyes, and made no reply.

" Silly !" said Renée, kissing her. " I have guessed it. I caught a few words here and there. Mamma is like a sieve. It concerns my noble brother, there !"

" Let us sit down ; may we ? I am tired."

And Naomi seated herself on the bench, in the very place occupied by her mother on the night of the theatricals.

" But you are crying ; what is the matter ?" said Renée, and she sat down beside her. Naomi let her head rest upon her friend's shoulder, and burst into tears—hot, salt tears, which Renée felt dropping on her hand.

K

"What is it? Tell me! speak to me! Naomi, come, my darling Naomi."

"Oh, you do not know," answered Naomi, in a broken voice, as if she were choking. "I will not—leave me alone—if you knew! Save me!"

And she threw herself despairingly on Renée's neck. "But I do love you," she said.

"What is it, Naomi? I understand nothing. Is it this marriage? Is it my brother? I insist upon your answering me; do you hear?"

"Ah, that is true; you are his sister—I had forgotten that. You do not know; I wish I were dead!"

"Dead! Why?"

"Because your brother is—"

She hesitated in presence of the horrible thing she was going to say, finished her phrase by a murmur into Renée's ear, and dropping her head on to the bosom of her friend she hid there the shame of her soul and the crimson of her cheeks.

"My brother? You say? You lie!" And pushing her away, Renée sprang to her feet and faced her.

"I?" And for answer Naomi gently raised to Renée her eyes, wherein truth shone like a light.

At that look Renée folded her arms. She remained for some minutes standing upright, silent, in an attitude which was resolute, energetic, and meditative. She felt in herself the strength of a woman, and almost the duties of a mother towards this child. Then she said: "But what does your father say? My brother has no title."

"But he is going to take one."

"Ah, he is going to give up our name. He is right."

XXIV.

"Hulloa! is that you? haven't you gone to bed yet?" said Henry to Renée that evening as she came into his room. He was smoking. He had reached that blessed moment when, his feet in slippers, resting on the chimney-piece, in a comfortable arm-chair, a man dreams his dreams as he lazily blows towards the ceiling the smoke of his last cigar.

He was dreaming of all that had happened to him during the last year. He was congratulating himself upon having played his cards so well. He was cogitating over that idea of the private theatricals, that he had seemed to throw out as a mere suggestion that evening, in the garden, his absence from the first rehearsals; the cold indifference which he had pretended to feel towards Naomi so as to reassure her, to lull her repugnance, to prevent her from refusing distinctly to act. He was thinking over that master-stroke wherein he suddenly exposed his love to the mother's jealousy in all the splendour of his theatrical surroundings, and which seemed as though it were dragged from his heart, in spite of himself, by the part that he was playing. All that had followed came back to him—the manner in which he had driven this last love to desperation, his manner during their last interview; and he felt a certain pride in thinking that he had arranged, combined, and foreseen all these circumstances which had been so naturally brought together and mingled by him with the passion of a woman of forty.

" It is I; I am not sleepy this evening."

And Renée, drawing a low chair up to the fire, sat down. " I want to have a talk such as we used to have in old days, do you remember?—when you had not your rooms in Paris. Ah, it was here that you accustomed me to everything—to a pipe, to a cigar! What talks we used to have when everyone else was in bed. We have laughed a great deal, and have made many silly jokes by this fireside. But now my brother is a serious man."

" Most serious," said Henry, smiling; " I am going to be married."

" Oh," said she, " that is not done yet. I beseech you." And, throwing herself on her knees, she took his hands: " See, it is I. Oh, you would not, for money! I am at your feet, you see. And, besides, it is unlucky to leave the name of one's fathers. That name is our blood. Henry —our brave, good father! Do not go on with this marriage, I entreat you—if you love me, if you love us all— oh, I entreat you!"

" What is this, are you going mad? What is the meaning of this scene? Come, I have had enough of it, get up!"

Renée got up, and looking her brother straight in the face, said:

" Naomi has told me all."

Her cheeks were scarlet. Henry was as pale as if someone had spat in his face.

" But you cannot marry her daughter," she cried.

" My dear child," replied Henry in a voice which, though cold, trembled, " it seems to me that you are meddling with what does not concern you, and you will allow me to say that for a girl—"

" Yes, I ought to know nothing about such mud, and I never should have, had it not been for you!"

"My dear child!"

And Henry advanced towards his sister. He was in one of those white passions which are terrifying. Renée. frightened, moved backwards. He seized her hand, pointed to the door, and said: "Go!"

For one moment, in the passage, he saw her support her self against the wall.

XXV

"You go first, Henry," said Monsieur Mauperin to his son. And as Henry tried to make his father precede him : "Go first," repeated Monsieur Mauperin.

After the lapse of half-an-hour, father and son descended together the steps leading from the office of the keeper of the seals.

"Well, you ought to be pleased with me, Henry," said Monsieur Mauperin, whose face was suffused with blood. "I have done what you and your mother wanted. You shall have this name."

"Father."

"It's done now. Let us say no more about it. Are you coming my way?" he asked, as he buttoned his great-coat with the military gesture wherewith old soldiers conceal their emotions.

"No, father, I would ask your leave to quit you. I have several things to do. I will come to dinner to-morrow."

"Very well—goodbye till then. You will do well to come—your sister is still poorly."

When he saw the carriage drive off with his father, Henry raised his head, looked at his watch, and walked to the Rue de la Paix with the easy, swinging step of a man who feels that the wind of fortune is blowing behind him.

At the corner of the Chaussée d'Antin, he turned into the Café Bignon, where several florid young men, who looked rich and provincial, were waiting for him.

During luncheon, the talk was about district meetings;

afterwards, on the boulevards, whither they went to smoke a cigar, they discussed the rotation of crops, drainage, lime-burning, and thence they rose to the elections, to the state of feeling in the country, to the chances of success of various candidates who had been mentioned, proposed, or suggested at agricultural meetings. At two o'clock Henry quitted these men, promising one of them an article upon his model farm, and went to his club, looked at the papers, and then began to write slowly in his pocket-book something that seemed to require very careful wording.

Thence he hurried to read a report to an insurance company, on to the directorate of which he had succeeded in pushing himself, thanks to the well-known mercantile reputation of his father. At four o'clock he jumped into a cab and made a round of visits to women who habitually received, and who had influence and connexions at the disposal of a man wanting a career. He remembered that he had not paid his subscription to the "Society for encouraging the good use of Sunday by workmen:" he paid it.

At seven o'clock, with friendly greetings on his lips, and his hand ready to be shaken, he ran up Lemardelay's staircase where the "Friendly Association" of his old schoolfellows was giving its annual dinner. At dessert he made a speech. recited the discourse which he had prepared at his club that afternoon, talked of the "brotherly agape, of an old family found again, of bonds between the past and the future, of help which should be given to old comrades who had met with undeserved misfortunes." He received loud applause, during which the orator withdrew. He looked in at the Debating Society of the Rue d'Aguessau, quitted it again. drew from his pocket a white tie, which he put on in the cab. and made his appearance at three or four parties.

XXVI.

THE blow which Renée had felt in her heart on leaving her brother's room, and under which she had staggered for a moment, left its traces in palpitations. She was unwell for a week or more. The evil yielded to gentle treatment, to a few doses of digitalis. But she remained sad, with a sadness that seemed incurable. Seeing her ill, and knowing the origin of her illness, Henry did all in his power to make up with her. He was unremitting in his attentions and his caresses, and seemed thereby to show his repentance. He had tried to enter again into the favour of that heart, to disarm that conscience, to appease that indignant spirit. But he always felt in her a coldness, a repugnance, a sort of hard resolution which caused him undefined terror. He understood that she had only forgiven the injury done to herself by his brutality : she had pardoned the brother and not the man.

One day her mother had promised to take her to Paris to amuse her, but as she was suddenly taken ill at the moment of starting, Henry, who had several things to do, proposed to take charge of his sister. They started. When they reached Paris, Henry stopped the cab which he had called at the station, at the Library in the Rue Richelieu : " Will you wait for me a minute ? " said he to his sister ; " I have a question to ask of the registrar of titles. By-the-way, why should you not come in with me ? You have always wished to see the manuscripts. They are in the same room. It will amuse you to see them, and I will meanwhile get my information."

Renée took her brother's arm, and they went together up to the room where the Manuscripts are kept. Henry placed her at the end of a table, found someone to bring her a Missal, and went to talk to a registrar in the bay of a window.

Renée slowly turned over the pages of her book. Behind her one of the attendants was warming himself. He was soon joined by another attendant who had just carried some books and papers over to the desk near which Henry was talking. And Renée heard this conversation take place about two feet from where she was sitting.

" Chamerot, do you see that little gentleman ? "

" Yes, the one at Monsieur Reisard's desk ? "

" Well he can boast of having got some very bad information ! He has just been asking whether there used not to be a family of the name of Villacourt, and whether it has died out. He has just been told that it has. Now, if he asked me, I could tell him a very different story, and that there ought to be some of them still. I don't know if they are the same. But certainly there were some when I left home, and one was a good strong fellow too, Monsieur Boisjorand. I remember that we had a fight once, and he could hit pretty hard. Their château is no distance from our house. From one of the towers one could see Saint Mihiel, and beyond that too. But even in my time it no longer belonged to them. Regular spendthrifts in that family— a queer kind of nobles ! They lived with the charcoal-burners in the woods at Croix-du-Soldat, near the Black Mound, like satyrs."

Saint Mihiel, the woods at Croix-du-Soldat, the Black Mound ; these words entered deep into Renée's mind.

" There, I have what I wanted," said Henry, gaily, as he came towards her. And he carried her off.

XXVII

DENOISEL had left Renée at her piano and was walking in the garden. As he returned to the house, he was surprised to hear her playing something which was not the piece she had been studying; then all at once the music stopped short, and he heard no more. He went to the drawing-room, and pushed open the door; Renée, seated on the music-stool, had buried her face in her hands, and was crying bitterly.

"Renée, my dear Renée, what is the matter with you?"

For a moment, sobs prevented Renée from answering; then she dried her eyes, as children do, on the back of her two hands, and said in a choking voice:

"It is—it is—too stupid of me. It is that thing of Chopin's, you know, for his funeral—his mass—that he wrote. Papa always forbids me to play it. But to-day, as there was no one in the house, and I thought you were at the end of the garden—I knew the effect it would have upon me, but I wanted to make myself cry over it; and, you see, I have had my wish. But isn't it stupid, eh? I who have such good spirits by nature."

"Come, come, you are not well, Renée. Something is the matter with you. People don't cry like that."

"No, no; I am quite well. I am as right as a trivet. Really, there is nothing the matter with me. Don't you think I would tell you if it were otherwise? It all comes from that horrid, stupid piece of music there. And to-day too, of all days, when papa has promised to take me to see

the ' Leghorn Hat'—a smile gleamed in her moist eyes at
these words—the ' Leghorn Hat' only think, at the Palais-
Royal!   I am sure I shall be amused!   Besides I only
care for plays of that kind.   Other pieces, dramas, senti-
mental plays.   For my part I think one gets so many
emotions of one's own that one need not go in search of
fresh ones.   And besides, an emotion which one feels in
common with everyone else is, to my mind, very like
crying in a pocket-handkerchief which does not belong
to one.   You are to come too, you know.   A real
bachelor party!   Papa has promised that we shall dine at
a restaurant.   And I promise you that I will, for this
occasion only, bring out again my old little girl's laugh, the
one I had when my English governess was here—Miss
——, do you remember? who used to wear orange-
coloured ribands, and get tipsy off Eau de Cologne!   Poor,
dear English woman!''

And, her fingers twitching at this recollection, Renée
gaily attacked a fantasia on the '' Carnival of Venice.''
Then stopping short, she said :

'' Have you ever been to Venice? ''

'' Yes.''

'' Is it not curious that there should be, in the world,
one place that one does not know, and yet which attracts
one and of which one dreams?   Some people feel it for
one country, others for another.   My one desire is to see
Venice.   Venice to my mind, now I am going to talk
nonsense, but Venice always appears to me to be the place
where all musicians ought to be buried.''

She replaced her hands upon the keys, but only touched
them lightly so as to produce no sound, as if she were
caressing, with the tips of her fingers, the silence of the
piano.   Then, letting them drop upon her knees she fell

again into her thoughtful attitude, and turning her head towards Denoisel, she recommenced.

"There is sadness in the air to-day. I don't understand why. But on some bright days one has no troubles, no worries, no sorrows before one. Well, all of a sudden one wants to be melancholy; one hunts up one's saddest thoughts. One feels that one must cry. Often I have gone to bed saying that I had a headache, and it was simply in order to bury my head in my pillow and have a good cry; and it has done me good. And in those moments one feels too much of a coward to shake oneself and get up. It is like the first feeling of a fainting fit; it is so pleasant to feel oneself going off."

Come, come, I am going to have your horse saddled, my little Renée, and we will go for a ride

"That's a good idea! But I warn you I shall go like the wind to-day."

XXVIII

"HOW can you help it! that poor Montbreton has four children, and not a large fortune," said Monsieur Mauperin, sighing as he folded up the newspaper in which he had just been reading the official nominations, and putting it on the table far away from him.

"Oh yes, that is what people always say. As soon as a man does anything low one is told: 'He has children.' One might almost fancy that in society people only have children for one purpose, to beg, and to do a heap of mean things. As though being the father of a family gave anyone a right to be a blackguard."

"Renée, Renée." said Monsieur Mauperin.

"No, it is quite true. I only know two kinds of people —those who are honest, and the others. Four children, indeed! That might excuse a father for stealing a loaf. In that case, Mother Gigogne would have had a perfect right to poison people. I am sure that Denoisel agrees with me."

"I? Not at all! I am strongly in favour of showing indulgence to married people, and to fathers of families. I should even like to see that indulgence extended to people with a favourite vice, a vice which may be rather expensive, but of which they are fond. As for other people who, having nothing to feed, nor wife, nor children, nor vice, sell themselves, ruin themselves, cringe, grovel, enrich themselves and abase themselves. Those people I give you to do what you please with!"

"I shall not talk to you any more," said Renée in a vexed tone. "All the same, papa, I do not understand how this does not make you jump, you who have always sacrificed everything to your opinions. What that man has done is disgusting."

"I do not say it is not. Only you are getting too excited, too excited."

"Yes, I am getting excited, and with reason! What? I see a man who owed everything to the late government and never had a good word for this one! and now he has gone over! All the same, your friend Montbreton is a wretched creature, a wretched creature!"

"Ah, my dear child, that is all very easy to say. When you have lived a little longer, life will make you more indulgent. You must be more gentle, my child—you are young."

"No, I have it in my blood. I am too thoroughly your daughter! I shall never know how to conceal my dislikes. I am made so, more's the pity! But whenever I see anyone whom I know, or for the matter of that. whom I don't know, fail in what you and all men call honour, well, then my feelings are too much for me. I feel as if I were looking at a toad! It makes me sick, it disgusts me. I trample upon it! Tell me, is a man honourable simply because he never does anything to bring him within the reach of the law? Is a man honourable who has committed in his life one action for which he blushes in solitude? Is a man honourable who has done things which, although he cannot be reproached or punished for them, nevertheless stain his conscience? To my mind there are worse meannesses than cheating at cards! And the indulgence of the world revolts me as though it were an accomplice. But there are such things as mean, dirty tricks! When I think of it, I feel almost indulgent towards criminals! At least they risk something. Their skin, their liberty are at stake! They play a fair game with good money; they do not commit infamies in gloves! I like that better! at any rate it is less cowardly!"

Seated on the sofa at the end of the drawing-room, her arms crossed, her hands burning, her whole body trembling, Renée thus spoke in a vibrating, sharp voice, which plainly showed all the anger she was feeling. Her eyes shone like fire out of the shadow which was cast upon her face.

"Your Monsieur Montbreton is a fine fellow!" she began again. "He has at least fifteen or sixteen thousand francs a year! If he had taken a less expensive house, or if he had not had his daughters dressed by Madame Carpentier."

"Ah, that deserves consideration," said Denoisel, "a bachelor with more than five thousand francs a year, or a married man with more than ten, can perfectly well afford to remain attached to an outgoing government. He can afford himself the luxury of regrets."

"And he will go on expecting politeness from you, shakes of the hand, salutes! Ah, it's too much! I hope that when he comes here, papa—I for one, shall leave the room."

"Let me get you a glass of water, Renée," said Monsieur Mauperin smiling. "You know that speakers—You were really fine during one moment. You were eloquent, it seemed to flow naturally."

"Oh, yes, laugh at me if you like. You know I am excitable, you always tell me so. And your Montbreton. But after all what does it matter! This gentleman is not one of us, is he? Ah, if anyone belonging to me did anything like that, anything dishonourable, anything—"

She stopped short. "I think," she resumed with an effort, and as if tears were rising to her eyes, "I think I could not love him any more. Yes, I really think my heart would close itself against him."

"Good, now the pathetic stop is turned on. Just now we had the little orator, here is the little girl now! It would be much better for you to come and look at this volume of caricatures that Davarande has sent your mother."

"Oh, show me!" said Renée, running towards him. And leaning on her father's shoulder, as he was turning over the pages of the book, she looked at two or three pictures; then turning away: "I have had enough of them. How can anyone find amusement in making things uglier than they have been made by nature! What a curious idea. In books, and in art, I am all in favour of the beautiful, and not of the hideous. And, besides, caricatures do not amuse me at all. They are like hunchbacks. A hunchback does not make me laugh. Do you like caricatures, Denoisel?"

"I' No; they make me cry. Really that sort of fun makes me miserable," answered Denoisel, taking up a review which lay on the table near the album. "To my mind it is a fossil family amusement. I cannot see a caricature lying on a table without thinking of a heap of lugubrious things: the spirit of the Directory, the drawings of Carle Vernet, and the gaiety of the middle-classes."

"Thank you," said Monsieur Mauperin, laughing, "and that is why you cut my 'Revue des deux Mondes' with a match, I suppose! Denoisel you are a queer fellow."

"Do you want a knife, Denoisel?" said Renée, and, plunging her hand into her pocket, she brought out a whole collection of odds and ends which she spread out on the table.

"By George!" said Denoisel, "your pocket is like a museum. There is enough in it to stock an auction-room. What are all these things?"

"Presents, from somebody. And they go everywhere with me. There is the knife you asked for," and, showing it to her father as she handed it to Denoisel: "Do you remember that one, and where you bought it for me? At Langres while we were changing horses. Oh! it is old now! This one," and she took up another, "you brought me back from Nogent. It has got a silver blade too, if you please. I gave you a halfpenny for it, do you remember?"

"If we are to begin making an inventory of everything," said Monsieur Mauperin, amused.

"And what have we here?" asked Denoisel, pointing to a little, worn, fat pocket-book, out of which peeped various ragged and dirty bits of paper.

"Ha, those are my secrets."

And picking up everything she had scattered about on the table, she put it all back into her pocket, with the pocket-book. Then, bursting out laughing, she hunted again, brought out the pocket-book, and, pressing the spring, spread out in front of Denoisel, on the table, all the little papers it contained, recognising them one by one: "See, that is a prescription given to papa when he was ill. That one is a poem he wrote for me two years ago, on my birthday."

"Come, come, pack up your reliquary. Hide all those things," said Monsieur Mauperin, as the door opened and Dardouillet came in. And with his hand he swept together all the papers.

"Oh, you are putting them all wrong," said Renée in an angry voice, as she replaced them in her pocket-book.

XXIX

A MONTH later, in the little studio, Renée said to Denoisel:
" Tell me, do you think I am very romantic ? "

" Romantic, romantic; first explain what you mean by
romantic ? "

" Oh, you know what I mean. I mean having ideas
not like other people, dreaming of a lot of things that can
never come to pass. For instance, a girl is romantic when
she finds it difficult to marry, as other girls do, a man
like other men, who has nothing extraordinary about
him, who comes in by the door, and who is presented to one
by papa and mamma, and who has not even saved one's life
at first sight, by stopping one's runaway horse, or by dragging one out of a river. You do not think that I am made
of that sort of stuff, I hope ? "

" No; that is to say I know nothing whatever about it,
and I bet that you know nothing about it yourself."

"Nonsense! Perhaps it is that I have so little imagination,
but it has always seemed to me so funny to have an ideal,
to dream of any one man ! It is the same with heroes in
novels; they never have had any attraction for me. They
appear to me too well educated, too beautiful, too accomplished. They are sickening, in short. But that is not
what I mean. Now you, if you were called upon to pass
all your life, side by side with a being—a being. "

" A being, what do you mean ? "

" Let me explain. With a man who did not in the least

respond to certain little delicate requirements of your nature, who did not seem to you poetical, who had not a scrap of poetry in him, but who, at the same time, redeemed all that was wanting to the other sides of his nature by a kind-heartedness, a kind-heartedness such as one does not often meet."

" So much kind-heartedness as that? Oh, I should not hesitate, I should take the kind-heartedness with my eyes shut! It is so awfully rare."

" You think highly of kind-heartedness, then?"

" I think highly of it, Renée, as one does of things one has lost."

" You? but you are so kind."

" I am not wicked, and that is all. Perhaps I should be envious, if I had more modesty and less pride. But as to being good; I am not good. Life cures you of that, as it does of childhood. One throws away one's heart, you see, Renée, when one sows one's wild oats."

" Then in your opinion, goodness—"

" Yes, the goodness that can resist men and experience, the kind-heartedness that I have met with in its virgin state, in some two or three middle-class people in my life, to my mind is the best and most divine thing remaining in man."

" Very well. But now let us suppose that a very kind-hearted man, such as you have mentioned, had feet which looked as though they were cut short in his boots, like a bit of cake? Supposing that such a man were fat?"

" Well, what of that? One looks neither at his feet, nor at his stomach; that is all. But I beg your pardon for having entirely forgotten."

" What?"

" Nothing; that you are a woman."

"Do you know that that speech is very uncomplimentary to my sex?"

Denoisel made no reply, and the conversation dropped.

Renée began again:

"Have you ever wished for a fortune?"

"Yes, frequently; but simply in order to treat it according to its deserts, to show that I have no respect for it."

"Why so?"

"Yes, I have often wished to be rich in order to display the contempt I feel for money, and I can remember having fallen asleep two or three times with the idea of going to seek a wife in Italy."

"In Italy?"

"Yes, there are more Russian princesses there than anywhere else. And as it is only Russian princesses who now-a-days can afford to marry a man without a sixpence. Besides I would have been satisfied with a princess who was rather pressed for money. I was not particular. I would have gone down with pleasure to eight hundred thousand francs a year, but that was the very least I would have taken."

"Thank you," said Renée, laughing. "And pray what would you have done with all that money?"

"It would have simply been like a stream running through my fingers. I would have done something dazzling, which I have never seen rich people do. I think all the arch-millionaires disgraceful. Do you see any difference in fortune between the life of a man with a hundred thousand francs a year and that of a man with ten thousand? But with me you should have seen. During a year I would have flung my million about recklessly, in all sorts of whims, and fancies, and follies. I would have bewildered and crushed Paris. I would have appeared before it like a sun, vomiting forth bank-notes. I would have defiled my money by all sorts of prodigality and extravagance, and at the end of a year, to the very day, I would have left my wife."

" Bah ! "

" Certainly ; to prove to myself that I did not love money. If I had not left her, I should have considered myself dishonoured."

" What extraordinary ideas ! I must admit that I have not yet reached such a height of philosophy as you. I should like a large fortune, all that it gives, the pleasures, the luxury, the horses, the carriages, and besides these, the delight of being able to snub people whom one does not like, to annoy them. I should enjoy being rich."

" I was right just now, Renée, when I told you that you were a woman, nothing but a woman."

XXX.

DENOISEL spoke as he thought. If he had sometimes wished for a large fortune, he had never envied one. He had a sincere and heartfelt contempt for money, the contempt of a man who is rich on little.

Denoisel was a Parisian, or rather he was the Parisian. Broken in to all the experiences of Paris, wonderfully trained in the great art of living by the rules of Parisian life, he was the man of that life: he possessed all its instincts, its feelings, its cleverness. He represented perfectly that modern personage, the civilised man, triumphing day by day, as in a forest of Bondy, over the price of things, over the dearness of capitals, as the savage triumphs over nature in a virgin forest. He seemed to have all the appearance and glitter of wealth. He lived among rich people, dined at their restaurants and clubs, shared their customs, joined in their pleasures. Through his relations, he was mixed up with some very large fortunes. All that money can open was open to him. He was to be seen at all the large subscription balls at the " Provençaux," at race meetings, and at first nights at the theatres. In summer he went to watering-places or to the sea, or to some gambling-place. He dressed like a man who keeps a horse.

Denoisel, however, possessed barely twenty thousand francs. Sprung from a family which was buried in old-fashioned ideas upon the subject of property, attached, and so to speak nailed to landed property, always talking of bankruptcy, and as mistrustful of the funds as a peasant used to be of a bank-note. Denoisel had shaken off the prejudices of his people. Without heeding the advice, the remonstrances, the anger, the threats of old and distant relations, he had sold the little farms which his parents left him. In his eyes there was no longer any proportion between the revenue to be derived from land and the expenses of every-day life. In his opinion, landed property might have done very well as a means of fortune in the days of which Paul de Kock wrote, when he said in one of his novels: " Paul was rich; he had six thousand francs a year." But since that time property had become, according to him, an anachronism, a sort of archaic possession whereof only the rich could afford themselves the enjoyment. So he sold, and made out of his land a little capital, which he invested, by the advice of a stock-broker who was a friend of his, in foreign funds, shares, and stocks, which doubled and tripled his revenue without incurring any risk to his bread and butter. Having thus made of his capital a sum without significance, except in the eyes of a lawyer, and which no longer interfered with his well-being, Denoisel arranged his life as he had arranged his fortune. He regulated his expenses. He knew perfectly well the cost, in Paris, of all that is ruinous, such as vanity, savouries at dinner, and cheap bargains. He was not ashamed to add up a bill before paying it. Out of doors he never smoked anything but cigars that cost him fourpence apiece; but at home he smoked a pipe. He knew how to find the best place for everything, of houses which open and treat their customers well during the first three months. He knew the cellars of all the restaurants; he would ask for Chambertin at such and such a place on the boulevard, and would

never call for it except there.   If he gave a dinner, he knew
how to arrange his bill of fare so as to command the waiter's
respect.   And he was, above all, capable of supping for a
few shillings at the Café Anglais.

In everything he showed the same understanding about
expenditure.   He was dressed by one of the best tailors in
Paris ; but a friend of his in the Foreign Office got over
from London for him, through the Embassy bags, all his
autumn clothes.   Had he a present to give either for a
wedding or the New Year, he knew what shop had just
received a cargo of pretty things from India or China, or
he remembered an old curiosity which he had seen in some
out-of-the way street, some old bit of Dresden or Sèvres, a
curio of some kind to which the recipient vainly tries to fix
a price, and of which he vainly dreams about the cost.

All that, in Denoisel, was spontaneous, natural, instinctive.
This continual victory which his Parisian intelligence gained
over daily life escaped altogether the miseries and meannesses of calculation.   It was a conglomeration of conditions which had happily come together in a happy existence,
and not the result of petty economies.   And while he was
so carefully regulating the use of his yearly fifteen thousand
francs, the man remained open and noble : he warded off an
expense, he did not bargain with it.

Denoisel lived on the first floor of a clean house, which
had a carpeted staircase.   He only had three rooms, but
the Boulevard des Italiens was at his very door.   And his
little drawing-room, which he had turned into a smoking-
room, was charming.   It was just one of those little sugar-
plum boxes that upholsterers in Paris make so admirably,
all lined and smiling with gay chintz, and with divans in it
as large as beds.   Denoisel wished that the absence of any
objects of art should complete the brightness of this room.

The hall porter waited on him, bringing him his cup of chocolate in the morning and doing his rooms. In the evening he would dine either at his club or at a restaurant, or with friends.

The smallness of his rent, the simplicity of his attendance and of his housekeeping, left Denoisel a great deal of that spare cash which the richest people are often without, and which is more necessary in Paris than anywhere else— pocket money. Nevertheless, sometimes that superior force, the Unexpected, would fall into the middle of his life, and would disarrange its equilibrium and the budget. Then Denoisel would disappear from Paris for some time; he would go and ruralise in some inn in the country, near a river, where he paid three francs a day, and spent nothing else except on his tobacco. Finding himself quite without money during two or three winters, he had emigrated, and having found a town like Florence where happiness costs nothing, and where daily life costs but little more than happiness, he had stayed there six months, lodged in an attic, eating truffles and Parmesan cheese at a restaurant, passing his evenings in the smartest opera-boxes, going to the balls given by the Grand Duke, made much of, run after, always wearing white camellias, and economising merrily all the time.

Denoisel spent little more on love than on anything else; as he had divested it of all personal vanity, he only paid his own price for it. However, on first entering life, it had been his only attraction, but it was an attraction which he had always kept under and within limits. He had wished to experience the pleasure of living like a lord with the most expensive woman in Paris. For this pleasure he allowed himself sixty thousand francs out of the hundred and eighty thousand that he then possessed, and he lived for

six months with the Génicot in the way that a man with a
hundred and twenty thousand francs a year, keeping a
woman who would give a tip of a hundred francs to a
postilion coming back from the races, might live. At the
end of six months he left this woman in love, for the first
time in her life, with a man who had paid her.

Tempered by this experience, he had thenceforward only
allowed himself temporary bonds. Suddenly, when he was
beginning to discover the monotony of venal love, there
had come upon him not a great desire for adventures, but a
great curiosity as to womankind. He began to pursue the
unexpected, the unlooked for, and the unknown. Actresses
all seemed to him the same courtesan, courtesans all seemed
more or less the same actress. What attracted him was
the unclassed woman, the woman who puzzles the observer
and the oldest Parisian. He often took long walks at
night, vaguely and irresistibly attracted by one of those
creatures who are neither all vice nor all virtue, and who
walk so prettily through the mud. Sometimes he was
dazzled by one of those beautiful Parisian girls, who seem
to make daylight as they pass, and he would forget himself
and stand looking for her long after she had disappeared
in the darkness of a side street. His vocation was to pick
stars out of the mud. Occasionally he would bring out of
her slum one of those marvels of the people of nature, would
make her talk, would look at her, would listen to her, would
study her, and then, when he was tired of her, he would
put her into circulation, and would amuse himself by bowing
to her when she passed him in her carriage.

Denoisel's appearance of fortune had secured him a good
reception from the world. He soon established himself in
society on a good footing, and people soon began to want
him on account of the gaiety he brought with him, the wit

that he scattered. and the kindnesses that he was always ready to perform. The friendship which he extended to foreigners, artists, and theatrical people, his knowledge of all the ins and outs of everything, made him invaluable on many occasions. Did a person want a box at a theatre, or permission to visit a prison or a private picture gallery, or a place in the assize court for a lady, or a foreign decoration for a man, he applied to Denoisel. On the two or three occasions on which he had acted as second in duels he had displayed determination, decision. a manly care for the honour as well as for the life for which he was responsible. The obligations which many people were under to him were in no wise diminished by the knowledge that he was a past master of the art of fencing. IIis character had gained him esteem. and he had come to be respected even by rich people. for whose millions, however, he himself had little reverence.

XXXI

· WELL, now, my wife wanted to have her portrait painted by Monsieur Ingres. You have seen it. It is not the least like her, but it is by Monsieur Ingres. Guess what he charged me for doing it? Ten thousand francs! I gave them to him, but I think it is a robbery; everyone wars against capital. What, because a man has a reputation, is he to charge me what he pleases? Is he to have no scale of charges, no tariff, simply because he is an artist? In that case he might ask a million! It is the same with the doctors who charge their patients according to their fortunes. Besides, does anyone know how much I have got? It is iniquitous. Yes, ten thousand francs; what do you think of that?"

And Monsieur Bourjot, who was standing near the fire talking to Denoisel, shifted his position from one foot to the other.

"Upon my word!" said Denoisel quite gravely, "you are right. All those people take an unfair advantage of their reputation. I can only see one way of putting a stop to it, which would be to decree a legal *maximum* for talent, a *maximum* for masterpieces. It would be very simple."

"Quite true," said Monsieur Bourjot, "that would be the way. And it would be perfectly fair, for really—"

The Bourjots had dined quietly that evening with the Mauperins. The two families were talking over the marriage, of which, in order to fix the day, they were only waiting for the expiration of the delay of a year after the first insertion of the name of Villacourt in the "Moniteur." Monsieur Bourjot had insisted upon this delay. The women were all talking of the trousseau, of the cashmere shawls, of the jewellery. Madame Mauperin, seated near Madame Bourjot, was contemplating her as she might have contemplated a person who had performed a miracle. Monsieur Mauperin's face was radiant with happiness.

Monsieur Mauperin had at last allowed himself to be dazzled by money. This honest, pure, severe, rigid, incorruptible man, had little by little, allowed this great wealth of the Bourjots' to filter into his thoughts, to form part of his dreams, to whisper to, and to touch his instincts, which were those of a practical and commercial man who was old, and the father of a family. He was seduced and disarmed. Since the success of his son's engagement, he had felt for him the sort of esteem that one feels for a talent or a fortune which suddenly reveals itself, and, without acknowledging the difference in his feeling towards him, he was no longer angry with him for changing his name. Fathers are human after all.

Renée, who, for some time past had appeared bored, sad, and moody, was almost gay that evening. She was amusing herself by blowing about the feathers which Naomi wore in her hair. The latter, idle and self-absorbed, her eyes half closed, answered by monosyllables the ceaseless chatter of Madame Davarande.

"Nowadays, everything is against money," said Monsieur Bourjot sententiously. "There is a league against it. Now, at Saunois, I have just finished making a road. Well, do you suppose they touch their hats to us? Not a bit of it. In '48 we gave them sacks of corn, and what do you suppose they said? 'That pig,' I beg your pardon, ladies, 'must be in a fright!' That was the only thanks I

got. I found a model farm, and ask the government to
send me a director for it; they send me down a red republican, a scoundrel who spends most of his time in blating
against the rich. And now I have on hand a tiresome
piece of business with our wretched municipal council.
I find work for them, do I not? We are the wealth of
the neighbourhood. Nevertheless, I feel positive that were
a revolution to break out, they would set fire to my house.
Oh, they would not care! You have no idea what a
number of enemies you make in a place by paying nine
thousand francs in taxes every year. They would burn us
without more ado. You saw them in February. Oh, the
people! I have changed all my old opinions about them,
and they are preparing a pleasant future for us too. I know
we shall be devoured by people without a halfpenny. I
prophecy. You will see. Those ideas often come to me.
If one had no children, for I don't care about money.

"What are you talking about, neighbour?" said Monsieur Mauperin as he came up.

"I am saying that I fear that some day our children will
have no bread, Monsieur Mauperin. That is what I am
talking about."

"You will prevent them from marrying!" said Monsieur
Mauperin.

"Oh, if Monsieur Bourjot is bringing out all his de-
spondent views, and beginning to talk about the end of the
world," said Madame Bourjot.

"I congratulate you, madame, on not having my
worries," said Monsieur Bourjot, bowing to his wife, "but
I assure you that, without being over-nervous, there is
plenty to make one uneasy."

"Certainly, certainly," said Denoisel, "I agree with
Monsieur Bourjot in thinking that property is threatened,

seriously threatened, dangerously threatened, first of all by envy, which is the fount of nearly all revolutions, and then by progress, which baptises them."

" But, sir, such progress as that will be infamous. For I am not suspected. I have been a liberal; I am one still. I am a soldier of liberty. I am a republican by birth. I am in favour of all progress. But a revolution against money would be barbarous. It would be a return to a savage state. We must have justice, and good sense. Can you imagine a state of society without property?"

" No more than I can a greasy pole without a silver cup."

" Do you mean to tell me," continued Monsieur Bourjot without overhearing Denoisel, and getting more and more excited, " that what I have gained by my hard work, and by my industry and honesty, what is mine, what I have acquired, the inheritance of my children, is not the most sacred thing in the world? I already regard taxation as an attack upon property."

" I entirely agree with you," said Denoisel in a tone of perfect good humour. " I quite agree with you, and I should be sorry," added he spitefully, " to paint things to you in blacker colours than those in which you already see them. But the first revolution was directed against the nobility, the next will be against the wealthy. They cut off the heads of all the fine old names, they will next suppress all the large fortunes. It was once a crime to be a Monsieur de Montomorency, it will soon be criminal to be Monsieur Fifty-thousand-a-year. That is evidently the direction which things are taking. I am specially qualified to speak to you upon the subject, as I am a most disinterested person. In the old days there would have been no reason to guillotine me, now I have nothing to lose. Therefore—"

" Allow me, sir," said Monsieur Bourjot with solemnity,

" You are jumping to a conclusion. No one deplores excesses more than I do. '93 was a great crime, sir. The aristocracy were abominably treated, and upon that point there can be but one opinion amongst honest men."

Monsieur Mauperin smiled, remembering the Bourjot of 1822.

" But now," continued Monsieur Bourjot, " the situation is no longer the same. Society is renewed. Its foundations have been restored. Everything is changed. The people had reasons, pretexts, if you prefer it, against the aristocracy. The Revolution of '89 was directed against privileges, which it is not for me to condemn, but which existed. That was a very different state of affairs. The people wanted equality. It was more or less legitimate, but at any rate there was some sense in it. But now, I ask you, where are the privileges? One man is as good as another. Have we not universal suffrage? You say : ' Money.' But every one can make money — all trades are open."

" Except those which are not."

" Well, at any rate, every one can attain to everything. Intelligence and hard work are the only requisites."

" And circumstances," said Denoisel.

" They can be created, sir! but look at society now. We are all sprung from nothing. My father was a cloth-merchant, wholesale, it is true, and you see—that is equality, sir, the real, true equality. There is no longer such a thing as caste. The middle-classes rise from the populace, the populace can rise to the middle-classes. I could have found a count for my daughter had I wished. But now, against fortune, we have all the bad instincts, the bad passions. Communistic ideas ; people declaim about misery. Well. I declare to you, that never has so much been done for the people as now. Comfort is making huge strides in France! People who never used to taste meat, now eat it twice a week. Those are facts. I am sure that our young economist, Monsieur Henry, will tell us,"

"Yes, yes," said Henry, "that is proved. In twenty-five years the increase in cattle has been twelve per cent. If you divide the population of France into twelve millions of townspeople, and twenty-four or twenty-five millions of country-people, you will find that the former consume, by the year and by person, about 65 kilograms, and the latter 20 kilograms, 26 centigrams. I will answer for the figures. What is quite certain is, that the most careful census shows, in France, since 1789, an increase of about ten years to the ordinary life of a man, and that progress is the surest proof of prosperity in a people. Statistics,"

"Ah, statistics, chief of inexact sciences!" interrupted Denoisel, who delighted in upsetting the ideas of Monsieur Bourjot with paradoxes—"But I admit everything; I admit that the life of the people has been lengthened, and that more meat is now consumed by them than there ever was before; but do you, on that account, believe in the immortality of our present social constitution? By means of a revolution, the reign of the middle-classes, that is to say, the reign of money was brought about; you say: 'That is over and done with; we must never have another; no other revolution would be lawful now.' That is very natural; but between ourselves, I do not see why the middle-class is to be the be-all and the end-all of modern society. According to you, once political equality is granted to all, social equality is accomplished; perhaps you are right, but you will have to persuade people whose interest it is not to believe it. One man is as good as another? doubtless, in the eyes of God, and every one in this nineteenth century has the right to wear a black coat so long as he has the wherewithal to pay for it. Shall I sum up modern equality for you in one word? It is equality in presence of the conscription : every one takes his chance, but three thousand francs give you the right to send some one to be killed in your place. You speak of privileges, and say truly that there are none now ; but the Bastille is destroyed, only it has left little ones behind. For instance, take a Court of Law ; and I am the first to recognise that it is there that a man's position, his name, his money, go for the very least and are not considered ; very well, suppose you commit a crime and are a peer of France ; they will spare you the scaffold and allow you to take poison. Observe that I think they are quite right. I only quote it to show you how fast inequalities grow ; and, upon my word! when I see how much ground they cover now, I wonder where there was room for any others. Hereditary rights say you? There is one of the things that the revolution hoped to have killed and buried, an abuse of the old state of things against which enough outcry was raised. I ask you now whether the son of a great political light does not inherit his father's name and all the advantages accompanying that name, his constituency, his acquaintances, his place in the world, his chair in the Academy? We are overrun with sons at present! We have got nothing else : they fill up every career ; their reversionary interests bar the road to every one else. Customs, do you see, are stronger than laws. You are money, and you say : ‘Money is sacred.’ Pray why? You say : ‘We have no caste.’ No, but you are already a new aristocracy whose insolence has already outdone the impertinence of the oldest aristocracies on the face of the earth. There is no court at this moment, and there never has been one in history, I believe, where one would have to put up with more contempt than in the office of some rich banker who has never accompanied to his door more than two people in his life ! You speak of bad instincts, of evil passions. What can you expect ? the middle-class rule is not likely to elevate minds. The upper ranks of society can digest and arrange matters ; the lower ranks cannot ; they have no ideas, only appetites. In former times when, by the side of money, there was something that was both above it as well as beside it, people could afford, in a time of revolution, not to demand money too abruptly, not to require the common change of coarse pleasure, they could satisfy themselves by changing the colours on a flag, or by writing a few words over a barracks, or by gaining some generous and hollow victory. But nowadays ! nowadays we know where is the heart of Paris ; they will storm the Bank rather than the Hôtel de Ville ! Ah ! the middle-class have made one grand mistake."

"Which is ?" asked Monsieur Bourjot, quite taken aback by Denoisel's outbreak.

"That of not leaving Paradise in Heaven, which was its proper place. The day on which the poor no longer consoled themselves by saying that the next life would make up to them for this, the day on which the people gave up looking for happiness in the next world was a bad day. Voltaire did a great deal of harm to the rich !"

"Ah ! how right you are !" exclaimed Monsieur Bourjot with enthusiasm. "It is quite clear ! All those black-guards ought to be made to go to church."

XXXII.

THERE were great rejoicings at the Bourjots', who had determined to announce, by means of a ball, the approaching marriage of their daughter with Monsieur Mauperin de Villacourt.

" What a good time you seem to be having! How you are dancing!" said Renée to Naomi, as she fanned herself with her pocket handkerchief in a corner of the big drawing-room.

" That is quite true; I never danced so much before," and Naomi, taking her arm, dragged her away into a smaller room.

" No, never," she repeated. And drawing Renée towards her, she kissed her. " Oh, how good it is to be happy!" And kissing her again with feverish excitement, she continued: " *She* no longer loves him! I am sure she does not love him any more! Formerly, do you see, she showed her love for him by the way she got up when he came in; she loved him with her eyes, with her voice, with her breath, with the noise of her gown! with everything! When he was not there, I felt, I cannot explain how, that her thoughts and her silence were loving him! A stupid creature like I! Are you not astonished that I should have noticed all that? But there are some things that I understand through this," and she laid Renée's hand on her gown of white moire antique, in the place of her heart, " and this is never wrong."

" And now you love him, yourself?" inquired Renée.

Naomi closed her mouth by laying upon it gently her bouquet of roses.

" Mademoiselle, you promised me the first polka." And a young man carried off Naomi, who, as she passed through the door, turned and kissed her hand to Renée.

Naomi's avowal had sent a thrill of pleasure through Renée. She was penetrated with the laughter of her love. She felt an immediate relief. In a moment everything changed in her eyes; and the thought, " She loves him!" carried before it all other ideas. She lost sight of the shame and of the crime that she had hitherto been only able to see in this marriage. She kept repeating to herself that Naomi loved him, that they loved each other. All the rest was the past; a past which they would both forget—Naomi by dint of forgiving it, Henry by dint of atoning for it. Suddenly a flash of memory came over her, a thought which caused her disquiet, a vague fear. But at that moment she was determined not to see any black clouds upon the horizon, nor anything threatening in the future. Chasing it away, she returned very quickly to Naomi and her brother. She thought of their wedding-day, of their household; and she seemed to hear little baby voices saying to her, " *Auntie!*"

" Mademoiselle, will you do me the honour of dancing any dance you like with me?"

It was Denoisel who stood bowing before her.

" We need not dance together, you and I; we know each other much too well. Come and sit here, and don't crumple my gown. Well! Why are you looking at me?"

Renée wore a gown of white tulle, trimmed with seven little flounces, and sprinkled over, here and there, with leaves of ivy and little red berries, which were repeated on

her gathered bodice and on the tulle trimmings of her
sleeves. A long wreath of ivy, dotted with the same little
red berries, was twisted round the plaits of her hair, and
fell on her shoulders in two green trails. Her head, somewhat thrown back, rested on the sofa. Her beautiful
chestnut hair, drawn to the front of her head, covered the
upper part of her shining forehead. A dark and tender
light, a soft and deep fire escaped from her eyes, which
were brown, veiled by their lashes, and swimming, and
from her glances, which were invisible. The light played
upon her cheeks. Shadow tickled the corners of her mouth,
and her lips, generally closed in a somewhat haughty little
pout, were, this evening, open and unclosed, and half showed
the smile of her soul. A reflection of light just touched
her chin; on her neck, a necklace of shadow seemed to
flicker at every movement of her head. She looked charming, her features lost in the brilliancy which fell from the
lustres, the shape of her face concealed in a child-like
happiness, as though in sunshine.

"You are very pretty this evening, Renée."

"Ah, this evening?"

"Well, in truth, during these last days you have looked
so bored and so sad. Pleasure suits you much better."

"Do you think so? Can you dance?"

"As if I had learned: very badly. But a minute ago
you refused me a turn."

"Did I really? I am very anxious to dance. Besides
we have lots of time. Do not look at your watch. I do
not want to know the time. So you think I am merry?
Well, you are wrong. I am not merry. I am happy,
very happy, there! Denoisel, when you are loitering
about Paris, you must have seen those old women in
white cotton caps, who sell matches at the street corners,

You will give a sovereign to each of the first five that you come across. I will pay you back. I have got some savings. Don't forget. Is the same valse still going on? Did I really refuse to dance with you? Well, henceforward I mean to dance everything without looking at my partners! They may be as ugly as you please, they may wear patched boots, they may talk to me about Shakespeare and the musical glasses, they may be too little or too tall, they may reach to my elbow, or I to their waists, they may have no ear for music, or they may have hot hands. I will take them all! That is how I feel to-night, and now say, if you can, that I am not good-natured."

A man's head appeared through the doorway of the little drawing-room.

"Davarande, come and give me a turn." cried Renée, and, as she passed Denoisel, she whispered to him: "You see I am beginning with the family."

XXXIII

"WHAT is the matter with your mother this evening?" Denoisel asked Renée. They were alone. Madame Mauperin had just gone upstairs to her bedroom. Monsieur Mauperin was going his rounds in the workshops, where the men were busy that night. "She seemed to be in a temper."

"In a horrible temper; out with it!"

"What is the matter?"

"Ah, that is the question." And Renée began to laugh. "I have just refused another offer; nothing more."

"Another? It seems to be a specialty of yours!"

"Oh, this is only the fourteenth; quite a moderate number still. And it is you who made me refuse it."

"I? What do you mean? What had I to do with it?"

Renée rose from her chair, buried her hands in her pockets, and began to walk up and down the drawing-room. From time to time she stopped short, and pirouetted on her heels, emitting at the same time a sort of whistle.

"Yes, you!" she repeated, coming back to Denoisel. "What should you say if I told you I had refused two millions?"

"Those millions must have been a good deal astonished at you!"

"I must say that I was not tempted. I don't wish to make myself out stronger than I am. I never pretend when I am with you. But, all the same, I was very nearly caugh tat one moment. It was Monsieur Barousse who had managed it all—very kindly. You will understand how they worked at me here. Mamma and Henry were for ever at me. I was worried the whole day long. And then, besides, I let myself dream a little too. At any rate, I slept very badly for two nights. Millions seem to bring sleeplessness. I must also say, to be just to myself, that all through it I thought a great deal of papa. Wouldn't he have been proud, eh? How he would have revelled in my two hundred thousand francs a year! You know how vain he is on my behalf. Do you remember his famous outburst: 'A son-in-law who would allow my daughter to go in an omnibus!' He was splendid! And then you come in—yes, you; your ideas, your paradoxes, your theories, all sorts of things that you have said to me. I remember your contempt for money; it gains upon me as I think about it. And one fine morning, bang! I kick over the traces. You are getting too much influence over me, my friend, decidedly."

" I, I am a fool. I am so sorry. I thought it was not catching. Really and truly it was I !"

" Yes, you, in a great measure, and also partly *he*."

" Ah !"

" Yes, partly Monsieur Lemeunier. When I felt that fortune was beginning to intoxicate me, when I had too great a desire to become Madame Lemeunier, I looked at him. Little did you think how truly you spoke to me the other day. I felt that I was a woman, and you don't know how much I felt it ! But against that, I saw how good he was. I can't give you an idea of his goodness. It was in vain that I turned him round and round again, studying him from every point of view, because at last, his perfection worried me. Well, I could find nothing! He was good wherever you looked at him. In that respect he was very different to Reverchon and the others! Can you believe that he said to me: 'Mademoiselle, I know that I do not please you; but let me wait until I displease you rather less.' He was too touching. There were days on which I felt inclined to say to him: 'How would it be if we were to mingle our tears?' Fortunately, when he made me feel inclined to cry, papa, on the other hand, made me feel inclined to laugh. Poor father! he did look so funny, half happy and half sad. I never saw such resigned happiness. His sorrow at losing me, and his happiness at seeing me make a good marriage, caused in his heart a curious mixty-maxty of feeling! Ah, well, it's all over now, thank goodness! Have you noticed how papa looks crossly at me whenever mamma is looking our way? But his crossness is all sham. In his heart of hearts I know he is very pleased with me. I can see that."

XXXIV

DENOISEL was in Henry Mauperin's rooms. They were sitting near the fire, smoking. They suddenly heard a noise of an altercation in the ante-room; and, almost immediately, the door was burst violently open, and a man entered roughly, pushing aside the servant who attempted to bar the passage.

" Monsieur Mauperin de Villacourt ? " said he.

" I am he, sir."

And Henry rose from his chair.

" Good. My name is Boisjorand de Villacourt." And with the back of his huge hand he marked Henry Mauperin's face with blood. At the blow, and bleeding freely, Henry became as white as the silk necktie which he was wearing. He stooped as if to spring upon his assailant; but he suddenly drew himself up, stretched out his hand towards Denoisel, who had thrown himself between them, calmly folded his arms, and said in his coldest voice :

" I think I understand you, sir. You are of opinion that there is a Villacourt too many in the world; and so am I."

The intruder, in presence of this calm man of the world, became confused, took off his hat, which, until then, he had kept on his head, and tried to stammer out a sentence.

" Will you be so kind, sir," broke in Henry, " as to leave your address with my servant ? I will send to you to morrow."

" What a tiresome business !" said Henry, when he was alone with Denoisel. " But where does this Villacourt spring from ? They told me there were no more of them. Hulloa ! I am bleeding," continued he, wiping his face. " What a lout ! George," cried he to his servant, " bring me some water."

" You will choose swords, will you not ? " asked Denoisel. " Give me a walking-stick. Now, listen to me. You put yourself on guard as far from him as you can, and engage very little of your sword. This man is hot-blooded, makes a rush at you, and you break with circular parries. And when you find yourself hard pressed, when he throws himself wildly upon you, you recoil on the right side of your left foot by turning on the point of your right foot, like that. He has nothing in front of him then, you catch him sideways, and spit him like a frog."

" No," said Henry, raising his head from the basin in which he was sponging his face, " no, not swords."

" But, my dear fellow, evidently this man is a sportsman ; he must be accustomed to handle fire-arms."

" My friend, circumstances alter cases. I have taken a name, which is always a ridiculous thing to do. A man appears and accuses me of having stolen it. I have enemies, in fact, I have a good many ; people will make a great talk about it. I must kill this gentleman ; that is evident ; it is the only means of clearing my position. Thereby I stop everything, the law-suit, the stories, the gossip, everything ! Why should you expect me to take the sword for that ? With a sword one kills a man who has had five years in a fencing-school, and who knows how to fence, who offers you his breast in the place in which you naturally look for it in a bout, but a man who does not know how to use his sword, who jumps, dances, treats it like a stick, I should wound him, and that would be all. And besides, I am rather good with the pistol. I have taken pains with it. You will do me the justice to acknowledge that I have chosen my accomplishments well. And besides, I want to hit him there," and he touched Denoisel just above the hip, "there, do you see? because, higher up, it is bad; the arm saves you, whereas here, you catch a whole lot of little machines of primary importance; there is especially that good bladder, and if you have the good luck to hit it, and it happens to be full, it means Carrel's peritonitis, my friend! So you will choose the pistol for me; a walking duel, do you understand? And I wish to have it kept as secret as possible, that no one should know anything of it beforehand. Whom will you take with you?"

"Suppose I take Dardouillet? He has served in the Mounted National Guard; I will make an appeal to his military instincts."

"Very good; he will do. Go first to my mother; she will be expecting me. Tell her I cannot go to see her before Thursday. We cannot have her coming in here just now. I shall not go out. I shall bathe my face so as to make myself more presentable. Is there a very bad mark? I shall have some dinner brought up to me here, and I shall devote my evening to doing the little writing that has always to be done on these occasions. By-the-bye, if you see this gentleman's seconds to-morrow morning, why should we not fight in the afternoon, at four o'clock? It is just as well to get it over. To-morrow, you will find me here all day, or else at the shooting-gallery. Make any arrangements you please about it, and thank you in advance. At four o'clock, eh, if possible?"

XXXV

THE name of the farm that Henry Mauperin had added to his patronymic, in order to ennoble it, happened by a curious but not unprecedented chance, to be the name of a seignorial property in Lorraine, and of a family once famous, but now so forgotten that it was supposed to be extinct.

The man who had just struck him was the last of the Villacourts, who took their name from the domain and castle of Villacourt, situated about ten miles from Saint Mihiel, and owned by them from time immemorial.

In 1303, Ulric de Villacourt was one of the three nobles who affixed their seals to the will of Ferry, Duke of Lorraine, at the express order of that prince. Under Charles the Bold, Gantonnet de Villacourt, who was taken prisoner while fighting against the Messinians, only obtained his liberty by giving his word not to mount a horse, or to carry warriors' arms any more; thenceforward he rode a mule, clothed himself in hides, and armed with a heavy iron bar, returned to the field braver and more terrible than ever. To Maheu de Villacourt, who married successively Gigonne de Malain, and Christine de Gliseneuve, between whom, until the time of the Revolution, he was to be seen represented in marble in the church of the Cordeliers at Saint Mihiel, Duke René gave permission to take eight hundred florins out of the contribution levied from the town of Ligny, to repay himself the ransom which he had had to pay after the disastrous battle of Bulgnéville.

Remacle de Villacourt, son of Maheu, was killed in 1476, in the battle given by Duke René, before Nancy, to Charles the Rash. Hubert de Villacourt, son of Remacle, seneschal of the district of Barrois, and baillie of Bassigny, followed Duke Anthony, in the capacity of standard-bearer, through the wars in Alsace; while his brother, Bonaventure, a monk of the strict order of St. Francis, became three times triennial superior of his order, confessor of the Dukes of Lorraine, Anthony and Francis; and one of his sisters, Salmone, was chosen abbess of Saint Glossinde of Metz.

Jean-Marie de Villacourt attached himself to the service of France. After the battle of Landrecies, the king knighted him and gave him the accolade. He was at once given the command of a body of three hundred foot soldiers, had an allowance made to him as the king's master-of-the horse, afterwards promoted to be captain of Vaucouleurs, and finally governor of Langres. He had married a sister of Jean de Chaligny, the master-founder of artillery in Lorraine, who made the famous culverin that measured twenty-two feet. His brother, Philibert, was captain of Charles IX.'s " reiters;" his brother Gaston was celebrated as a duellist; it was he who killed Captain Chambrulard with two blows of his sword, behind the Carthusian Church in Paris, and in presence of four thousand people. Jean-Marie had still another brother, Agnus, who was canon of Toul and archdeacon of Tonnerrois; and a sister, Archangel, who was abbess of Saint-Maur, at Verdun.

Then came William de Villacourt, who took part against Louis XIII. He was obliged to surrender at discretion with Charles de Lenoncourt, who defended the town of Saint Mihiel, and he shared with him four years of imprisonment in the Bastille. His son, Charles Mathias de Villacourt, married, in 1656, Marie Dieudonnée, daughter of Claude de Jeandelincourt, master of the salt mines at Château-Salins. By her he had fourteen children, of whom ten were killed in the service of Louis XIV.; Charles, captain in the Regiment du Pont, killed at the siege of Philisbourg; John, killed at the battle of Nerwinde; Anthony, captain in the Normandy regiment, killed at the siege of Fontarabia; James, killed at the siege of Bellegarde, where he happened to be by special leave of the king; Philip, captain of grenadiers in the dauphin's regiment, killed at the battle of Marsaille; Thibalt, captain in the same regiment, killed at the battle of Hochstett; Peter Francis, commanding the Lyons regiment, killed at the battle of Fleurus; Claude Marie, commanding the Périgord regiment, killed at the passage of La Hague; Edme, lieutenant in his brother's regiment, killed at his side in the same affair; and, lastly, Gerard, knight of the order of St. John of Jerusalem, killed in 1700 in a fight between four galleys of the true faith against one Turkish man-of-war. Of the three daughters of Charles Mathias, one, Lydia, married the lord of Majastre, governor of Epinal; the two others, Bertha and Phœbe, died unmarried.

The eldest son of Charles Mathias, Louis Aimé de Villacourt, who had served for eighteen years and had quitted the service after the battle of Malplaquet, died in 1702. His son quitted Villacourt, established himself in Paris, took to gambling, and lost the remains of a fortune already seriously undermined by the failure of a lawsuit commenced by his father against the d'Haraucourts. He went on playing in the hope of recovering his fortune, ran more deeply into debt, and returned to Villacourt, married to a person of the name of Carrouge, who had kept a gambling-hell in Paris. He died in 1752, owning scarcely anything except the walls of his castle, leaving a name tarnished, and whose honour was waning.

Of the two children of this marriage, a son and a daughter, the latter became maid-of-honour to the empress-queen; the son remained at Villacourt, leading in a paltry and ignoble manner the life of a country squire. At the time of the abolition of privileges, in 1790, he renounced his seignory, and took to living on a footing of equality and companionship with the peasants until 1792, the year of his death. His son, John, lieutenant in the Royal Liège regiment in 1787, chanced to find himself in the skirmish at Nancy, emigrated, went through the campaigns of 1792 to 1801 in the Mirabeau regiment, which was afterwards called the Roger de Damas, and in the Bourbon grenadiers in Condé's army. On the 13th of August, 1796, he was wounded in the head at the battle of Oberkamlach. In 1802 he returned to France, bringing with him a wife whom he had married in Germany, and who died leaving him four sons.

His wound had resulted in cerebral weakness which was almost softening of the brain. Little by little, disorder increased in the house without a housekeeper, and the open table that he kept forced him gradually to sell the little land which still belonged to the castle. Bit by bit, the structure itself was falling away. It was no longer repaired, and there was no money wherewith to pay the workmen. The wind blew through it, the rain came in everywhere. The family gradually retreated, going from room to room, finding shelter wherever the roof was sound. But this did not trouble him in the least; he would sit sunning himself on an old stone bench in the orchard, near an old sun-dial, the hours on which had long since been effaced, and after two or three cups of brandy he would amuse himself by calling over the hedge to any passers-by, and inviting them to come in and drink with him. Meanwhile misery and ruin were on the increase in the castle. Of the plate there only remained a silver salad-bowl, out of which an old horse named Brouska, which had been brought from Germany by the emigrant, and which was allowed to wander in perfect liberty through the ground floor of the house, used to eat.

The four sons grew up as the castle was going to pieces, n the wind and the rain, in hardships, neglected, abandoned by their father, and receiving the most desultory lessons from the parish priest. Living the life of peasants, taking part in their work and in their games, they became real peasants, and the most renowned both for strength and courage in the neighbourhood.

At the death of their father, the four brothers agreed to sell to the first purchaser all that remained of the stones of their castle, in consideration of a few hundred francs where-with to pay the most pressing debts, and an annual sum of five hundred francs to be paid until the death of the last of them. Then they dived into the woods which surrounded the property that had been theirs, and lived with the wood-cutters and like them, making of their huts their dwellings, making love to the same women as they did, and peopling the forest with a bastard race which was a cross between Villacourt and nature, and whose very language was not even French.

A few former comrades-in-arms of John de Villacourt had, indeed, after his death, tried to do something for his children. People were interested in this name which had fallen from such a height to such a depth. In 1826, the youngest of them was brought to Paris, being little more than sixteen years old. The little savage was dressed, and was presented to the Duchess d'Angoulême; he put in two or three appearances in the drawing-rooms of the Minister for War, who was related to his family and very anxious to serve him; but at the end of a week, feeling himself stifled in those drawing-rooms and in those clothes, he bolted like a young wolf; he returned straight to his lair, and never left it afterwards.

Of the four Villacourts but one was alive twenty years later; it was he. His three brothers had all died violent deaths successively, one from health, one from drink, and the last from blows, beaten and thrashed out of life. Surrounded by the bastards they had left, this survivor of the Villacourts held, in the woods, the position of a tribal chief when, in 1854, the law was passed relating to shooting. The laws, the guards, the verdicts, the fines, the confiscations, the slavery of sport, that is to say of his life, the fear of yielding to anger and of sending a bullet through a keeper, all helped to disgust him with his country, with France, with that corner of the earth which no longer belonged to him.

The idea occurred to him to go to America in order to be at liberty, to have plenty of room, and to hunt in virgin forests without any gun licenses. He went as far as Paris, meaning to embark at Havre; however, he had not sufficient money to defray the cost of the voyage. He fell back upon Africa, but there again he found France, with its administrations, its police, and its gamekeepers. He obtained a concession and made a clearing, but he was not suited to that work. Besides, the country and the climate tried him; in the heat of the sun and the unhealthiness of the soil, his strong woodland constitution broke down. At the end of two years he returned.

When he entered his hut, at the Black Mount, he found the only thing that had arrived during his absence—a newspaper. It was a number of the "Moniteur," and was already about a year old. He took it to light his pipe, and, as he twisted it up, his eye fell upon a mark in red pencil, which caused him to open it. He read at the place which was marked:

"Monsieur Mauperin (Alfred Henry), better known under the name of *Villacourt*, intends to take the necessary steps, in the office of the keeper of the seals, to obtain the authorisation to add to his name that of Villacourt, and to call himself, henceforward, *Mauperin de Villacourt*."

He got up, walked about, snorted, then sat down again, and slowly lighted his pipe.

Three days later he was in Paris.

At the first moment of reading the newspaper, he had felt as though he had received a cut from a whip in the face. Then, he told himself that he was being robbed of his name, and that that was all, that his name was no longer of any value, belonging as it now did to a poor scoundrel like himself. But this philosophical condition of mind did not last long: the idea that he was being defrauded of his name had, little by little, come back to him more painful, more bitter and more irritating. After all, he had nothing left but that, he could stand it no longer, and off he started.

By the time he arrived he was in a frenzy of passion. His first thought was to go and thrash Monsieur Mauperin. But when once he found himself in Paris, in the streets, in presence of the crowd, and of this large number of people, the shops, the passers by, the noise, he was as dazzled as a wild beast when he is first turned loose in a circus, whose fury vanishes and who stops short after his first spring.

He went straight to the Law Courts, and in the Salle des Pas Perdus he addressed himself to one of the men in black who are always leaning against the pillars, and told him what had occurred. The man in black told him that, as the delay of one year had expired, he could do nothing but make an appeal to the Council of State against the decree authorising the addition of the name, and gave him the address of a lawyer who practised before the Council of State and the Court of Appeal.

Monsieur de Villacourt flew direct to the lawyer. He found a cold, polite man, wearing a white tie, who, leaning back in his leather arm-chair, listened, with his eyes closed, to all his story, his titles, his rights, his indignation, and the crackling of the parchment deeds that he was crumpling up in his nervous fingers. On his listener's face no sign appeared. When Monsieur de Villacourt had finished, he thought he had not been understood, and would have recommenced, but the lawyer stopped him by a gesture and said: "Sir, I think you will win your case."

"You think! Are you not certain?"

"A lawsuit is always a lawsuit, sir," said the lawyer with a smile which exhibited so much scepticism that it froze Monsieur de Villacourt, who was just going to fly into a fresh passion. "But, in my opinion, sir, the chances are all in your favour, and I am prepared to undertake your case."

"There, then," said Monsieur de Villacourt, laying on the writing-table the bundle of papers. "I am much obliged to you, sir."

He rose and bowed.

"I beg your pardon, sir," said the lawyer, seeing him go towards the door. "I must point out to you that in cases of this kind, in an appeal to the Council of State, we are not only the advocates but also the attorneys of our clients. There are certain expenses connected with enquiries, and the examination of papers. I am obliged to ask you, if you wish me to undertake your case, to leave with me a sufficient sum to cover them for me. Oh, it is not serious, only five or six hundred francs; five hundred, we will say, if you like."

"Five or six hundred francs! What!" exclaimed Monsieur de Villacourt, reddening. "I am to be robbed of my name, and then because I do not happen to have seen the newspaper in which the man who robbed me gave me warning of his intention, I am fined five or six hundred francs to make the scoundrel give it me back! Five or six hundred francs! sir," said he, letting his arms fall, and hanging his head. "I have not got them."

"I regret it sincerely, monsieur, but the formality is indispensable. Oh! you cannot fail to find them. I am sure that among the descendants of those families that are related to yours, you cannot have any difficulty. On occasions like this people cling together."

"Sir, I know nobody: and, besides, the Count de Villacourt will ask for nothing. On my arrival I had three hundred francs. I paid forty-five for this coat in the Palais-Royal, on my way to see you. This hat cost me seven francs, my bill, at my lodging, will, I suppose, come to about twenty francs. I must put aside five-and-twenty for my return journey. Could you not do with the remainder?"

"I am sorry I cannot, sir."

Monsieur de Villacourt put on his hat, and left the room

Just as he reached the door of the ante-room, he turned round abruptly, came back through the dining-room, and, opening the door of the study: "Sir," said he, in a hollow voice, which he tried to restrain, "can you give me, for nothing, the address of Monsieur Henry Mauperin, called de Villacourt?"

"Certainly; he is a lawyer. I can find it for you directly. Here it is, Rue Taitbout, number 14.

It was immediately after this that Monsieur de Villacourt appeared in Henry Mauperin's rooms.

XXXVI

THAT evening, when Denoisel entered the Mauperins'
drawing-room, he found them unusually gay. A look of
happiness was on every countenance. Monsieur Mauperin's
good humour sparkled with smiling malice in his eyes.
Madame Mauperin's face beamed with expansive pleasantness and secret contentment. Renée, dancing about the
drawing-room, brought into it, with her girlish spirits, the
movement, the life, and almost the fluttering of the wings of
a bird.

"Hulloa! Denoisel," exclaimed Monsieur Mauperin.

"Good evening, sir," said Renée, in an impertinent little
voice.

"Have you not brought Henry?" asked Madame
Mauperin.

"He could not come. He will come the day after
to-morrow, without fail."

"That is very nice! How sweet it is of you to have
come this evening," continued Renée to Denoisel, using
little endearments to him as though he were a child whom
she wished to make laugh.

"So you have come at last, you bad fellow! Ah!
my boy—"

And Monsieur Mauperin, squeezing his hand, winked in
the direction of his wife.

"Yes, yes, come here, Denoisel," said Madame Mauperin,
"Sit down there and tell me whether what I hear of you is

true. It seems that you were seen, a few days since, driving in a brougham in the Bois de Boulogne."

And she stopped as a cat does when it is drinking milk.

"There, your mother is started now!" said Monsieur Mauperin to Renée. "I must warn you, Denoisel, that my wife is in tearing spirits to-day."

Madame Mauperin had dropped her voice. Leaning over towards Denoisel, she told him a long and questionable story. Nothing was to be heard save a few words interspersed with stifled laughter.

"Mamma, you know that laughing in corners is forbidden. Give me back my Denoisel, or else I shall begin to tell stories to papa."

"Oh dear, oh dear, how stupid it is, is it not?" said Madame Mauperin when she had finished her story, and still bursting with laughter, with that laughter of old women who are amused at a rather free story, and which is so pleasant to listen to.

"What spirits you are all in this evening!" Denoisel remarked.

"As merry as crickets," said Renée, "so we are. And mean to be as merry as this to-morrow, and the next day, and always. Don't we papa?" And running towards her father, she seated herself on his knee like a little girl.

"Darling!" said Monsieur Mauperin. "Look, Madame Mauperin, do you remember? This was her knee when she was a little child."

"Yes," answered Madame Mauperin, "and Henry had the other."

"I think I can see them now," continued Monsieur Mauperin. "Henry was the girl, you, Renée, were the boy. To think that fifteen years have passed since then! How it used to amuse you when I passed your little fingers over the scars of my sword-cuts. You wretched children! You used to laugh."

And turning to Madame Mauperin: "My dear wife, you had your share of trouble with them. All the same, Denoisel, home life does one good; upon my word, it is the heart that makes the children!"

"So, here you are at last," said Renée; "we do not mean to let you go again, Denoisel, your room has been pining for you too long."

"I am very sorry, my dear Renée, but really, I have business in Paris this evening. I assure you I have, really and truly."

"You! business! What swagger!"

"Stay with us, Denoisel," said Monsieur Mauperin. "Madame Mauperin has a whole collection of stories like the last one she told you, and you shall hear them all."

"You will stay, won't you?" said Renée. "We will have great fun. I will not touch the piano. I will not put too much vinegar in the salad. We will make lots of puns. Come now, Denoisel."

"I accept, for next week."

"Wretch," said Renée, turning her back upon him.

"And Dardouillet?" asked Denoisel. "he is not here this evening?"

"Oh, he is sure to come," said Mauperin. "Though all the same he may not. He is hard at work, and has just had a fresh fit of posts and rails. I believe he is moving his mountain into his lake and his lake on to his mountain."

"Yes, but he can't do that in the evening."

"Oh, no one knows what he does in the evening," said Renée. "He is full of mystery is Monsieur Dardouillet. But how queer you look to-night, Denoisel."

"I?"

" Yes, you. You do not look sprightly; you are not sparkling at all. What is wrong with you?"

" Denoisel, something is the matter with you," said Madame Mauperin.

" Nothing whatever, madame," answered Denoisel. " What should be the matter with me? I am not at all sad. I am only tired. For the last week Henry has made me fetch and carry for him. He wanted the benefit of my taste in choosing his furniture."

" That is true," said Madame Mauperin, whose face had become perceptibly brighter, " that is true, the day is getting near. The 22nd. Ah! if anyone had told me that two years ago! I am afraid of being too happy that day. And only think, Mauperin, what it will be when we have grand-children!" And she gently closed her eyes at the idea of her future grand-motherhood.

" It will be difficult for me to spoil them, after you, mamma!" said Renée. " Do you know that I am going to be extremely beautiful that day, Denoisel. I have a new gown; I tried it on yesterday; it fits me like a glove. By the way, papa, have you a new coat?"

" I have my old new coat."

" Oh! you must get one even newer than that, to give me your arm. Ah, how stupid I am, you will not give it to me. Denoisel, I engage you for a country dance. We are going to give a ball, are we not, mamma?"

" A ball, and everything else!" said Madame Mauperin. " People may not consider it a smart thing to do, but so much the worse. I mean to have a real wedding, a return from church such as we had on our wedding day, do you remember, Monsieur Mauperin? Every one shall dance, and eat, and drink."

" That's right!" said Renée, " we will make all our work-people tipsy! and Denoisel, too! Perhaps that will cheer him up!"

"Meanwhile, I don't see Dardouillet yet," said Denoisel rising.

"What in the world are you so anxious to see Dardouillet for, this evening?" asked Monsieur Mauperin.

"Yes, that is true," said Renée. "It requires explanation. Explain at once, Denoisel."

"How inquisitive you are, Renée. A mere trifle. Nothing at all. I want him to lend me his terrier for a rat-fight, at my club to-morrow. I have made a bet that he will kill a hundred in two minutes. Thereupon I am off, good night!"

"Good night!"

"And my son, I shall see him the day after to-morrow, without fail?" inquired Madame Mauperin, as Denoisel was leaving the room.

Denoisel bowed, and made no answer.

XXXVII.

ON arriving at Dardouillet's house, at the other end of the village, Denoisel rang. The door was opened by an old housekeeper. "Has Monsieur Dardouillet gone to bed yet?"

"He? Not likely," was the answer, "he is doing the same as usual. Wandering about the garden somewhere: you will easily find him." And she opened the long window of the dining-room.

A brilliant moonlight, illuminated the garden which was absolutely bare, square as a pocket handkerchief, and ploughed up like a field. In a corner, on a little mound, stood a black outline, its arms crossed, motionless; one might have been taken for a ghost in one of Biard's pictures. It was Monsieur Dardouillet.

He was so absorbed as not to notice Denoisel until the latter was close upon him.

"Ah, it's you, my dear Monsieur Denoisel," said he, "I am delighted. Look!" and he pointed to the freshly turned earth. "What do you think of that? There are some lines! It is all as soft as possible, do you see?"

And he passed his hand through the air over the imaginary outline of his hill, as though he had been caressing the ideal crupper of a horse.

"Monsieur Dardouillet, pardon me!" said Denoisel, "I have come on business."

"Moonlight, now remember that, if ever you have a garden. That is the only light by which to inspect one's work properly; by daylight one does not allow for the embankments."

"Monsieur Dardouillet, I speak to you as to a man who has worn a uniform. You are on good terms with the Mauperins. I come to ask you to serve as second to Henry."

"A duel?"—And Dardouillet buttoned up the black coat that he wore, winter and summer alike. "By George!" said he, "one cannot refuse those services."

"I must carry you off, then," said Denoisel, taking him by the arm. "You shall sleep at my house. We must get it over quickly. It will be done to-morrow, or next day at latest."

"Very good!" said Dardouillet, casting an eye of regret upon a line of posts which had just been planted, and whose shadows lay on the ground in the moonlight.

XXXVIII

On leaving Henry Mauperin, Monsieur de Villacourt remembered that he had no friends, no seconds. It had not occurred to him until that moment. He remembered two or three names which used to crop up now and again in his father's stories. He tried to find, by means of the streets, the houses to which he had been taken as a child when he came to Paris. He knocked at several doors; but either the owners had changed, or would not see him.

In the evening he returned to his humble hotel. He had never felt so much alone in the world. As he was taking the key of his room, the mistress of the hotel asked him if he would not taste her beer, for the good of the house, and, opening a door in the wall, showed him into a café which ran along the ground floor of the hotel.

On the hooks round the wall swords and cocked hats were hanging. At the end of the room, through the thick clouds of smoke, he could see uniforms revolving round the patched cloth of a billiard table. A seedy-looking little waiter, in a white apron, ran hither and thither, bewildered and half out of his wits, slopping the coffee over the "Army Gazette" which was lying on the tables.

Near the counter, a drum-major was playing at backgammon with the master of the establishment in his shirt sleeves. From all sides voices called to each other and answered back in the guttural voice peculiar to soldiers: "To-morrow I am on duty at the theatre." "I've got a week's leave." "Gaberiau, who is verger at Saint Sulpice now?" "He was put forward for examination at the last inspection." "Who is on duty at the Bourdon music-hall?" "Imagine a fellow blowing out his brains when he hasn't a single punishment marked against him!"

They were all "Gardes de Paris," from the neighbouring barracks, awaiting the nine o'clock tattoo.

"Waiter! a bowl of punch, and three glasses!" said Monsieur de Villacourt, seating himself at a table occupied by only two soldiers.

When the punch was brought, he filled the three glasses, pushed one towards each man, and rising:

"I drink your good health, gentlemen!" said he, saluting them with his glass. "You are soldiers. I have to fight a duel to-morrow. I have nobody to stand by me, but I feel sure that I see two seconds before me now."

"What do you say, eh, Gaillourdot?" said one of the men turning to his comrade, after looking into Monsieur de Villacourt's eyes. The other, without answering, took his glass and clinked it against that of Monsieur de Villacourt.

"Good! to-morrow morning at ten o'clock. Room 27."

"Done with you!" said the soldiers.

Next morning, just as Denoisel was starting with Dardouillet to go to Monsieur Boisjorand de Villacourt, his bell rang, and the two soldiers entered. Their directions being to agree to everything, conditions, weapons, distances, the arrangements for the duel were very soon completed. It was settled that they were to fight with pistols, at a distance of thirty-five paces, with power to each adversary to advance ten steps. Denoisel, in Henry's name, asked that everything should be got over as quickly as possible. Monsieur de Villacourt's seconds were going to make the same request: they had leave merely for a theatre, and could act for Monsieur de Villacourt only till midnight. The meeting was to take place at four o'clock at the ponds of Ville d'Avray.

Denoisel hastened to secure the services of a young surgeon with whom he was acquainted. He then went to a livery-stable and secured a comfortable and well-lined carriage in which a wounded man might travel safely. He then went to Henry's rooms and learned that he had gone out. He hastened to the shooting gallery, and found him there, amusing himself by firing at little packets of four or five matches hung on a thread and which he exploded by striking them with a bullet.

"Oh, that is nothing," said he to Denoisel, "I believe that the wind caused by the bullet makes them go off; but look at this."

And he showed him a cardboard target, into the bull's eye of which he had placed a dozen bullets.

"This afternoon, at four o'clock, as you wished," said Denoisel.

"Good," said Henry returning his pistol to the attendant, and stopping with his fingers two holes in the cardboard some little distance from the others: "There," said he, "were it not for those two bad shots, that target would be worth framing. Ah, I am glad it is to be to-day."

And he raised his arm with the gesture familiar to a man accustomed to shoot and who is preparing to fire, and shook his hand for an instant so as to drive all the blood out of it.

"Do you know," he continued, "that the idea of this duel did not worry me in the least till this morning when I was lying in bed. That devilish horizontal attitude. I don't think it is good for one's courage."

They lunched at Denoisel's, then they began to smoke. Henry was gay, and frank, and talked a great deal. The surgeon arrived. They all four got into the carriage.

U

Halfway (they had kept silence until then), Henry impatiently threw his cigar out of the window.

"Give me a cigar, Denoisel, a good one. Do you know that it is very important to smoke a good cigar before one shoots? To shoot well, one must not be nervous—that is a primary condition. I began my day by taking a bath. If you feel the least bit shaky—now, for instance, nothing is so bad as driving. The horses pull your arms off, and after that I defy you to shoot straight. Your fingers are always stiff afterwards. And what rubbish novelists talk when they describe a man driving up to the ground and flinging the reins to his servant. What one wants is to live a healthy life, that is certain. I never saw any one shoot so well as an Englishman whom I know, but then, he goes to bed at eight o'clock, drinks no stimulants, and takes a little constitutional every evening. Every time that I have been to the shooting gallery in a hard carriage, my targets have suffered. By-the-way, this is a very good carriage of yours, Denoisel. Well, and it is just the same with one's cigar: a cigar which burns crooked wants to be looked after, and every moment it is necessary to raise one's arm to one's mouth, and that wearies the hand, whereas a good cigar, ask any man who shoots, puts your nerves in a good state. There is nothing better than that rhythm of the arm which takes it out of one's mouth and puts it back regularly. It is slow, it is regular."

They arrived at the place.

Monsieur de Villacourt and his seconds were waiting on the road between the two ponds.

The ground was white with the snow that had fallen all the morning. The wood stretched to the sky its naked arms, and far away, some black rows of trees streaked a red and wintry sunset.

The party went as far as the Montalet road. The paces were counted, Denoisel's pistols were loaded, the adversaries took their places. Two walking sticks, laid on the snow, marked the limit of the ten paces which each combatant was entitled to advance.

Just as Denoisel was conducting Henry to the place which had fallen to him by lot, and as he was pushing back for him a corner of his shirt-collar which had risen above his necktie—"Thank you," said Henry to him, in a low voice, "my heart is beating a little under my arm-pit, but you shall be pleased with me."

Monsieur de Villacourt pulled off his coat, tore off his necktie, and threw everything far away from him. His shirt, which was wide open, showed his strong, muscular chest, which was covered with black and white hair.

When the combatants had received their pistols, the seconds withdrew and took up their position side by side.

"Forward!" cried a voice.

At this word, Monsieur de Villacourt advanced, walking without trying to efface himself. Henry, remaining motionless, let him take five steps. At the sixth, he fired.

Monsieur de Villacourt fell, sitting on the ground.

The seconds then saw the wounded man lay down his pistol, apply his two thumbs with all his strength to the double hole the ball had made as it passed through his stomach, and then smell his thumbs.

"They don't smell of d——! He's missed me! Go back to your place, sir!" he cried in a loud voice to Henry, who, thinking that all was over, had turned to go away; and picking up his pistol, he began to advance the four steps that separated him from the walking-stick, dragging himself along on his hands and legs. On the snow behind him he left traces of his blood.

When he reached the stick, he rested his elbow on the ground, and took long and careful aim.

" Fire! and have done with it!" cried Dardouillet.

Henry, who had made himself as small as he could, covered his face with his pistol, and stood waiting. He was pale, but his face was proud. The pistol went off; he oscillated for a second, then fell at full length, his face to the ground, and his hands, at the end of his outstretched arms, clutched at the snow with their stiffening fingers.

XXXIX.

According to his custom, Monsieur Mauperin had gone straight into the garden when he was dressed, and he suddenly saw Denoisel coming towards him.

"You here, so early?" said he, in astonishment. "Where did you sleep?"

"Monsieur Mauperin," began Denoisel, taking his hands.

"What? What is the matter?" asked Monsieur Mauperin, foreseeing a misfortune.

"Henry is wounded."

"Dangerously? In a duel?"

Denoisel hung his head.

"Wounded? Ah! he is dead!"

Denoisel only replied by throwing himself into Monsieur Mauperin's arms and embracing him.

"Dead!" repeated Monsieur Mauperin mechanically; and his hands opened as though they were letting go of something. Then tears mingled with his words: "And his mother! Henry! Oh my God! One never knows how much one loves them! At thirty!"

And choking with sobs, he fell upon the bench. After a minute: "Where is he?" he asked.

"There." And Denoisel pointed to the window of Henry's room.

From Ville-d'Avray he had brought the body back to Dardouillet's house whither he had summoned on some invented pretext Monsieur Bernard, to whom Monsieur

Mauperin entrusted a key of his house; and, in the dead of night, while the household was asleep, the three men, having taken off their boots, had lain the corpse upon the bed.

"Thank you!" said Monsieur Mauperin; and, making a sign that he could talk no more, he rose.

They walked thus, in silence, four or five times round the garden. From time to time, Monsieur Mauperin's eyes filled with tears; but he shed none. Every now and again, words seemed to rise to his lips, and then to fall back, unspoken, into his heart. At last, in a voice, broken yet deep, breaking with an effort this long silence, Monsieur Mauperin said sharply to Denoisel, without looking at him: "Did he die well?"

"He was your son," answered Denoisel.

The father, on hearing this, raised his head, as though he received strength to shake off his grief.

"Come," said he, "now we have our duties to do. You have already done your's sufficiently."

And he pressed Denoisel to his heart, crying the while over his hair.

XL.

" THESE things are as bad as murders!" said Barousse to Denoisel, as they followed the body to the cemetry. " Why did you not arrange the matter ? "

" After a blow in the face ? "

" After as well as before," said Barousse peremptorily.

" Go and say that to his father ! "

" Oh, of course, a soldier ! But you, bless my soul, you have never been in the army, and you let him go and be killed; for, in my eyes, you killed him ! "

" Look here ! leave me alone, Monsieur Barousse."

' I take a reasonable view of things. I have been a magistrate." Barousse had been judge in the Commercial Court. " And a duel ! You have on your side the law-courts, justice, everything. But it is contrary to all laws, human, and divine, do you see that ? What ! a scoundrel gives me a box on the ear, and I am to let him kill me as well ! Ah ! I can promise you one thing, and that is that if ever I am on a jury and we have a case of duelling be-fore us—for in my eyes a duel is a murder—duellists are murderers. Besides it is a cowardice."

" Which everyone has not the courage to commit, Mon-sieur Barousse. In that respect, it is like suicide."

" Oh, if you are going to take up the cudgels for suicide," said Barousse; and breaking off the discussion, he continued in a melancholy voice: " Such a good fellow ! Poor Henry ! And besides there are Mauperin, and his wife, and his daughter; a whole family in tears. No, I cannot restrain myself when I think. A child whom I have seen——"

As he spoke, Barousse had taken his watch out of his pocket and looked at it: "Just my luck!" said he, suddenly breaking off, "I am sure it will have been sold. I shall have missed the 'Assembly at a concert,' a splendid proof! Before the dedication!"

Denoisel brought Monsieur Mauperin back to La Briche, and, immediately on his arrival, the latter went up to his wife's room. He found her in bed, the shutters closed, and the curtains drawn, buried and stupefied in the blackness of her sorrow.

Denoisel went into the drawing-room, where he found Renée, seated on a sofa, sobbing, with her handkerchief up to her mouth.

"Renée," said he, taking her hands, "someone killed him."

Renée looked at him and dropped her eyes.

"That man need never have known anything about it. He read nothing, he saw nobody, he lived like a wolf. It is not likely that he subscribed to the 'Moniteur,' is it? Do you understand me?"

"No," stammered Renée.

She was trembling.

"Well, it was some enemy whose hand threw that paper in his way. Of course you cannot understand such treachery, naturally! But I tell you that that is what happened. One of his seconds showed me the passage, scored with a red pencil."

Renée had risen from her seat, her eyes dilated with terror: her lips moved, she opened her mouth, she would have cried: "It was I!" But suddenly, pressing her hand to her heart as to a sudden wound, she fell senseless on the carpet.

XLI.

DENOISEL came every day to inquire after Renée's health. When she was somewhat better, he felt surprised that she expressed no desire to see him. Was he not accustomed to be received by her when she was in bed, poorly, like a friend who really belongs to the family? And in all her former illnesses, was it not he who had been always sent for at once by her, her jester, the buffoon whose mission it was to cheer her convalescence and to bring back her healthy laughter? He sulked, and then returned to the charge. But Renée's room remained closed to him.

One day he was told that she was too tired; Another day that she was engaged with Abbé Blampoix. At last, after a delay of a week, he was admitted.

He expected an effusive greeting, one of those demonstrations of sick people in whom rises the wish for strength when they see those to whom they are attached. Her heart, he said to himself, would jump to his neck.

Renée shook hands with him, coldly, without any pressure, and said to him the same words as she would have said to any one else, and at the end of a quarter of an hour, she closed her eyes as if she were sleepy.

This coldness, which to him was inexplicable, left Denoisel in a state of irritation mingled with bitterness. He felt wounded and humiliated in the oldest, the purest, and the sincerest of his affections. He tried to think what could have set Renée against him. Had Barousse been putting ideas into her head? Was she avenging the death of her brother upon the man who had acted as his second in the duel? And as one of his friends who had a yacht at Cannes, proposed a voyage in the Mediterranean, Denoisel decided he would go.

Renée, on her side, had been afraid of Denoisel. She could remember nothing but the beginning of the attack that she had had in his presence, the instant which had preceded her fall and her fainting fit. She had seemed to feel that her brother's blood was stifling her, and that a cry was rising to her lips. Had she spoken? Had her secret escaped from her unconscious mouth? Had she told him that it was she who had killed Henry, she who had sent that newspaper? Had her crime burst from her? When Denoisel came in, she fancied that she could see that he knew all. The feeling of awkwardness which came over him and which had its origin in her, the coldness which he caught from her, helped to confirm her in this belief, in the certainty that she had spoken, and that it was a judge who was sitting near her. When her mother wished to leave her for a minute, during his visit, she clung to her with a terrified gesture.

The idea occurred to her that she could easily defend herself by saying that it was a fatality, that by sending the paper she had only intended to produce an action, to prevent her brother from taking that name, to break off his marriage; but then she would have also been obliged to say why she had done all that, and why she wished to destroy the future and the fortune of her brother; she would have had to acknowledge everything. And the bare idea of having thus to defend herself, especially before the man, whom, of all others, she esteemed, terrified her and made her feel cold: all that she could do for him whom she had killed, was to leave his memory in peace, and his death in silence.

When she heard of Denoisel's departure she breathed more freely: she fancied that now her secret was her's only.

XLII

RENEE was getting better. A few months later, she seemed to be cured. Every appearance of health returned to her. She no longer suffered any pain. She no longer even felt the discomfort that suffering leaves in the organs attacked by it, or in the life attempted by it. All of a sudden, her illness reappeared. When she went upstairs, she used to feel as though she were choking. The palpitations of her heart returned with renewed violence and frequency; then once again, all was quiet, as sometimes happens in cases of deep-seated illnesses, which seem as though they had, for a time, forgotten the sufferers.

At the end of a few weeks, the doctor from St. Denis, who had charge of the case, called Monsieur Mauperin aside and said to him: "Something in this case puzzles me. The state of your daughter is not quite clear to me. I should like to have the assistance of a doctor who has made a special study of illnesses of this kind. Those affections of the heart are sometimes so treacherous in their movements."

"Yes, those affections of the heart. You are quite right," murmured Monsieur Mauperin.

He could say no more. His ancient notions of medicine, the desperate doctrines of the school of his day, Corvisart, the motto of his work on the heart: "*Hœret lateri lethalis arundo*," all that, suddenly, flashed through his mind, distinctly. He fancied he saw again those books with their pages full of terror.

"The chief danger," continued the doctor, "of these illnesses is that they are always of long standing. They have generally gained so much ground before we are called in. They are accompanied by premonitory symptoms of which even the patient is often unaware. Now, your daughter has always been very impressionable from her childhood upwards, has she not? Torrents of tears at the slightest word of reproach, her face flushing for nothing, and immediately afterwards, her heart beating a hundred to the minute, great excitement for the smallest trifles, her brain very active, outbursts of passion almost like convulsions, inclined to be feverish at very little? Am I not right? She brought passion into everything, into her friendships, her games, her dislikes, did she not? Yes, yes, all children in whom this organ predominates, and who have an unhappy tendency to hypertrophy, have the same symptoms. Tell me, has she, to your knowledge, recently had any great emotion, or great grief?"

"Yes! Oh, yes! Her brother's death!"

"Her brother's death, yes, no doubt," said the doctor, without appearing to attach great importance to the information: "but I mean, perhaps, a disappointment in a love affair for instance?"

"She?"

Monsieur Mauperin shrugged his shoulders: "Disappointed. God bless me!" And half joining his hands, he raised them in the air.

"Well," said the doctor, "I only asked you to satisfy my mind. Accidents, in such cases, only have the effect of developing the germ of the evil and of accelerating its steps. The physical influence of the passions upon the heart is a theory. It has had much doubt thrown upon it during the last twenty years, and rightly, according to my view. The idea that the heart breaks in a fit of rage, or in any great moral upheaval—"

Monsieur Mauperin interrupted him: " Then a consultation, you think, you believe, do you not ? "

" Yes, Monsieur Mauperin, it will be much better, do you see. It will tranquillise every one, you as well as me. I suppose we had better have Monsieur Bouillaud. He has the best reputation."

" Monsieur Bouillaud," repeated Monsieur Mauperin, mechanically, nodding his head in token of agreement.

XLIII

It was five minutes past noon.

Monsieur Mauperin, seated near Renée's bed, was holding his daughter's hands in his. Renée's eyes were fixed on the clock. "He will soon be here," said Monsieur Mauperin. She only answered by slowly dropping her eyelids; and in the silence of the room one could hear, as in the night, the breathing of the patient, and her heart beating as loudly as a watch.

An imperious, clear, and distinct bell sounded in the house. Monsieur Mauperin felt as though it rang in his body. A shiver passed all through him, even to the tips of his fingers, like the pricking of needles. He went to the door.

"It was some one who mistook the house, sir," said the footman.

"How hot it is!" said Monsieur Mauperin to his daughter, as he reseated himself. He was quite pale.

Five minutes later, the servant knocked at the door. The doctor was waiting in the drawing-room.

"Ah!" said Monsieur Mauperin.

"Go!" said his daughter; and then she called to him: "Papa!" He came back to her.

"Is he going to examine me?" she asked, looking frightened.

"I do not know; I do not think so. Perhaps he will not consider it necessary." said Monsieur Mauperin, feeling for the handle of the door.

Monsieur Mauperin had brought the doctor upstairs and had left him alone with his daughter.

He was in the drawing-room, waiting.

He had walked up and down, he had sat down. He had studied the pattern of the flowers in the carpet. He had been to the window and had drummed upon the glass with his fingers.

Everything seemed suspended in him and around him. Had he been there an hour or a minute? He did not know. He was going through one of those periods of life which cannot be measured by the ordinary divisions of time.

He had felt that his whole existence had flowed towards his heart. The emotions of a life-time were compressed for him into an instant which seemed eternal.

He felt giddy, as a man does who, in a dream, falls over a precipice, and who is in an agony lest he should go on falling for ever. All sorts of dark thoughts, of confused anxieties, of miserable terror, rose from the depths of his stomach and seemed to collect and buzz in his temples. Yesterday, to-day, to-morrow, the doctor, his daughter, her illness, all these whirled round and round in his head, mixed themselves up in his mind, and mingled with a physical sensation of sickness, uneasiness, terror and cowardice. Then, suddenly, an idea occurred to him. He had one of those lucid intervals which, at such moments, come into the soul. The doctor was there; he could see him placing his ear against Renée's back; and he was listening with him. He seemed to hear the creaking of a bed, as though some one were being turned round on it. It was all over, he was coming, but no one came!

He began to walk about again; he could not remain still. He felt impatient and irritated. He thought that he was being kept waiting a long time; and then immediately afterwards, he said to himself that it was a good sign that a great physician would not merely waste his time and that he would have already come down stairs if he had found that he could do nothing. Flashes of hope crossed his mind; his child was saved; when the doctor came in he would see, by his countenance, that she was saved. He watched the door; no one coming yet! Then he told himself that there would be lots of precautions to take; that perhaps she would be always delicate, that many people lived with palpitations of the heart. And the words, the terrible words: *"to die,"* besieged him all this time. He drove them away and repeated to himself, for the hundredth time, his former ideas of convalescence, cure, health. He thought over all the people he had known, who had been ill, but who, nevertheless, were still living. And notwithstanding all this, he unceasingly repeated to himself: "What is he going to tell me?" He thought the doctor's visit would never end. And then, he would shudder at the idea of seeing the door open. He would have liked to remain for ever in that position, and not to know anything. At last hope took entire possession of him.

The door opened.

"Well?" said Monsieur Mauperin to the doctor, who appeared on the threshold.

"Courage, sir," replied the doctor.

Monsieur Mauperin raised his eyes, looked at the physician, moved his lips, but without emitting any sound: his mouth was quite dry.

The doctor explained to him at great length the illness of his daughter, its gravity, and the complications against which they had to guard; then he wrote a long prescription, saying to Monsieur Mauperin, as he named each ingredient: "You understand?"

" Perfectly," replied Monsieur Mauperin with a stupefied look.

" Well, my darling child, and so now we are going to get quite well ! "

These were the words with which Monsieur Mauperin greeted his daughter on entering her room.

Really ? " said she.

" Kiss me."

" What did he say to you ? "

" See, look at me ! " And Monsieur Mauperin smiled. But he felt death in his heart.

" Ah ! " said he, suddenly jumping up and pretending to hunt for his hat. " I must be off to Paris to have your prescription made up."

XLIV

AT the railway station he caught sight of the doctor just as he was getting into a carriage. He got into another. He felt that he had not the strength to speak to him or to look at him.

On reaching Paris, he went to a chemist's. They told him it would take three hours to make up the prescription. He said: "Three hours!" but all the same he was glad that it would be so long: he had lots of time to spare before returning home.

When he got into the street, he walked straight before him. He had no connected ideas, but he felt a constant pulsation in his head, like the pulsation of neuralgia. His feelings were deadened, as though he were under the influence of a kind of torpor. He saw nothing except the legs of the passers-by and the wheels of the carriages.

His head seemed to him to be both heavy and empty. Seeing other people walk he walked also. The crowd carried him forward, and tossed him about, as it were, in a whirlpool. Everything looked dark to him, and the same colour as things do the day after a night of intoxication. The light and the noise of the streets appeared to him as only a dream. Had it not been for the white trousers of a policeman, which occasionally caught his eye, he would not have known that the sun was shining.

He did not care whether he turned to the right or to the left. He had no wish for anything, no courage for anything. He was surprised at the activity that surrounded him,

people hurrying, walking fast, going somewhere. For some hours past he had been without an object, without an interest. The world seemed to him to have come to an end. He felt like a dead man over whose grave all the life of Paris was passing. He thought over all that may happen to a man and tried to find something therein which could move him, or even touch him, and he found no despair so deep as his own.

Sometimes, as though answering some one who had asked for news of his daughter, he said out loud: "Oh! yes, very ill!" and, as he said it, he felt as though it had been said by a person near him. Often, a young work-woman, with no shawl, with a rounded waist, a fine girl, pretty, and rejoicing in the strength of her class, passed before his eye: he would cross the street so as not to see her. At one moment he would fly into a passion with every one who passed him by, with all these useless living people, who were not beloved as his daughter was, and who had no need to live.

He found himself in a public garden. A child came and laid some mud pies on the skirt of his long coat; others, emboldened, approached him with the impertinence of sparrows. Then, little by little, amazed, laying down their spades, they left off playing and began to look timidly and gently, with the eyes of little men, at this big gentleman who seemed so sad. Monsieur Mauperin rose and left the garden.

His tongue felt parched, and his throat was dry: he entered a café.

Just opposite to him was a little girl in a straw hat and white frock. The child's little legs were visible, the flesh of her solid little calves showed between her drawers and her open-worked socks. She was fidgetting about on her father's knee and did nothing but climb and jump about over him. She trampled his knees with her feet. A little cross danced up and down on the pink skin of her neck. Her father said to her continually: " Be quiet, do ! "

Monsieur Mauperin closed his eyes : his own six-year-old daughter appeared before him ! And pulling towards him an illustrated paper, he leaned over it, and tried to fix his attention upon the pictures, and, at the last page, he stopped at the acrostic.

When Monsieur Mauperin raised his head, he wiped his brow with his handkerchief. He had guessed the acrostic :

" *Against death there is no appeal.*"

XLV.

THEN began for Monsieur Mauperin the painful life which those lead who hope for nothing and who can only wait, a life of terror and of anguish, a life of despair, filled with starts, a life spent in listening for death, a life which makes one fear the noises in the house, and which makes one fear one's own silence, which makes one fear a sound in the next room, or the voices which one hears and which seem to be coming towards one, which makes one dread the look of the face that opens the front door to one when one returns home, and of which one asks, by a look, whether all are still alive in the house.

Like all people who are in constant attendance upon a sick person who is dear to them, he buried himself in the bitterness of the reproaches he heaped upon himself. He increased his grief by accusing himself, by saying that it was his fault, that he had not done all that he ought to have done, that she might perhaps have been saved if he had sent for a doctor sooner, if, at such and such a time, in such a month, on such a day, he had thought of such a thing.

At night, the heat of his bed seemed to increase the fever of his sorrow. Out of the shadows, the silence, the solitude, only one thought rose before him, only one image; his daughter, and always his daughter! His imagination excited itself in its anxiety; his terrors became too strong for him, and his sleeplessness ended by taking the intensity of the painful sensations of a nightmare. In the morning he woke up in a cowardly manner, or else, like a man who is half asleep and instinctively turns his back upon the light, he buried himself again in sleep, drove away his first thoughts, tried not to remember anything and to escape for a moment longer from the entire consciousness of his existence.

Then the day came with its tortures, and the father was obliged to hold himself in, to conquer himself, to be merry, to answer all those smiles of suffering, those melancholy sallies, those failing illusions which look forward to the future, those heart-breaking words with which the dying comfort themselves and try to inspire hope into those who are round them. She would say to him in her weak, tender voice, which was gradually disappearing: "How happy one feels when one is not in pain. I am going to enjoy my life when I am quite cured again." And he would answer: "Yes," and swallow down his tears.

XLVI

SICK people believe in places where they will be better,
and in countries which can cure them. There are places,
nooks, and memories which come back to them, bringing to
them a smile from home, and the softness of the cradle.
Like the fears of a child in the arms of its nurse, their hopes
fly away into some country place, some garden, or, it may
be, the village where they were born, and which will not
allow them to die.

Renée began to think of Morimond. She said to herself
that, once there, she would suffer no more. She felt it, she
was certain of it. The house at La Briche had brought
her misfortune. She had been so happy at Morimond.
And this idea increased in her, it grew more fixed and
more keen in proportion to her longing for change, and the
need of change that suffering often causes. She spoke to
her father and teased him about it. It would not upset
anything; the refinery could do quite well without him;
Monsieur Bernard, his manager, was a man in whom he
had every confidence, and who could do everything; they
would come back in the autumn. " When are we to start,
dear father ? " she repeated this question every day, with
increasing impatience.

Monsieur Mauperin yielded. His daughter so often
promised him that she would be quite well there, that he,
at last, allowed himself to believe it; in her wish, he
fancied he saw an inspiration sent to a sick person. The

doctor whom he consulted said : " Yes, perhaps the country may do her good," like a man accustomed to these longings of dying people, who think they can distance death by going rather farther away.

Monsieur Mauperin made haste to put all his affairs in order, and they started for Morimond.

The pleasure of starting, the excitement of the journey, the nervous strength which it gives to the weakest, the fresh air blowing in through the open carriage window, supported the invalid as far as Chaumont. She reached it without being over-tired. Monsieur Mauperin made her rest there one day, and the next morning he placed her in the best carriage he had been able to hire in the town, and they went on to Morimond. The road was a bad, country road. The journey was painful and tedious. By nine o'clock it had begun to be hot. By eleven, the sun scorched the leather of the carriage. The horses sweated, panted, and could hardly get along. Madame Mauperin nodded in her seat with her back to the horses. Monsieur Mauperin, seated beside his daughter, held against his side, with his arm, a pillow upon which she leaned, and against which she fell after each jerk. From time to time she asked what o'clock it was and said, " Is that all ?"

At length, towards three o'clock, they drew near. They had only another league to travel. The sky was clouded over, it was cooler, the dust fell, and the earth breathed again. A water-wagtail began to fly along in front of the carriage, resting upon the heaps of stones about every thirty yards. A row of elms grew by the side of the road, the fields began to be divided by hedges. Renée seemed to improve with her native air. She raised herself, and resting on the door of the carriage, leaning her head on the back of her hand after the manner of children in a

carriage, she began to look about her; she seemed to be
breathing in all she saw. And as the carriage proceeded,
she said: "Look, the big poplar at the Hermitage is
broken! There is the pond where the little boys used to
fish for leeches! There are Monsieur Richet's cornel-
trees!"

At the little wood, near the village, her father had to
get down to pick her a little flower from the edge of a
ditch, which she pointed out to him.

The carriage passed the inn, the first houses of the
village, the smith's forge, the great walnut tree, the
church, the clockmaker who also sold antiquities, Pigeau's
farm. All the villagers were at work in the fields. Some
children stopped teasing a wet cat in order to watch the
carriage pass. An old man, sitting on a bench in front of
his house, in the sun, wrapped in a woollen comforter and
shivering, touched his cap. Then the horses stopped. The
door opened. A man who was waiting at the foot of the
steps took Mademoiselle Mauperin in his arms and carried
her into the house.

"Ah!" sighed he, as he lifted her. "Our poor young
lady; she weighs no more than a bundle of sticks!"

"How d'ye do, Chrétiennot! how d'ye do, my old
friend," said Monsieur Mauperin, as he shook hands with
the old gardener who had served him so many years.

XLVII

THE next day, and those which followed it, she had delicious waking moments when the day which was beginning, the morning of the sky and of the earth, mingled themselves, in her dawning thoughts, with the early morning of her life. Her first recollections came to her with the first songs that reached her from the garden. The nests, in waking, re-awoke her childhood.

Supported, almost carried, by her father, she insisted upon seeing everything, the garden, the espaliers, the meadow in front of the house, the shady canal, and the pond with its stagnant water. Gradually she recognised the trees, the alleys, as one remembers things seen in a dream. Her feet carried her, of their own accord, along the old paths which had almost disappeared, but which she had followed as a child. The ruins appeared to her older by the years that had passed since she had seen them. She recognised places in the grass where she had lain as a little child, and which had been under the shadow of her baby frock. She found the place where she had buried a little dog. He was white, and was called " Jewel." She had been very fond of him. She saw her father carrying her on his arm round the orchard, after she had been given physic.

A thousand memories also came back to her from the house. Corners of the rooms seemed to her like old play-things which she might have lighted upon in a lumber

room.   It was a pleasure to her to hear again the creaking
and plaintive old weathercock on the roof, which, with its
noise, had so often calmed her childish dreams and terrors.

She appeared to revive, to get better.   The change, her
native air, and her recollections seemed to diminish her
sufferings.   This lasted for some weeks.

One morning her father was standing beside her on one
of the paths, and was watching her.   She was engaged in
cutting off the dead flowers from a large white rosebush.
Under her broad-brimmed straw hat, her thin little face
had all the light of the day and the softness of the shade.
She went merrily from one bush to another; the thorns
caught her gown as though they would play with her.
And at each snap of her scissors, a dead rose, earth-
coloured, resembling the corpse of a flower, would fall to
the ground from a branch whereon the little living roses,
with their pink hearts, were hanging.

Suddenly, breaking off from her work, Renée threw
herself into her father's arms: "Ah, papa, how I love you,"
she exclaimed ; and burst into tears.

XLVIII.

FROM this day forward, the improvement began to disappear. Little by little, she lost the healthful colour which touched her cheeks with the last kiss of life. She no longer felt the pleasant restlessness of convalescence, or the wish to go here and there which had so recently made her take her father's arm. The gaiety which comes from forgotten suffering, the merry chatter of returning hope, rose no longer from her soul to her lips. She was lazy about speaking, and about answering. "No, I want nothing; I am quite comfortable." Those were the only words which fell from her mouth now, and they were said with an accent of suffering, sadness, and patience. Her low spirits weighed her down. They felt like a heavy weight on her bosom, which her breathing could scarcely remove. A feeling of discomfort, a vague feeling of pain spread itself all through her being and enervated her, took from her all her vital energy, destroyed in her every wish to move, and kept her crushed, bowed down, and without strength to rise and shake it off.

Her father decided her to allow herself to be cupped.

XLIX.

SHE took off her muslin scarf with those slow movements of sick people, so slow as to be almost painful. Her shaking and trembling fingers sought her buttons and the shoulder-straps of her chemise to take them off. Her father and mother helped her to undo the flannel and the wadding in which she was wrapped, and her poor little body, appearing from among the linen which she pulled up and held firmly against her chest, was quite naked and quivering with modesty and emaciation.

She watched her father, who was lighting the candle, twisting up paper, and preparing the claret glass, with that disturbed look that arises from the terror the body feels for the fire or the iron that is being prepared for it.

" Am I right here ? " she asked, trying to smile.

" No; put yourself like this," answered Monsieur Mauperin.

She turned herself round on the chair on which she was sitting, placed her two hands on the back of it, rested her cheek on her hand, gathered up her legs, crossed her feet, and, as it were, kneeling and crouching in the little arm-chair. She presented her shoulders, and her bones seemed to be coming through the skin. Her hair, which had come down, fell over her back and cast its shadow on her. Her shoulder-blades stood out. Her back-bone showed all its knots. Below the shoulder-strap of her chemise, which had fallen to the bend of her arm, a miserable little elbow peeped out.

"Well, father?"

He was standing there, nailed to the place, not knowing what he was thinking about. At the sound of his daughter's voice, he seized a glass; then he suddenly remembered that he had bought those glasses for the dinner on the day of Renée's christening. He lighted a piece of paper, threw it into the glass, and turned over the glass while he closed his eyes. Renée drew a sharp breath from the pain, a quiver ran through all her bones; and then she said: "Oh! well, I expected it would have hurt more."

Monsieur Mauperin let go of the glass, which slipped and fell; the blister had not risen.

"Another," said he to his wife.

Madame Mauperin brought him one slowly.

"Give it here!" said he, roughly, taking it from her.

The perspiration was standing on his forehead, but he no longer trembled. This time the vacuum was made; the skin wrinkled all round the glass, and rose within it, as though drawn up by the piece of charred paper.

"Oh, father, do not lean so heavily," said Renée, whose lips were clenched. "Take away your hand."

"I am not touching it," said her father. "Look;" and he showed her his hands.

Renée's white skin was still rising in the glass, and was therein becoming red, spotted, and purple. After the blisters had been put on, it was necessary to take them off again, and, in order to do this, it was necessary to draw the skin against one of the sides of the glass, and to rock it over towards the other side. Monsieur Mauperin was obliged to make two or three attempts to do this, and to lean heavily on the poor skin which seemed so near to the bones.

L.

ILLNESSES do their work secretly, their ravages are often hidden. Then suddenly there appear those horrible external changes, which gradually alter the features and efface by degrees the person, and produce, by the first touch of death, the semblance of a corpse in the body that one loves.

Every day Monsieur Mauperin looked at his daughter, as though to find something which he missed and which no longer existed in her; her eyes, her smile, her movements, her walk, her dress, which used to stand out proud of its young mistress of twenty; her youth, which was like an atmosphere about her, and which breathed upon you as she passed. All those things were being veiled, were fading, vanishing, as if every symptom of life were passing from her. She no longer imparted life to all she touched. Her clothes fell in miserable, scanty folds upon her, as the clothes of old men do upon their bodies. Her step was slow and her heels no longer rang as she moved. Her gestures seemed to have become awkward, her caresses had lost their grace. All her movements had shrunk; she huddled them up to herself like a person who is cold, or who fears to take up too much room. Her arms, which hung down by her sides, looked like wet wings. She scarcely resembled her former self. And when she walked in front of her father, her back bent, her waist weak, her arms pendant, her gown hanging loosely about her, it seemed to him as though she were no longer his daughter; he remembered her as she had been!

A shadow had fallen round her mouth and seemed to enter into it whenever she smiled. The mole on her hand, near her little finger, had increased in size and had become quite black.

LI

" MOTHER, to-day is Henry's birthday."

" I know," said Madame Mauperin, without moving.

" Suppose we go to Our Lady of Maricourt?"

Madame Mauperin rose, left the room, and returned with her bo net and shawl.

Half-an-hour later, Monsieur Mauperin helped his daughter out of the carriage before the big door of the church at Maricourt. Renée went to a little chapel and there found, on a marble altar, the little miraculous, wooden Madonna, quite black, to which, as a child, she used to pray with a feeling of terror. She sat down upon one of the school-children's seats, which were always there, and murmured a prayer. Her mother, standing beside her, looked round the church and did not pray. Then Renée rose, and refusing her father's arm, crossed the church with a firm step, and went up to a little side-door which opened into the churchyard.

" I wanted to see if that were still there," said she to her father, pointing to a bunch of artificial flowers which was hung up amongst a number of other "ex voto" offerings.

" Come, my child," said Monsieur Mauperin, " do not stand about too much. Let us go home now."

" Oh, we have plenty of time."

In the porch stood a stone bench, on which the sun shone.

"It is warm." said she, laying her hand on it. "Give me my plaid, and let me sit here a minute. I shall have the sun on my back. There."

"It is very unwise," said her father.

"Oh, just to make me happy." And when he had arranged her comfortably, she leaned upon him, and in a voice as gentle as a sigh she said : "How bright it is here!"

The lime-trees, alive with bees, were murmuring gently. Some hens were picking and scratching in the short grass. At the foot of a wall, near some carts whose wheels were all white with dried mud, and on the trunks of some trees that had been barked, some chickens were playing, and some ducks were sleeping, rolled up into balls. The church seemed to be full of dead voices, the blue sky was reflected in its windows. Pigeons were continually flying in and out of the hollows in the carvings and the holes in the old masonry. The river rushed foaming past; a white colt ran down to it, madly excited.

"Ah!" said Renée, after a few minutes, "we ought to have been made of something else. Why did God see fit to make us all of flesh? It is horrible!"

Her eyes had fallen upon some pieces of ground which were raised here and there in a corner of the graveyard, and which were half hidden by two rows of barrel hoops of which a trellis had been formed, and over which the convolvulus was climbing.

LII

HER illness had not produced in Renée any of the quickness of temper, or of the changeability of mind, or the nervous irritability which so often puts some of the patient's sufferings into the hearts of those who tend them. She let herself be pleased by everything that came. Her life seemed to ebb away from her without any effort on her part to retain her hold upon it. She had remained affectionate and gentle. Her wishes had nothing in them of the unreasonableness of caprice. The shadow that enveloped her was a shadow full of peace. She let death rise over her white soul, like a beautiful evening.

But, nevertheless, there were moments in which nature woke in her, in which her mind bent under the weakness of her body, in which she listened to the blows which were gradually undermining her life. Then she would become profoundly silent. She would have long periods of alarming meditation and of silent immobility, during which she resembled a statue. She passed long hours without ever hearing the clock strike, and gazing, with a steady and fixed look, into space, a little beyond her foot. And now her father never obtained a look from her! Sometimes, after she had drooped her eyelids two or three times, she would hide her eyes by half shutting them, and he saw her sleep, with her eyes half open. He would talk to her, he racked his brains to think of anything that could amuse her, he invented jokes for her, in order to try and make

her listen to him and to be aware that he was there ; in
the middle of a sentence he would see the attention, the
thoughts of his child wander away from him, and the
light of intelligence itself go out of her countenance.   He
no longer felt the warmth of old days in his affection.
Near her he felt cold now.   It was as though her illness
were robbing him, day by day, of a little of the heart of
his child.

LIII

SOMETIMES also, Renée let fall some of those words wherewith sick people bewail themselves, words which seem to bear in them the coldness of death.

One day, while her father was reading the paper to her, she took it from him in order to read through the list of marriages; and after an instant, "Twenty-nine! How old that one was!" said she, as though to herself. She was reading the deaths.

Monsieur Mauperin made no answer; he walked up and down the room, and then went out.

Left by herself, Renée got up in order to shut the door which her father had left ajar, and which was banging. She fancied she heard a groan in the passage; she looked but could see nothing; she listened, all was silent, and she was on the point of shutting the door when she again thought she heard the sound. She went out into the passage, and walked as far as her father's room; the noise came from there. The key was not in the lock: Renée bent down, and through the keyhole she saw her father lying on his bed, weeping, and shaken with sobs, burying his face in his pillow in order to stifle his tears and his despair.

LIV.

RENÉE would not make her father cry any more.

Next day she said to him :

"Look here, papa. We leave here, don't we, at the end of September? That is quite settled. We will travel about everywhere, spending a month here, a fortnight there, just as the spirit moves us. And then I want you to take me to all the places where you have fought. A little bird once told me that you had been in love with a princess. Shall we go and look for her? It was at Pordenona, was it not, that you received these great sabre wounds?"

And, taking her father's hand in her two hands, Renée touched with her lips the hollow, white marks made by the finger of Glory.

"I shall expect you to explain everything to me," continued she, "it will be pleasant for you to fight all your battles again in company of your daughter. And if one winter is not enough for us, why, bless me, we will stay two! And then when I am all right again, you see, my sister and I are quite rich enough, and you have slaved quite long enough, and then you shall sell the refinery and we will come and settle here. We will spend two months of every year in Paris, just to amuse ourselves, and that will be quite enough for us, will it not? As you will want occupation you shall take back the farm you have let to Tétevuide's son-in-law. We will have some cows, and a fine poultry yard for mamma : do you hear, mamma ? I shall be out of doors the whole day, and I shall end by becoming too well, you will see ; and besides we will always have a few people staying here—one can do that in the country without ruining oneself, and we shall be perfectly happy, you see if we are not ! "

She talked of nothing but plans, journeys, and the future. She spoke of it as of a thing that was settled, and that was quite within her reach. She was the personification of hope in the house ; and she hid away so carefully the possibility of her death, she made so good a pretence of wishing to live, that Monsieur Mauperin when he looked at her, and listened to her, began to dream with her of the years that awaited them, and that were all to be crowned with peace, tranquillity and happiness. Sometimes even the sufferer herself was taken in by the pictures she drew, and by her own fibs, and forgetting herself for a moment, she would say to herself in a low voice : " All the same, suppose I were to get well."

At other times she would gently turn towards her past. She told stories, anecdotes of what had happened, her words described all the joys of her childhood that once again were passing before her eyes. She seemed to be raising herself in her agony to kiss her father for the last time with all her youth. She said to him :

" Oh, my first ball-dress! I can see it now, it was made of pink tulle. The dressmaker did not come; it was raining, and there was no cab to be had. How you did run! And how funny you looked when you came back with the box under your arm ! You made me all wet when you kissed me. I remember."

Renée was quite alone, and had to depend entirely upon herself in her attempts to keep up the spirits of her father and her own spirits. Her mother, certainly, was near her, but since Henry's death she had been plunged in a silent apathy. She remained silent, indifferent, as it were, taken out of herself. She passed days and nights by her daughter's side, never complaining, patient and unvarying, ready to do everything, docile, humble as a servant, but there was always something mechanical in her tenderness. All the soul had gone out of her caresses, and all her affection was of the kind that only touches the body : nothing remained to her of motherhood, save the hands.

LV.

RENEE once more dragged herself, with her father, as far as the first trees of the little wood. Against an oak, in a certain place just on the fringe, she let herself down and sat upon the moss. From the fields around her, a smell of hay, of grass, of honey, and of sunshine came to her. The breath of the woods came to her, damp with the coolness of its springs, and with the moisture of its overgrown paths. Out of the depths of the silence rose a deep and many-tongued rustling, a winged buzzing, filling the ear with its noise which resembled the incessant sound of a bee-hive, or the infinite murmur of the sea. Round Renée, near her, there appeared to be a great living atmosphere of peace, in which everything was moving, the fly in the air, the leaf on the tree, the shadow on the bark, the tops of the trees in the sky, the barren oats by the road-side. Then, out of this buzzing there came a breath, or a sigh; a breeze, which had sprung up afar off, threw, as it passed, a shiver over the trees, and the blue of the sky, above the quivering leaves, seemed more motionless than before. The branches swayed gently to and fro, a breath passed over the temples and the neck of Renée, a sigh kissed her and refreshed her. Gradually she allowed the consciousness of her physical existence, the feeling and the fatigue of living, to slip from her and to escape her; a delicious languor overcame her and she seemed already half detached from her being, and ready to be absorbed in the divine sweetness that surroun-

ded her. Now and then she squeezed herself against her
father, as a child does who is afraid of being carried away
by a gust of wind.

In the garden there was a bench made of stone and
covered with moss. After dinner, towards seven o'clock,
Renée liked to go and sit there, stretching herself out,
leaning her head back, and, her ear tickled by a spray of
volubilis, she would remain gazing into vacancy. They
had reached those beautiful days in summer which die
away in evenings of silver. Insensibly, her ideas and her
eyes would lose themselves in the infinite whiteness of the
darkening sky. As she watched, more light, more brightness would seem to reach her from the dying day, more
brilliancy and more serenity would seem to fall upon her.
Deep caverns seemed to open therein for her, in which she
fancied she could see the light of myriads of stars, pale as
the twinkling of a taper. And, presently, tired out with
gazing into this radiance which was gradually being extin-
guished, blinded by the sunbeams, she would close her eyes
for an instant before the abyss over which she was leaning,
and which seemed to be calling her away.

LVI

"MOTHER," said she, "have you not noticed how smart I am? Look, see all the trouble I have taken on your account."

And lazily twisting her arms round her head, like a crown, she leaned back among her pillows and stretched herself prettily on her couch, her waist supple, her body in an attitude of coquettish and painful grace.

She thought that it made her look ill to remain in bed and to be buried under the sheets. She would not stay there, and put forth all her last strength to get up. She dressed towards eleven o'clock, slowly, painfully, heroically, stopping to take breath, resting her arms wearied with combing her hair. She threw over her head, a little veil of point-lace; she put on a peignoir of white cashmere, wadded and lined, which fell in large folds. On her little feet she wore open slippers, with bunches of real violets that Chrétiennot brought her every morning, in place of rosettes. And in order to keep up the appearance of life that sick people preserve as long as they are up and dressed, she remained until the evening in this white, virginal and perfumed toilet.

"Oh! how odd it is to be ill!" said she, casting her eyes over herself and into the room. "I only like pretty things now." They are a pleasure to me at present. I could not wear anything ugly. Do you know, I have a great longing. Do you remember that little water-jug, mounted in silver, which was so pretty, and which we saw in that jeweller's shop in the Rue Saint-Honoré, when we came out between the acts of the play at the Français? If he have not sold it, if it be still there, you must get it for me. Oh, I feel that I am becoming recklessly extravagant; I warn you. I want to arrange everything here. I am becoming difficult to please, in all sorts of ways. My ideas are getting grand, and you know I used not to care before. Now, I have eyes for myself, and for everything that surrounds me, and such eyes! There are colours which positively hurt me; should you have ever believed that? And others which are quite new to me. That comes of being ill, of course: it is so ugly to be ill! It makes one love all that is beautiful more than ever!"

Other senses seemed to come to Renée together with all the refinement, the coquetry, and the love of beauty that death brings. She became, and she felt herself becoming, more of a woman. Under the languor and the softening influences of illness, her heart, which had always been affectionate, albeit somewhat masculine and violent, became softer, gentler, and more peaceful. Little by little, the manners, the tastes, the ideas of her sex reappeared in her. Her mind underwent the same transformation as the rest of her. She lost her quickness of judgment and her boldness of language. It was very rare that one of her old expressions passed her lips: if it did, she would say, smiling: "Ah! that is a remains of the old Renée!" She called to mind words she had used, her former boldness, her tone in speaking to, and her familiarity with, young men: she would not have dared to do it again. She was astonished at herself, and could not recognise herself. She had given up reading both serious and amusing books: she only cared now for works that made her think, books which put tender ideas before her.

When her father talked to her of the coursing meetings she had been to, and of those which she would attend in the future, the mere idea of being on horseback frightened her: she felt like some one who is just going to fall off. The emotions, the faintness that she ·felt in the country, were quite new to her. Hitherto, she had never occupied herself with flowers; now they were as dear to her as human beings. She, who used to be bored with needle-work, now undertook to embroider a petticoat elaborately, and took pleasure in the work. She was gradually waking up and being born again in the memories of her girlish life. Her thoughts travelled back to the comrades of her childhood, or her girlhood, to friends she had had, to places where she had been with grown-up women, to faces which had knelt in the same row with her when she made her first communion.

LVII.

As she was looking out of her window one day, she saw a woman sit down in the dust in the middle of the village street, between a stone and a rut, and undress her baby. The child, lying on his stomach, the upper part of his body in shadow, was moving his little legs, crossing his feet, kicking in the sunlight; the sun was whipping him tenderly, as it does whip naked children. Sunbeams caressed and tickled him, and seemed to throw at his feet the roses out of a basket in a Corpus Christi procession.

When the mother and child moved away, Renée remained looking out of her window.

LVIII

"Do you see," said she to her father, "I never could love any one; you have spoiled me. I felt so certain beforehand that nobody would love me as you did! I saw so many things pass over your face, so much happiness, when I was there! And when we used to go about together, were you not proud of me? Did you not delight in giving me your arm? Ah, father, it would have been useless for any one else to try to love me. I should never have found my papa in any one else; you have spoiled me too much!"

"But all the same, that will not prevent my darling from finding a handsome young man, one of these fine days, when she is quite strong again."

"Your handsome young man is still a long way off!" answered Renée, smiling with her eyes. Then she went on : " It may seem curious to you, does it not, that I have never wished to be married ? Well, I will tell you this, it has been entirely your fault! Oh, I don't regret it! What did I want ? I had everything. I never pictured any other happiness to myself, I never thought of it. I did not want to change, I was so happy as I was! But, pray, what more could I wish for ? The life I led near you was so sweet, and my heart was so happy! Yes, perhaps," said she, after an instant's silence, " if I had been like other girls, with dull parents, with a father unlike you, yes, no doubt, I should have done as all of them have done. I should have wished to be loved, I should have wished my married life to be what I had dreamed it might be. But all the same, I must say, that it would have been very difficult to me to fall in love. It has never been my way, and it has always made me laugh a little. Do you remember when my sister and Davarande were engaged? How I teased them! Do you remember, they ended by calling me 'the wretch'? All the same, I have had my feelings like every one else; my day-dreams, and my fancies. Otherwise I should not have been a woman. But it was simply like a tune running in my head which excited me a little. It came and went in my imagination, but it never rested on the head of any one in particular, never. And besides, as soon as I left my room, it was all over. If there were any one there, I could only use my eyes; I only thought of looking in order to laugh later on, and you know how your naughty daughter could look! You should have—"

"Sir," said Chrétiennot, opening the door, "Monsieur Magu is below, and wishes to know if mademoiselle can see him."

"Oh, father," said Renée in a tone of entreaty, "don't let me see the doctor to-day. I do not want him. I am quite well. And then he snuffles too much! Why does he snuffle so, papa?"

Monsieur Mauperin could not help laughing.

"I will tell you. It comes from driving about in a dog-cart in winter to pay his visits. As his two hands are occupied, one with his reins, and the other with his whip, he has got into the habit of never using his handkerchief."

LIX

" Is the sky blue everywhere, father ? Look out and see," said Renée one afternoon to her father, from her couch.

" Yes, my child," answered Monsieur Mauperin from the window : " it is a beautiful day."

" Really ? "

" Why ? Are you in pain ? "

" No; only I fancied there were some clouds about, and that the weather was going to change. It is curious, when one is ill, to feel how near the sky seems to be to one. Ah! I am a splendid barometer now."

And she began to read the book that she had laid down while she was speaking.

" You will tire yourself with reading, my darling. Let us talk a little. Give me the book," and Monsieur Mauperin stretched out his hand to take the volume which she passed to him. On opening it his eyes chanced upon some pages which he had folded down some years before, so that she should not read them ; the forbidden pages were still folded.

Renée seemed to go to sleep. The storm which had not yet appeared in the sky, was already brewing in her. She was suffering from an intolerable heaviness which weighed her down, and at the same time her whole being was in a state of nervous tension. The electricity which was in the air, had got into her system and was exciting her. A great stillness, which seemed to have come from the horizon, had spread itself over everything, and the heavy atmosphere that lay over the whole country had filled her with an overwhelming restlessness. She watched the clock, without speaking, and kept clasping and unclasping her hands,

" Yes, you are quite right," said Monsieur Mauperin,
" there is a black cloud over Fresnoy. How fast it is
travelling! It is coming in this direction, and will soon be
here. Would you like me to shut the windows, the shutters,
everything, and ring for lights? Then my pet will be less
frightened."

" No," said Renée, hastily, " no lights; let us keep the
daylight. No. no; besides I am not afraid now."

" Oh, it is still far away," said her father, for the sake of
saying something: his daughter's speech made him fancy
he saw tapers burning in the room. .

" Ah. here comes the rain," said Renée, in a tone of
relief, " this rain is like dew. One seems to drink it. does
not one? Come and sit here. quite close to me."

Large drops fell one by one; then the rain poured down
from the sky as if some one above were emptying a huge
water-jug. The storm enveloped Morimond. The thunder
pealed and crackled. The country appeared, at one moment,
to be on fire, at the next to be buried in darkness. And
continually the lightning. playing into the dark room,
covered with its pale radiance the sick girl, who lay there
all clothed in white. motionless. her eyes closed, and seemed
to throw a winding sheet over her body.

The storm ended in a final peal of thunder, so violent,
and so close that Renée threw her arms round her father's
neck and hid her face on his shoulder.

" Silly, it is all over now," said Monsieur Mauperin.

She, like a bird which timidly draws its head from under
its wing, raised her eyes towards him, and still holding
him tightly embraced, said with a smile in which some
regret seemed to be mingled: " Ah. I thought we had all
died together!"

LX

ONE morning, on coming in to see Renée, who had passed a bad night, Monsieur Mauperin found her dozing. At the sound of his footsteps, she half opened her eyes, and turning round slightly, said:

"Ah, is it you, papa!" And she murmured a few confused words, amongst which her father could distinguish the word "journey" several times repeated.

"What are you saying about a journey?"

"Yes,—I feel as if I had come from a long way off, a very long way off, from a country of which I have even forgotten the name."

And opening her eyes wide, she stretched out her hands upon the sheets, and seemed to be searching in her memory for the place where she had been, and whence she had come. A confused recollection, a pale remembrance remained to her of spaces, tracts of country, unknown places, of all those worlds and limbos whither sick people go during the last few nights they spend on earth, and whence they return quite astonished, bewildered with the glimpse that they have had of the infinite, as if during their forgotten dream they had heard the first flutter of the wings of death!

"It is nothing," she continued, after an instant, "it was the opium that did it; they gave me some last night to make me sleep."

And, shaking herself a little, as though to get rid of her thoughts: "Hold the glass for me, so that I may tidy myself. Higher than that. Oh, how awkward you men are!"

She puffed out her hair by passing her thin hands through it. She arranged her lace scarf which had come untied.

"There, now," said she, "talk to me. I want to be talked to." And she almost shut her eyes while her father talked to her.

"You are tired. Renée; I will leave you," said he, seeing that she did not seem to be listening.

"No, I am in some pain. But go on talking, it amuses me."

"But you are not listening to me. What are you thinking of, my dear little girl?"

"I am thinking of nothing. I was trying to remember. Dreams are so curious. It was—I don't know. Ah!" she exclaimed, at a sharp twinge of pain.

"You are suffering?"

She made no reply.

Monsieur Mauperin could not restrain a movement of his lips, and he cast a rebellious glance upward.

"Poor father!" said Renée to him, after a pause. "But see, I am resigned. No, you must not be so angry as that with pain. It was sent to us for a good reason; we are not made to suffer simply for suffering's sake."

And in a broken voice, stopping to take breath at every moment, she began to point out to him the good side of suffering, the springs of tenderness that it opens in us, the refinement and the sweetness of character that it gives to those who accept it with patience and do not allow it to make them bitter. She spoke to him of all the miseries and the littlenesses that are driven out of us by suffering, of that instinctive irony that we lose, of the unkind laugh that it takes from us, of the pleasure we no longer take in the small troubles of others, of the kindly feeling towards every one that it produces in us. " If you only knew how silly wit seems to me now," she said. And Monsieur Mauperin overheard her thanking suffering for having come to her as a proof of her election. She spoke of the egotism and of the earthly matter in which we are wrapped when we are in health, of the hardness which is produced by the comfort of our bodies, and she said that, in illness, there is a freedom and a deliverance, an interior lightness, and that our aspirations are taken upwards and away from ourselves. She spoke of suffering as removing from us our pride, as reminding us of our weakness, as humanising us, as making us one with all who are in pain, as making us feel the need of charity in ourselves.

" And besides, without suffering," she added, " we should miss one thing! Sadness!"

And she smiled.

LXI.

"My friend, we are very miserable," said Monsieur Mauperin to Denoisel, who had just jumped out of a dog-cart, a few evenings later. "I had a presentiment that you would come. She is asleep now; you shall see her to-morrow. Oh! you will find her sadly changed. But you must be hungry," and he led him into the dining-room, where supper had been hastily laid.

"Come, Monsieur Mauperin," said Denoisel, "she is young; at her age there are always resources."

Monsieur Mauperin put his two elbows on the table, and the tears ran slowly from his eyes.

"But, Monsieur Mauperin, you see she has not been given up by the doctors. There is still hope."

Monsieur Mauperin shook his head, made no answer, and continued to weep.

"She has not been condemned?"

"But can't you see that she has!" burst out Monsieur Mauperin at last, "and that I do not wish to tell you so. One is afraid of everything, you see, when one has got to this state, and I fancy that some words are capable of bringing about events; and that word, I believe, has the power to kill my daughter! And besides why should not a miracle be performed! The doctors have spoken to me of miracles. She still gets up, and that is a great deal. I have noticed an improvement during the last two days. And besides two in one year, it would be too hard! Oh, it would be too hard! But you are not eating, you eat nothing," and

he put a large slice on to Denoisel's plate as he spoke.
"We must be men, you see. What news have you from
Paris?"

"None; I know nothing. I have just come from the
Pyrenees. It was Madame Davarande who read me one
of your letters, but she has no idea of how ill her sister is."

"Have you any news of Barousse?"

"Yes; I met him on my way to the railway-station. I
wanted to bring him with me, but you know that nothing in
the world would induce Barousse to leave Paris for a week.
He must have his walk on the quays every morning. The
idea of missing an engraving with an entire margin!"

"And the Bourjots," asked Monsieur Mauperin, with an
effort.

"They say that Mademoiselle Bourjot will not marry."

"Poor child! She loved him!"

"As for her mother, it seems that her state is very bad
indeed. I hear of excesses of all kinds, of madness even.
They are talking now of shutting her up in an asylum."

LXII

"RENEE," said Monsieur Mauperin next morning on entering his daughter's room, "There is somebody downstairs who very much wants to see you."

"Somebody?" And she looked hard at her father for some time. "I know who it is; it is Denoisel. Did you write to him?"

"Not at all. You never asked to see him. I did not know if it would give you pleasure. Does it vex you?"

"Mother, give me my little red scarf, there in the drawer," she said, without answering her father. "I must not frighten him." And when her scarf was tied in a bow, she said : "Now bring him here quickly."

Denoisel came into the room, which smelled of the vague perfume of young sick people, and which impregnates a room with the smell of a faded bouquet, and of dying flowers.

"It is good of you to have come. See, I have put on my red scarf for you; you used to like me in it."

Denoisel bent over her hands and kissed them.

"Here is Denoisel," said Monsieur Mauperin to his wife at the end of the room.

Madame Mauperin did not seem to heed him. Then, after a minute, she rose, went up to Denoisel, gave him a cold kiss, and returned to the dark corner in which she had been sitting.

"Well! and how do you think I am looking? I am a good deal changed, am I not?" And without giving him time to speak, she went on: "You see, I have a naughty father, who insists upon thinking I look ill, and who is so obstinate! I tell him in vain that I am much better. He declares I am not. When I am quite cured, you will see that he will always want to treat me as an invalid."

And observing that Denoisel was looking at her wrist, which was visible through the unbuttoned cuff of her night-gown:

"Oh," said she, hastily buttoning it up, "I am a little thinner than I used to be, but I shall soon get my feathers back. Do you remember the funny story that always used to make us laugh so much, papa? The day we dined with the farmer at Breuvannes with Têtevuide, you remember? Imagine, Denoisel, the good man had been keeping some crawfish for us for two years. Well, just as we were sitting down to table, papa said to him: 'By-the-bye, where is your daughter, Têtevuide? I insist upon her dining with us. Is she not here?' 'Yes, sir.' 'Very well, then, tell her to come, or I will not eat a morsel.' Thereupon the father goes into a neighbouring room, and we hear sounds of voices and tears, which last about a quarter of an hour. He comes back alone and says: 'She dare not come; she says that she is too thin!' But look here, papa, poor mamma has not been out of my room for two days. Now that I have a sick-nurse, you must oblige her to take some fresh air."

"Ah, my dear Renée," said Denoisel, when they were alone, "you do not know how much pleasure it gives me to find you like this, in such good spirits! It is a good sign; and you are going to get better now, and I say it, with the care of your good father, of your poor mother, and of your stupid old Denoisel, who, with your permission, is going to establish himself here."

"You, too, my kind friend? Look at me!"

And she stretched out her hands so that he might help her to turn a little on one side, in such a manner as to look straight at him, and to bring her face into the daylight: "Can you see me well now?"

The smile had died away from her eyes and from her lips. Life had all at once fallen from her face like a mask.

"Yes," she continued, lowering her voice, "It is nearly over, and I shall not have much longer to wait! Oh, I wish it might be to-morrow! I cannot go on much longer as I am doing at present. I cannot go on keeping up the spirits of every one in this house; my strength is exhausted, and my one desire is to have done with it all. He does not see me as I really am, you understand. I cannot kill him beforehand, can I? When he sees me laugh, he knows that I am condemned, but he remembers nothing, he sees nothing, he knows nothing! Well, all I can do is to go on laughing! Ah! those who can die as they please are the happy people; to be quiet, to have finished with it all, to die, at one's own pleasure, in a corner, with one's head against the wall—that would be pleasant—it would be quite easy to die like that! But the worst is over now; and you have come, too, and will encourage me. If I fail, you will be at hand to support me. And after, after I am gone, I count upon you. You will stay with him during the first few months. Ah! do not cry," she exclaimed, "you will make me cry too!"

There was an instant's silence.

"Already six months since my brother's funeral," recommenced Renée. "We have only met once since then. Do you remember the terrible fit that I had?"

" Yes, yes, I remember it well," answered Denoisel. " I have often thought of it since. I can see you now, poor child, making that gesture of horrible suffering, while your lips tried to speak, to call out, without being able to pronounce a word."

" Without being able to pronounce a word," said Renée, repeating his last words. She closed her eyes, and her lips moved as though in prayer. Then, with an expression of joy that astonished Denoisel, she said to him: " Ah, how happy I am at seeing you again, my dear friend! Together we shall have lots of courage, you shall see. And we will take them in finely, poor people! "

LXIII.

THE heat was stifling. In the evening they used to leave open the windows in Renée's room, and not light any lamp, so as not to attract the moths which frightened her very much. They talked, and, as the daylight faded, their words and thoughts gradually fell into the solemn strain that twilight, with its unspoken dreams, often brings. Soon all three would become silent ; they would sit, breathing in the cool air, thinking of the evening. Monsieur Mauperin would hold his daughter's hand, which he pressed from time to time. Darkness came on. The whole room became dim. Lying on her couch, Renée's outline, in her white peignoir, gradually disappeared. Then a moment would come in which nothing was distinguishable, in which the room seemed confounded with the sky, and then Renée would begin to talk in a low and penetrating voice. Her words were now gentle and lofty, now tender, grave or passionate : at one time they seemed as though they were singing the last song of a pure conscience, and again they seemed to fall round her, on her listeners, like the consolation of an angel. Her thoughts raised themselves as she forgave everybody and everything ; sometimes, her words seemed to reach their ears as though they came from beyond this world, from above this life, and, by degrees, a kind of awe, born of the solemnity and of the darkness of these moments of night and of death, would fall upon the room wherein Monsieur Mauperin, his wife, and Denoisel listened to all that dropped from these dying lips.

LXIV.

THE walls were papered with a pattern of bunches of wild flowers, ears of corn, corn-flowers, and poppies. A sky was painted on the ceiling, light, a sky of early morning, full of fleecy clouds. Between the door and the window stood a *prie-Dieu* of carved wood, with a cushion of worsted-work; its place seemed familiar, and it kept discreetly in its corner, like an old friend. Above it, glistened a holy water stoup of polished copper, representing the baptism of Christ by St. John. In the opposite corner, a little book-case hanging to the wall by cords of silk, showed the backs of the books leaning against one another, and a few English books bound in cloth. In front of the window, which was wreathed in creepers that seemed to dip their leaves in the sunlight, a looking-glass framed in blue velvet stood upon a dressing-table covered with silk and lace, and among several bottles with silver tops. The chimney-piece, which stood a little back from the room in a corner, was surmounted by a glass framed in velvet of the same shade as that on the dressing-table. On one side of the glass, hung a miniature of Renée's mother when a girl, with a string of pearls round her neck, and on the other a daguerreotype of her mother in somewhat later life. Above it a portrait of her father, in uniform, painted by herself, leaned forward, and seemed to watch over the room. A rose-wood wash-hand-stand bore, in front of the fire-place, the last caprice of the poor child, the silver-mounted jug and the Dresden basin that she had asked for. A little

further on, near the second window, hung all the sporting
recollections that Renée had brought home in the pockets
of her riding habit, her whips, a Pyrenean whip; a stag's
foot, mounted with blue and orange ribands, showed, on a
card hanging from it, the day and place of the death.
Beyond the window, stood a little writing-table, which
had belonged to her father when he was at the military
school. It was littered with the boxes, the work-baskets
and all her last New Year's Day presents. The bed con-
sisted entirely of muslin. At the head of it, and as it were,
under the shelter of its curtains, all the prayer-books which
Renée had had since her childhood, were arranged on an
Algerian shelf, from which hung her rosaries. Then there
was a chest of drawers, on which stood a thousand trifles,
little dolls' houses, little glass toys, little sixpenny bits of
jewellery, toys won at lotteries, fairs, even down to some
animals made of crumb of bread, with their legs made of
matches, a whole museum of trifles whereof girls make up
the sum of their lives and the greater part of their hearts.

The room was brilliant with sunlight. The southern
sun filled it with warmth and radiance. Near the bed, on a
little table arranged as an altar and covered with a linen
cloth, two candles burned, their flames flickering in the
golden sunshine. A silence, broken only by sobs, made
audible the heavy tread of the country priest, as he left
the room. Then all was still, and the tears ceased around
the dying girl, dried momentarily by the miracle which
was exhibited in her last agony.

In a few minutes, illness and all the signs of suffering
and anxiety had completely vanished from Renée's thin
face. A beauty of ecstasy and of supreme happiness, in
presence of which her father, her mother and her friend
had fallen on their knees, had succeeded it. The sweet-

ness, the peace of a vision had fallen upon her, Her head seemed to have arranged itself upon her pillows, under the influence of a dream. Her eyes, wide open, seemed to be looking into infinity, her expression gradually took the fixed look of eternity.

Every feature shone with a blessed look of hope, A remains of life, a last breath hovered round the corners of her mouth, motionless, half-open and smiling. Her complexion had become quite white. A silvery whiteness imparted to her skin and to her forehead a pallid splendour. One would have said that with her head she was already touching another day more glorious than our own : Death approached her like a light.

It was the transfiguration which frequently accompanies death from disease of the heart, which seems to bury the dying in the beauty of their souls, and to carry heavenwards the countenance of the youthful dead !

LXV.

THOSE who travel far afield have perchance met in cities or among ruins, one year in Russia, the next in Egypt, two old people, a man and a woman, who seem to go straight in front of them without looking and without noticing. They are Renée's parents; her father and mother. They are alone. The only child who remained to them, Renée's sister, died in her confinement.

They sold everything and went away. They now care for nothing. One country takes them on to another country, from one hotel bedroom they migrate to another hotel bedroom. They move about here and there like things which have been uprooted and thrown to the winds. They wander hither and thither, exiles upon earth, flying from tombs, and the abodes of the dead, which nevertheless attract them, trying to wear out their misery by the fatigues of travelling, dragging their bodies from one end of the world to the other in the hope of exhausting them.

THE END.

www.ingramcontent.com/pod-product-compliance
Lightning Source LLC
Chambersburg PA
CBHW031333070726
47496CB00018B/1847